I0680561

Hollywood

The Richard Jackson Saga, Volume 3

Ed Nelson

Published by Ed Nelson, 2024.

Table of Contents

Other books by Ed Nelson

The Richard Jackson Saga
Book 1 The Beginning
Book 2 Schooldays
Book 3 Hollywood
Book 4 In the Movies
Book 5 Star to Deckhand
Book 6 Surfing Dude
Book 7 Third Time is a Charm
Book 8 Oxford University
Book 9 Cold War
Book 10 Taking Care of Business
Book 11 Interesting Times
Book 12 Escape from Siberia
Book 13 Regicide
Book 14 What's Under, Down Under?
Book 15 The Lunar Kingdom
Book 16 First Steps
In the Richard Jackson World
Mary, Mary
Stand-Alone Story
Ever and Always
Cast in Time
Book 1, Baron
Book 2, Baron of the Middle Counties
Book 3, Count
Book 4, Earl
Book 5, Earl of the Marches

Dedication

This work is dedicated to my wife Carol for her support and help as the first reader and editor.

Bellefontaine High School Class of 1962 just because.

Professionally edited by Janet E. Rupert

Copyright © 2019

Quotation

That's the way it happened, give or take a lie or two.

James Garner as Wyatt Earp, describing the gunfight at the OK Corral in the movie *Sunset*.

Chapter 1

We were back at school on Monday, the fifth of January. Before the Christmas vacation started, it seemed like it would be long. Now that it was finished, it seemed to have gone too fast or too short. The only good thing about being back in school was that we could see each other's new clothes. We were all about the same age and growing, so ninety percent of our presents were clothes.

It wasn't so critical for the guys. Girls needed to stay in the mainstream of fashion, or they were whatever girls were when their clothes weren't the current styles...frumpy, odd, or weird. I don't know. Having heard enough giggling over the years, I knew that having the wrong clothes could be a social disaster. No matter how new the clothes were.

Guy's clothes didn't change that much, so it wasn't the same problem. Jeans were jeans; khakis were khakis. The brand name didn't matter.

With guys, what mattered was your haircut. The jocks wore a flattop. A college cut was required for those who thought of advanced education or were trying to look preppy. Rebel types wore their hair the same as Elvis, heavy on the grease, long sideburns, and ducktails until the Army drafted him.

The last haircut you wanted was a pineapple. This was a lock of hair left in front, and the rest cut down with a number two guard on the clippers. At the start of summer, this is the haircut parents would get their small kids to last the season. Melvins, dorks, and nerds kept their hair this way.

Then, of course, it needed to be kept trimmed, so there was the Saturday ritual of a trip to the barbershop. We didn't think or talk about it. We just did it. You had to keep it above your ears in what was called a white wall. If you wore glasses, the last thing you wanted was the hair to go over the sidebars. They had raised the cost of a haircut to fifty cents last year, so this was serious upkeep.

I kept my college cut trimmed every Saturday if I could. If I let it go for two weeks, Mum would tell me I needed a dog license. If I missed a Saturday, I almost always went on Monday and never past Tuesday.

The most interesting girls were those who switched to a new bra style. The ones that stuck out a lot were called "Nose Cones". That or "Headlights". Of course, any bra was also called an over-the-shoulder boulder-holder. Yes, we freshmen had a lot of class.

Boy's heavy sweaters with reindeer were the in thing this year. I didn't have one, but I thought they were okay.

Restarting classes was the usual commotion. It was like we had never been to school before. Two weeks off, and we had forgotten everything we had learned this year. We were into the fourth week of this six-week grading period. The first semester exams would start in two weeks, so teachers would start reviewing for the tests next week.

I have been carrying straight A's, so it wasn't a dreadful prospect, but I was still going to be prepared. I had already gone over the material that would be presented this week, so I started my review a week early. This should give me a firm foundation for taking the tests.

At lunchtime, the usual gang was at our table. We all shared what we got for Christmas. Tom Wilson told us about an aunt who had knitted him a sweater. The only problem was that one arm was about two inches longer than the other. His mom forced him to wear it when his aunt visited. It wasn't that funny, but the way Tom described it, we were all in stitches.

Tom and Tracy had matching sweaters to show they were a couple. Cheryl and I hadn't exchanged presents. We were in sort of no man's land. We liked each other and had done things together but hadn't been on an official date. Yet, at the same time, other people treated us as a couple.

I decided to move things forward and asked Cheryl if she would like to watch a movie on Friday. She accepted quickly and then asked me what was playing. I had no idea.

Tom Morton told us it was *North by Northwest*, an action movie with Cary Grant. I liked the action part, and Cheryl liked Cary Grant, so it sounded good. I had done the right thing on cue from the looks Cheryl and Tracy exchanged.

The rest of the school day was spent getting back into the swing of things. There was no big news or gossip from over the holidays, so that was a good thing.

I went home and did my practice typing. I realized that I had plateaued at forty words a minute without errors. This was respectable, considering I wasn't going to be a secretary. A professional would do a hundred words a minute or more.

Typing achieved, I had to find some other skill to master. Later, I realized that I had a good basic knowledge of Spanish. At least I could carry on a conversation. My understanding of grammar left something to be desired.

Mrs. Hernandez was back from Miami, and she was vibrant. Visiting her relatives had done her a world of good. She told us that more and more Cubans were continually fleeing to Miami.

She told us that there were now parts of the city where Spanish was the only language heard. Until the mess with Castro was taken care of, it wouldn't change. She thought it might be as long as five years until most people could return to Cuba.

That sounded like a long time to be in exile. Then I remembered the outcomes of World War II and other wars and thought they might be lucky if it was only five years. On a more cheerful note, all this conversation was in Spanish and was very rapid. Even Mary, who didn't understand the gist of the conversation, understood the words. She told us they should call a taxi if they wanted to go home. Eddie told her it would have to be a water taxi.

She replied, "Then Mr. Jingles could take them home!"

Dad had some interesting news at dinner. He had inquired about the ownership of the four houses on Bellefontaine Island. They had all been for sale for back taxes. He had purchased them for five hundred dollars each. We now owned the entire island!

We planned to check the houses out this Saturday. We would probably have to tear them down and build one cottage. It also brought up what we were going to do with the boathouse. It was way oversized for one family's boat or boats, but now we didn't want to sell it and share our island.

After dinner and helping with the cleanup, I finished typing more copies of the last Blackhoof papers. Tomorrow Mr. Redfoot will be stopping by our house. We had been told to expect him around four o'clock, so I would be home from school.

That night I didn't feel like reading. I was thinking about summer fun at the lake with a speedboat and a new cottage to stay at; this balanced against working on a steamship for the summer and seeing the world. I fell asleep quickly. Having to get up and go to school left me tired.

Chapter 2

At least, that's what I thought when I woke up on Tuesday.

The boilers must have been working overtime because the school was so warm it was hard to stay awake. All the teachers knew this, so they worked with us.

As Mr. Hurley said, "If I nod off while giving a lecture, it must be terrible listening to it."

In the afternoon it had cooled down enough that we survived the day. I heard that Miss Bales set a record for how many kids she gave detention to.

At lunch, I found out that Cheryl and I were going on a double date with Tom and Tracy. They wanted to see a movie, and apparently, it would be better received by the colonel if we doubled for our first date.

Tom would be driving, so I could be in the backseat with Cheryl. If we didn't double date, we would have to get a ride with a parent. I bet the colonel hadn't thought of that.

After school, I went straight home. I was looking forward to meeting Mr. Redfoot. I wondered if he would be wearing full regalia. When the doorbell rang, I was first there.

A gentleman holding a briefcase was standing outside in an overcoat, fedora, and business suit. He introduced himself as Alex Redfoot of the Shawnee tribe. He asked if Richard Jackson was available.

I invited him in and introduced myself and the rest of the family. As he shook hands all the way around, I inspected him. He was nothing like I thought he would be.

He had high cheekbones and dark hair going grey. It looked like he had a good suntan for this time of year. His features were strong but not over the top. Since I knew he was of Indian heritage, I could see it. He would have been just another man on the street if I hadn't known.

We invited him to the kitchen and offered him coffee. He turned it down, explaining he wanted to see the items and didn't want any liquids near while examining them. I had set the box out on the kitchen counter. Mum had picked up several pairs of disposable white cotton gloves at the pharmacy. Mr. Redfoot and I donned a pair each.

I opened the container and set each of the medals out on the table. He extracted the photographs that had been sent to him from his briefcase. Before he started, he said a phrase that I didn't understand since it wasn't in English, but that wasn't a surprise.

He explained, "I was afraid I was on a fool's mission. I will check everything, but I know it is real. I was giving thanks."

He then carefully examined everything, even to the extent of pulling a magnifying glass out of his case. He compared everything to our photographs and then to another set he had brought. He explained that these were pictures of known examples of the actual medals from various museums.

"No one museum has a collection of all the medals. They are individually rare. As a collection, I can't even begin to guess."

He then proceeded to review the letters. I gave him a typed copy of each of the letters. He asked who had done this. When I explained that I had read and typed out the copies, he just nodded his head and continued his review.

He looked at each of the letters, which he compared to photographs of similar documents signed by each author.

He showed us other known copies of the various signatures that, in every case, matched the signer of each letter but that a secretary had written the main text.

He explained what was expected of this sort of letter. It wasn't a personal letter but a government letter. The signer would have stated a need for the letter and a general thought on its contents. He would have then reviewed the letter before signing it.

In the case of the king of England, it would have been presented for his signature, and he would have done so without even reading it. Running a large empire didn't give the king time to review anything involving natives outside his colonies.

After he had finished reviewing everything, he placed the medals back into the box. The box was removed from the kitchen table. Then he took us up on the offer of coffee. Eddie and Mary had lost interest and were watching TV by this time. Denny had chocolate milk while we drank our coffee.

Mr. Redfoot asked me, "Rick, according to your letter, you were the one who made this historical discovery. Would you tell me how it came about?"

I then related the entire chain of events. Wanting to write about the Ohio tribes and then learning of the *Bellefontaine Gazette* from Mrs. Rupert. How when reading it, I realized that if Chief Blackhoof had ever received the Jefferson Medal, it had probably been part of the theft.

I continued with the set of lucky circumstances that had me at the Manary Blockhouse and discovering the hidden compartment.

"Rick, I think the Shawnee were the lucky ones. The discovery was lucky but being found by someone of your ethics is the truly lucky portion. I have to ask you again. What would you like from this?"

"I have thought this through and discussed it with my parents. The satisfaction of returning this treasure to where it belongs is all I desire."

"Have you thought about how it should be handed over and the discovery made public?"

"We thought," sweeping my hand around to indicate the whole family, "that we would have my parents hand them to you in our lawyer's office tomorrow. That way, it would be a witnessed, signed transaction. No question that we are giving this to the Shawnee tribe and not a personal gift to Mr. Alex Redfoot. No offense meant, but I realized after reading about Captain Lewis that the white man does not have a monopoly on dishonest people."

"None taken. Actually, I feel more comfortable doing it that way. This keeps everything honest and above board. I will have a signed and witnessed handover to the tribal elders, so I cannot be accused of any misconduct later. These are worth a fortune on the collectors' market."

"How will you announce the discovery?" Dad inquired.

"We will tell the world we found them in our archives. We just won't tell how long they were there. Since your letter, we checked, and we have a box marked Blackhoof that contains some of his possessions."

"We will state that we recently opened the box and found these in the contents. Not specifying the contents were placed there several days earlier. This will keep all the other potential claimants at bay."

Mr. Redfoot continued, "I think the Shawnee owe Mrs. Rupert a small debt. Do you think she would like to have a true trade tomahawk and a peace pipe?"

"She would be thrilled. How will you explain to her why she is receiving it?"

"It will be a vague letter stating that it is for her work in preserving the tribal history of the Shawnee Indians in Ohio. There will be a letter of authenticity for each item and the thank you letter signed by our principal chief."

After those arrangements, my parents will meet Mr. Redfoot at Eugene Burke's office. As he was leaving, he handed each of us his business card.

"I should have done this when I first arrived."

The card read "Chief Alexander Redfoot, Shawnee Tribe, Head Curator, Shawnee Tribe Heritage, and Cultural Museum".

That evening, I read more about Natty, Uncas, and Chingachgook. It was a shame that Wah-ta-Wah died.

Chapter 3

Tuesday was a bright clear day, a wonderful day to be alive. It was still the middle of winter, but there was a hint of warmth in the air. Dad called this the January thaw. I ran for my full five miles and could tell it. The winter downtime had hurt my stamina.

At breakfast, we discussed our day. Mum and Dad visited our lawyer's office to turn over the Shawnee artifacts. After that, they had to attend a closing on another unit that we had purchased. Later in the day, they were jointly interviewing several young ladies to staff the office downtown.

Dad had tried to take care of the office himself, but he had to be out maintaining units, clearing new units, or looking for housing to purchase. He was rarely in the office. This defeated the purpose of the office. Two part-time employees took care of electrical and plumbing issues.

The family was still doing the cleanups and painting new units, but that was getting to be a bit much. Denny had stepped up and was making himself some serious money helping Dad on the weekends and after school. One weekend Dad paid him fifteen dollars for all his help.

He was spending some of his money on new clothes. He was in junior high, where the boys wore blue jeans and checked shirts. He was looking increasingly preppy with khakis, pinstripe shirts, and a pullover sweater. The number of telephone calls for him from girls had also increased.

The only interesting thing in school was when I made a mistake in World History. The question was, "What is the old name of Istanbul?"

I replied, "Baghdad."

I was accused of reading too many *Arabian Nights*. I had to blush on that one.

At lunch, we talked about the upcoming double date on Friday. This took us a minute. After that, the two Toms and I talked about basketball. Ohio State was in a rebuilding year. We figured they would do good to break even for the season.

They did have a fairly good forward by the name of Bob Knight. He was okay, probably one of those who would play basketball in college, and then you would never hear of him again.

While we discussed the fine points of Ohio State Basketball, the girls discussed what they would be wearing on Friday. I half-listened. It was interesting. I never knew it was so important to wear the right clothes at the right time. Sure, a tux for prom, a suit, and a tie for other special events, but anything else clothes were just clothes.

After school, I returned home to a different world. My parents were sitting in the kitchen, and my father looked like hell. There was no other way to put it. Something had hit him emotionally and hit him hard.

Mum looked up as I entered the door and said, "Jack just learned his father has died."

I didn't know what to say.

Dad looked up, so I did say, "Sorry, Dad."

I didn't know my grandfather Ross Jackson. He lived in Princeton, Indiana, where he ran and owned a feed mill until he retired. My grandmother Anna and Ross had divorced in the early 1920s. He then married a lady named Florence and had two sons named Ross Junior and James with him. They would be in their mid to late twenties now.

She didn't want any of his sons from his first marriage around, so we had never visited. I understand that after the war, Mum and Dad and I lived with them for a summer, but I remember nothing about it. Mum says Florence never made her welcome, and she was glad to leave.

Dad and his father had not spoken in almost ten years, but it still hit Dad hard. At least Florence had called and let him know. From what I had been told about her, she might not have. The funeral was on Friday, and we would be going. We would drive over on Thursday, stay in a hotel, attend the funeral on Friday, and return home late Friday night.

I know it was selfish, but my first thought was that my date with Cheryl was ruined. As soon as I thought that, I set it aside. The date was just delayed. The family was more important than my date. Dad needed us with him so we would be there.

I did call Cheryl and let her know what was going on. She sounded a little disappointed but understood.

At dinner, Dad explained to everyone his family situation. We would attend the funeral but not spend time with his stepmother or stepbrothers. After dinner, he took me aside.

"The other kids won't notice, but none of my other brothers will be there."

"Why is that?"

"There is no way to sugarcoat this. I am the only natural son of Ross Jackson by Anna Jackson. She and Ross's marriage was truly one of convenience. I don't think they even liked each other."

"Why did they get married?"

"She was pregnant with their child. They got married, and then the child, Cloyd, died from influenza, which was quite common in those days. The child was the only reason they got married, and when he died, what little semblance of marriage they had died. They stayed together because divorce was almost impossible early in the century."

"How do you know that you are Ross's son?"

"Blood tests, and he acknowledged it. They tried to make a go of it at one point. It didn't work out, and they were finally divorced in 1927. I was seven years old at the time and remembered us packing and leaving.

"We went from a nice house in Princeton, Indiana, to a shack outside Patalaska, Ohio. That was the beginning of hard years for us. The Depression hit soon after. Ross did send money, and Mom worked, but we never had anything."

"Ross got remarried in 1930. Anna remarried in 1932, and I never got along with her new husband, Jim Warren. He is Wally and Jim's father. After the war, Mum and I needed a place to stay until I could find work. Jim Warren wouldn't let me stay at his house. I called Ross, and he let us come over Florence's objections."

"What was Florence's problem?"

"Money. Granddad Ross's feed mill was worth a lot in those days. She wanted it all for her sons."

That explained why I never really knew my American grandparents. Grandma Anna would come to our house when she was alive; now, I understand why we didn't go to hers. Granddad Ross never visited us. What a messed-up family my dad had.

I didn't know my English grandparents because they were so far away. They still sent packages to us kids on Christmas and birthdays. There would be a knit item from Grandma Newman. These were always a hoot since she didn't know our sizes. There would be a book, English candy, and, best of all, English comics. I loved *Beano*.

Thinking of the *Beano* comics made me pull out my old ones and reread them. I needed some lighter thoughts tonight. I had to laugh at the antics of the *Golliwogs*.

Chapter 4

Wednesday started drearily. All my classes seemed slow, no matter how busy I kept. Mum had given each of us boys a note for our school offices to let them know we would be out Thursday and Friday. The only good thing on Wednesday was lunchtime.

Each of the kids there said words of sympathy. Cheryl had talked to Tracy about our double date, and word had spread. I told them I didn't know my grandfather, having not seen him since I was little. One neat thing was that Tammy Woodstock had joined us and sat next to Tom Wilson. I guess his serious side was working!

I told everyone about our plans and that we would return on Saturday.

Tom Morton asked, "Could we do an afternoon matinee on Sunday?"

I replied, "I don't see why not. I'll check at home to be certain but let's plan on it if everyone can go."

I hadn't planned to start something but the next thing I know, Tom and Tammy are included in our plans. The backseat would be crowded with four of us in the back. This created major dress questions. So many that Tom Wilson and Tammy changed seats so the girls could plan their apparel.

Tom Wilson reverted to the class clown. He pointed out that Mr. Watkins's tenth-grade English teacher room is on the ground floor. His desk, if tipped sideways, would fit through one of the classroom windows. He had hall duty at lunchtime. If he were distracted, several people could hand his desk out the window to others waiting. Then the desk could be taken anywhere.

Now, this was all theoretical discussion, of course. We debated what to do with the desk.

Tom Morton came up with, "One of the emergency exits for the auditorium is just down the way. If someone opened that door, we could leave it at the center of the stage."

Then I had to open my big fat mouth. "We could do it before a school assembly. It would be close timing, but wouldn't it be neat if the desk sat there when they opened the curtains."

That led to further planning questions. How many people would it take? We figured six; two in the classroom, two outside, and one person to open the auditorium door. Then there would be one person to ensure that Mr. Watkins didn't come back into the classroom. The two in the classroom would go out of the window and help move the desk.

There was a concern about the desk drawers. It was a big old wooden desk with three drawers on each side and a center drawer for pens and pencils. We didn't want those to come open and dump their contents. We decided to take the drawers out and leave them if they were not locked. Any that were locked would stay as they wouldn't be in danger of coming open.

We decided we had a plan. Not that we would ever do such a thing, but it was neat to think of it. With a plan this well thought out, what could go wrong?

We got so engrossed in our planning that we hadn't noticed that the girls were listening. Their dress plans had been settled quickly.

Tammy said, "I'll be in the hall. I'll let out a screech if Mr. Watkins starts towards his room. When he asks, "I'll tell him I saw a mouse."

Tracy joined with, "I'll be at the auditorium door."

Then Cheryl added, "Rick and I can be in the classroom to lower the desk to the two Toms."

Tammy then asked, "What if the window won't open?"

Oops!

Tom Wilson volunteered, "They open them every spring when it gets warm, so we know they work, but I will test it the morning of."

So, we had a plan and team in place. Not that we ever intended to do anything. At least, that's what I thought at the time.

We had canceled Spanish that night as we all had to pack for our trip on Thursday. Dad called a hotel he knew of in Princeton and made reservations for two rooms. He also went down to the Sohio station and picked up the latest road maps for Ohio and Indiana to plan our trip.

It looked like we would be taking good old US Route 40 through Indianapolis, then turning south at Terra Haute on US 41, going through Vincennes, and making a left turn on Indiana 64 to go to Princeton.

At dinner, I asked if there was any problem with me going to the movies on Sunday afternoon. There wasn't, so I called Cheryl to let her know after dinner. She would talk to everyone else.

That night I started a new series of two books that I had checked out of the library at school. They were based on a concept used during the nineteenth century.

It was the story of people registered at birth in a business venture or trust where all dividends go to a charity. When only one member remained alive, they would receive the entire principle, which would be a fortune.

In this story, there was a three-year registration period, so there was a three-year variance in the entrants' ages. The list of all entered was made public. No one paid attention for the first fifty years.

It started to get interesting as the number alive dwindled. After seventy-five years, it started to get dangerous. At ninety years, it was only plain murderous. The participants by this time were too old and decrepit to do anything, but their heirs were continually active. Today these are officially banned. I did wonder what happened unofficially.

Chapter 5

Thursday, we were up and on our way after a quick breakfast. It would be a long day. As we traveled along Route 40 that day, I pointed out sites from my summer vacation. Where the sheriff had stopped me in Urbana, the parade route followed in Springfield, spots I had slept in fields along the way. Denny and Eddie paid attention to all this. I don't think my trip seemed real to them until I could show them where I had been.

Of course, we counted cows along the way. You lost your count when you passed a cemetery. Since Eddie and Mary were in the middle, it was decided by Mum that Mary would lose her count for any on the left and Eddie on the right.

That would give either Mary and Denny the same count or Eddie and me. That would be decided by each of us having a bonus spot. Mine was a firehouse. Denny's a high school, Eddie a grade school, and Mary a service station. I think Mum stacked the deck for Mary.

We stopped for lunch in Indianapolis at a new hamburger chain named McDonald's. Their burgers were fairly good with their special sauce. It is a shame they didn't have any indoor seating. We were ready to get out of the car by then.

We did stop at a Sinclair gas station where a kid filled the gas tank, checked the air in the tires, added a quart of oil, and cleaned the windows. We all used the restrooms there. Dad paid and gave a quarter as a tip. Mum thought this was too much but didn't make much of it.

We made it to Vincennes at around three o'clock. It had been a long day, and we still had a way to go. I noticed a war memorial at the courthouse. It was one of the tallest ones I had seen outside a large city like Columbus or Indianapolis. We were just past it when Dad had to stop for a pedestrian in a crosswalk.

As we stopped, I looked to my right. I was sitting behind Mum on her side of the car. Looking up slightly, I saw smoke pouring out of a partially open window.

"Dad, stop the car. There is a fire!"

I exited our car as quickly as I could. I checked out what was in front of me. There was an open jewelry store and a doorway that appeared to open to stairs that went to the apartments above the store.

Eddie had got out behind me. I gave him the change in my pocket and pointed him toward a payphone on the corner.

"Call the fire department. Tell them you are across from the courthouse."

He ran off. Denny had followed Eddie out of the car. I told him, "Get the people out of the store."

I ran over to the door that appeared to open to a staircase. It did, and I ran up the stairs two steps at a time. Two doors opened to rooms over the jewelry store. I laid my hand on the first door. It was hot. The paint on the outside of the door was starting to bubble.

I ran to the next door and pounded on it. No one answered immediately, so I pounded harder and shook the doorknob. The door came open, and a young lady with an infant in her arms was standing there. I didn't give her a chance to say anything,

"There is a fire, and we have to get out."

I started to pull her out the door.

She said, "Wait for my daughter."

I rushed into the apartment; there was a three-year-old watching TV. I grabbed her and ran for the door. The mother had already started down the hall after she saw I had the girl. I could see smoke coming from the other door. It was about to burn through.

I took running strides and passed the door. As we were about halfway down the stairs, there was a roar as the fire burned through the door and had new oxygen available. We came out of the building and ran across the street. Dad had pulled the car around and parked on the other side. He was just getting out. The whole incident would take longer to tell than it took me to go up and down those stairs.

We came to a stop in the car. The young woman looked like she didn't understand what was happening. It must have been a shock. A stranger almost drags you out of your home, and it explodes in flame.

The three-year-old I was still holding wanted her Mommy and wanted her now! Mum took the infant, and the young lady picked up her daughter. We could hear the sirens as the firetrucks approached.

Denny came up and reported, "I cleared the store. An old man in the back didn't believe me, so I carried him out."

That made me do a double-take as I realized my middle brother was not so little anymore.

Eddie told me, "I called the fireman as you wanted. Can I keep the rest of the change?"

A police car came screaming up to the fire. Lights, sirens, and tires were squealing. When the cop hit the brakes, I didn't know if he could stop or not. He stopped, jumped out of his cruiser, and looked around. He saw us and ran towards us. The young lady ran to him. From the way they hugged, I figured out they were married.

They pulled apart. He had taken the three-year-old, and she retrieved the baby from Mum. She told her husband what had gone on. Just as she was telling him, the interior of the building collapsed. This started a whole new pillar of flame. Firemen were unrolling the hose and hooking it up as fast as possible.

I heard someone yell, "Turn in a general alarm. We will need every unit in town."

A man in a business suit joined us. It was the young lady's father. He introduced himself as Jim Hobbs, and this was his daughter Melissa and her husband, Bill Rose. The little girl was Ruth and her baby brother James.

By this time, Mary had come out of the car and was sharing her doll baby with Ruth. As little kids can do, they shrugged the whole thing off and decided it was teatime.

Melissa sobbed as she said, "Bill, what are we going to do? We didn't have much, but we've lost it all."

Bill replied, "Dear, remember when you insisted that we buy a renters policy for our apartment, and I didn't think we needed it. You were right, and I was wrong. Thank goodness we bought it."

Bill turned to Jim and asked, "Is it okay if I take Melissa and the kids to your house."

"Of course it is. Martha would kill me if they went anywhere else."

The family went to the police car and got in. I noticed that Ruth had acquired a doll baby. I asked Mary, "Do you know she has your doll?"

"I gave it to her; she lost her dolls in the fire, and she needs one now."

"Good move, squirt. I will buy you another one."

Maybe she isn't the spoiled brat I thought she was. Well, at times, she was, but she was going to be okay.

The whole street by now was a tangle of hoses. It didn't appear that we would be leaving for a long time.

Jim turned to us and said, "Now, what are your names? You have saved my daughter and her family, and I don't even know you yet."

Dad introduced us all.

About that time, a man in a suit came up. He asked, "Mr. Mayor, I'm told these people saw the fire and helped everyone out. I will need their statements. We are treating this as arson until we know differently."

Sergeant Dixon was businesslike in his questions but very polite at the same time. It was quickly established that I saw the fire, arranged for the call, had the store vacated, and brought the young family out of the burning building. Somehow it all sounded like more than it was.

By this time, a small group of people was standing around us. One stood out. I knew the type. Who else goes around with a cameraman taking pictures of everything? He stepped forward after Sergeant Dixon was finished. He introduced himself as John Taggart of the *Indiana Sun-Commercial,* the local paper.

Before he could even ask the first question, Mayor Hobbs told him to be nice to the heroes. The mayor put so much force into that statement it made you wonder about their relationship.

It sounded more like, "Be nice, or I will rip your heart out!"

Mr. Taggart didn't seem intimidated but was gentle in his questions anyway. While we were being questioned, the photographer had us three boys pose for a picture. Mr. Taggart wanted to know where we were from and what we were doing in town. When he, the mayor, and everyone standing around heard that we were on the way to our grandfather's funeral, they backed off and quieted down.

Dad handed the newsman his card and told him, "We will be home late Saturday."

Dad turned to the mayor and continued, "Is there any way we could get our car out and get moving? It is getting late, and we need to get to Princeton."

The mayor hustled over to the fire chief, and we shortly were on our way to Princeton.

Of course, the kids chattered like crazy about the fire and what we had done. Even though we were all there and watched what each other had done, it still had to be replayed.

Dad commented, "Rick, this is the first time I have seen you in action. I know of all the things you have done, but never have I seen anyone look at a situation and take the right actions as quickly as you did."

"Thanks, Dad," I replied. "When I saw a problem, the world seemed to slow down as I looked around. When I saw what needed to be done, things started moving quickly again."

Mum chimed in, "During the war, we saw that all the time. Some people can process events faster than others. Normally we don't notice it, but when lives are on the line and seconds count, those who react stand out."

After that initial outburst of talk, we all became quiet. Eddie fell asleep, and Denny looked tired. I felt like I had run a marathon and just wanted to sit. When we got to the hotel in Princeton, we checked in, went to bed, and went to sleep.

Chapter 6

We had two rooms with double beds. Mum, Dad, and Mary in one room, Denny, Eddie, and I in the other. After getting cleaned up, we went down for breakfast. We were all slow starters this morning. I think yesterday's traveling and the fire took a lot out of us.

When we were finished, it was still early. Visiting hours at the funeral home started at ten, and the funeral was at one. To help pass the time, Dad took us on a tour of Princeton. It was a nice town, but not that big. The most interesting sight was the Jackson Feed Mill. What was interesting was that a crew was painting over the name on the side of the building.

Dad stopped and asked them what was going on. One of the men told him that the mill had been sold to some large corporation and that the name was changing. Dad shared this with Mum, and she asked him if that bothered him. He told her that it didn't. He had never counted on receiving anything from his father.

After riding around for almost an hour, we returned to the hotel and changed into suits and ties. Mum came out in a nice dress, a dark blue.

She turned around and asked, "Do I look okay?"

All of us guys said yes.

Mary said, "Mum, the seam on your left stocking is not straight."

We all looked, and of course, the kid was right.

"Thank you, Mary. We women have to stick together. Men don't notice anything."

Mary looked over, stamped her foot, and said, "Men!"

Thus, the training of another woman started. Now I know why men don't stand a chance.

We signed the guest register at the funeral parlor. There was a small crowd already. Ross had been in business in Princeton for many years. He was continually active in town affairs and was well known.

From the comments, I heard everyone liked him. Several farmers told of how he had carried them through some tough times.

The recent widow, Florence, was there dressed in black. When she saw Mum and Dad, she came right over. She thanked them for coming. She kissed Mum on the cheek and hugged Dad. She was introduced to each of us. She told Mary she was darling.

She introduced two very well-dressed men who had joined her. They were Ross Junior and James, her sons by Ross. They didn't seem extremely interested in meeting us. Indifference would describe their attitude. They would be my half-uncles, but I suspected I would never be close to them.

Dad started, "I see the feed mill has been sold."

James quickly asked, "What business is it of yours?"

No, I wouldn't be close to them.

"Why, none of my business. I was just commenting," replied Dad.

If one knew what to look for, you would have seen the tightening of Mum's jaw.

"Just want to make sure that you are not trying to claim something that isn't yours," said my surly uncle.

Ross touched his arm and said, "Jim, you don't need to start trouble where there isn't any. There are the Bannermans. We need to say hello."

They left without any other comments.

Florence shook her head sadly. "Jack, I'm sorry. This has been a very rough time for us. Ross was diagnosed with cancer just a month ago. He went quickly. Then we just found out that the feed store was deeply in trouble. Ross had to write off too many bad debts over the years."

"The last straw was when the bank called his loan the day he died. We had to arrange a quick sale to pay everything off. We lost a lot of money. There is just enough to pay off the loans. The house is paid for, so I have that. Other than that, I have nothing but social security. The boys will have to find work somewhere. It won't be easy on them as they have never held a job."

Wow! What had they been doing all their lives? It may have been impolite, but I asked Florence.

"They have always had the money at hand, so they played golf, tennis, raced cars, went to dinner and shows in Evansville, the things that young men of means have always done."

"Fops," Mum commented.

No one asked her what a fop was, so it dropped.

Dad was approached by the funeral director, who asked to speak to him for a minute. Dad stepped aside to listen, nodded his head, and came back.

"Rick, you and I will be pallbearers."

As Dad was listening, the funeral director handed him an envelope which Dad slid into his inside jacket pocket.

We paid our respects at the casket and then left. We went back to a restaurant next to the hotel.

During lunch, Mum asked, "What was that envelope the funeral director slipped you?"

"I don't know; he just handed it to me without comment."

At that, Dad retrieved and looked at the envelope.

"It is from Dad's attorney's office."

As he was telling us, he opened the letter using a table knife as a letter opener. He read it through slowly, cleared his throat, and read it to us.

> "Dear Jack. I'm dying of cancer. As one of my sons, I want you to know I have always loved you and respected what you have done with your life. Because of my relationship with Anna, we never had the opportunity to be close.

Now, as I find I am dying much sooner than expected, I find that I'm not leaving the world as a successful businessman but as an overall failure. Somehow it doesn't mean that much right now.

You have probably met your two half-brothers by now. They aren't worth the gunpowder to blow them up. Florence had her way of raising her young 'gentlemen'. Young louts are more like it.

When I found I was dying, I inquired about how you were doing in Bellefontaine. It was very pleasing to learn that you and Peg are doing well and that your children have such good reputations. You and yours will have to carry on the good Jackson name. I know those other two won't.

The only thing I can leave you is a family mystery. There is a small container buried twenty-five feet from the northwest corner of the San Toy jail. It is down about four feet. Maybe you can figure out what it means. It is connected with the Rowlands. I and my father, John, both studied it for years and could not come up with what it was talking about. It may be worth something, and it may be nothing. Go with God, your father.

Ross Jackson."

That was the only time that I saw a tear in my father's eye.

We attended the funeral and laid my grandfather to rest. It was a dull January day, very appropriate for a funeral. Attractive young ladies there accompanied my two uncles.

As we were leaving, I heard one of the women tell Uncle James, "Well, call me if you can come up with the money to go out. If not, I will find someone else."

Florence came over and spoke to Mum and Dad.

"Jack and Peg, I know I haven't always been the kindest to you. However, we are family and need to pull together during this financial emergency. When you stop by, I want to talk to you about a loan."

Dad and Mum exchanged looks. Even I could understand what was said.

Dad replied to Florence. "I'm so sorry we won't be stopping by the house. We have to get back to Bellefontaine as soon as we can. Why don't you write with what you need, and I will see if we can help?"

She had no choice but to accept what Dad told her. She gave a weak smile and thanked us once again for coming to the funeral. We headed to our car, which was parked next to the hearse. It blocked the line of sight from other cars. As we were getting in our car, we all heard very clearly.

"Mother, did you get the money? If not, we will have to cancel our trip to Europe!"

We piled into our car and returned to the hotel. We went upstairs and packed while Dad checked us out.

Once we were in the car, he told us, "We will get a room in Vincennes. It is too long of a drive to try to make it home tonight."

Mary made the only comment about Ross's family.

"That lady didn't smell very nice at all."

Dad snorted and chuckled, and that was the end of that.

We got to Vincennes in good time and found a room at a motel outside of town. We ate dinner at a little diner across the street. We watched TV on the little sets in our room.

I read more about life gambles and how the descendants got greedier and greedier as they got closer to the final payout. I wouldn't have believed family could be like that at one time. Now I knew better.

Chapter 7

Saturday morning, after breakfast at the diner, we headed home. We got to downtown Vincennes near where the fire was, when a police car turned on its lights behind Dad.

He muttered, "What now?" while pulling over."

The policeman was Bill Rose from yesterday. He was all smiles, "Sorry if I scared you, folks. The mayor had us on the lookout for you. He would like to speak to you at his house if it wouldn't be too much of an imposition."

There was no reason not to, and our trip was ahead of schedule, so we followed the police car to the mayor's house. The patrolman must have called ahead because the family was waiting at the door.

We were welcomed in like favored members of the family. After taking our hats and coats, we settled into the kitchen with our choice of coffee or hot chocolate. Mayor Hobbs handed us each a copy of the *Indiana Sun-Commercial*. The headline was, "Deadly Fire Kills".

The story proceeded to tell that one person didn't make it out of that inferno. He was in the first room. I must have got a sick look on my face because the mayor spoke up.

"Rick, Mr. da Costa was known to smoke in bed and was an advanced alcoholic. He was dead before you ever went up those stairs."

I still wondered.

Mum gasped, "Rick, have you looked at the pictures?"

As I said, "No," I looked at the front-page picture. I never noticed, but the *Sun- Commercial* photographer must have been there when I came out of that building. The picture showed me coming out of the doorway with the girl in my arms.

I was looking up, so it was a good shot of my face. Behind me, smoke was curling up the doorframe behind me, and flames were shooting down the stairs.

Other than the fact it was me, it was the most incredible action shot I have ever seen. The look on my face was of such intense concentration there is no doubt I would have run through a brick wall to get out of there. Further inside the paper were additional pictures of my brothers and me.

When the reporter interviewed us, I gave a concise description of what occurred when I went upstairs. He asked how I knew to check the doors for heat before opening them. I told him about Boy Scout training. Eddie let him know that I had just passed Eagle. That was in the paper.

Mr. Hobbs informed us that the whole family would receive the keys to the city of Vincennes and be recommended for our actions for an Indiana State Award of Heroism. They would keep us posted on events and would like us to come back for the presentations. He also told us the photograph was so dramatic that the AP had picked it up, and the story would be in many newspapers. Oh, joy!

Mary and Ruth played with dolls at the other end of the table. Melissa told us she had hunted for a Barbie Doll to replace Mary's. She couldn't find them anywhere. When she inquired about a local store carrying the Mattel brand, they made a phone call and found out that our area was a test market. Sales in the test area had been tremendous so that the doll would be released nationwide in March.

Mary heard all this and said, "It's alright. I have other dolls at home. Rick promised he would buy me one when he could. I know he will."

Of course, I had to reaffirm the promise, which was no problem. As we got ready to leave, the two little girls hugged and promised to write to each other. Their Mums exchanged addresses.

On the way out of town, we were accompanied by the police with lights and sirens. After that quick trip, the rest of the drive seemed slow. While driving, I asked Dad about the Rowlands that Ross had referred to in his letter.

"They are relatives of your grandmother Anna. Though I suppose with the way families intermarried back then, it could be both sides. Anyway, John Rowland's brother is your great-great-great-grandfather."

Dad continued, "John was a Rocky Mountain fur trader in the early 1820s. He moved to what is now New Mexico in 1823. He and his business partner William Workman got tangled up in several attempts to overthrow the Spanish there. In 1840 they were connected somehow to the Republic of Texas. They were such known troublemakers the Spanish governor of Santa Fe threw them out.

"Rather than heading back to the United States, they led the first Americans into California. They ended up with large land grants, but none of that is still in the family except for about a hundred acres in the City of Industry, which the direct descendants own. You now know as much as I do.

"When we get a chance, we will dig this up, whatever it is."

"Dad, won't they object if we start digging holes right outside of the town jail?"

"Hardly, Rick. It is a ghost town. That is another story for later."

Talk about the fire, the funeral, the family we had never met before, and what was buried in San Toy kept us occupied for the whole trip home. It was late when we arrived back in Bellefontaine.

Sunday, we went to church as a family. Cheryl and her parents were there. We didn't have a chance to talk.

After lunch, I went over to Tom Morton's, and we piled in his car and went to pick everyone up. We went directly to the movie. It was a great action story, and the girls loved Cary Grant, so all was well. We stopped at Don's for a hamburger after the movie.

Cheryl had been smiling and happy until we arrived at the restaurant.

"Rick, I have been dreading this. Dad got word late Wednesday. We knew his posting here was only temporary. He was up for promotion. It requires Congressional approval. Congress was holding up all promotions over some sort of budget dispute. Because of this, Dad couldn't go to his new command. They had a problem with the existing commander in Bellefontaine and needed a temporary replacement.

"Dad was given the assignment as squadron commander here, which is normally a major's or lieutenant colonel's slot. He was supposed to take over a fighter group in California, but it was all messed up with the timing. So now he has been appointed to a job in the Pentagon. He reports next week, and Mom and I will follow up in two weeks. This is the life of an Air Force brat. This will be the sixth time I have moved since the first grade."

The rest of the date was almost in a haze. I was numb. Would I never have a regular girlfriend?

I shared the Hawthorn's impending move with my parents. They didn't appear to think this was the disaster that I saw. Mum wanted to talk about who we should invite to my Eagle ceremony, which was coming up in two weeks.

Chapter 8

Monday was hectic. The morning started at home with the usual routine. When I hit the school door, it began. The *Columbus Dispatch* had picked up the Vincennes fire story in its supplement. The picture of me carrying out Ruth took up half the page. There was no doubt that it was me. Someone had already placed a copy of the paper in my trophy case.

Kids kept coming up to me and wanting to know the full story. Why I don't know. If they had read the paper, they would know the full story. What topped the cake was when I was asked to autograph a copy of the paper. I did it, but this was getting out of hand.

For one of the few times in my life, I was glad to hear the bell ring to start class. That lasted for about two minutes. Every teacher had to recognize me and my heroic feat. For God's sake! I carried a little kid down the stairs!

Lunch was a mixed bag. The gang wanted to talk about the fire and Cheryl's leaving. We agreed that it sucked having to leave in the middle of the school year. That part didn't seem to bother Cheryl. She had done that many times.

It was leaving people behind that bothered her. I liked to think that leaving me was on that list. We tried to console her by pointing out that we would leave many people behind as we got older, like when we graduated high school and college.

I guess it is easier to say than life because she didn't look any more cheerful. We agreed that we would write her a weekly group letter updating her on how the class fared this year. We knew it would be pointless to continue it after that, but it would give her some closure on this episode in her life.

I won't say school lessons themselves were boring, but when you are constantly ahead, everything being presented is blasé. The sense of discovery in learning was mostly in the study hall. I had few connections with my classmates. I was working at a different level than they were. While they were memorizing facts for a test, I was delving into the whys of events.

After reading additional accounts, what was presented as straightforward in our textbooks was seldom straightforward. There were fifteen different interpretations if I read ten accounts of an event.

I found that "why" something happened varied more than "what" happened. Even what happened seemed to be more an average of the witnesses rather than concrete facts.

I reread the *Columbus Dispatch* story with this in mind. They described the photograph of me coming out of the stairwell as focused and resolved on saving the child. I remember very clearly feeling relief that I hadn't stumbled coming down the stairs.

When I walked into the house after school, the first words out of Mum were "I'm glad you're here. George Weaver will be here shortly for an interview."

"I will like that. There is an issue I need to clear up."

Mum inquired about it. Why did she laugh when I told her?

"You think people will listen to your version of events? The picture says it all. You are a brave lad saving that young girl. Anything else will be viewed as false modesty."

When Mr. Weaver showed up, the conversation and interview went exactly as she predicted. He heard me out and then shook his head.

"Rick, live with it. You did a heroic deed. We need our heroes."

That ended my quest for truth in reporting. Like beauty, it appeared to be in the eye of the beholder.

As the interview ended, Mary came in and said, "*¿Cómo estás, hermano.*"

"*Estoy bien, hermana pequeña,*" I replied absently.

Mr. Weaver asked, "Does your whole family speak Spanish?"

"Just the kids are formally studying," Mum told him.

This led to a discussion of why, where we were learning, who our teacher was, and all the other details. He told us that it could be an interesting piece of local interest. He would stop over and speak to Mrs. Hernandez. When he learned, she was Cuban, you could see the wheels turn. Mr. Weaver saw himself as Our Man in Havana!

For dinner, Mum made several pizzas. This was a new addition to our meal list. It was good, but the anchovies were too salty. Maybe she could skip them next time. Unfortunately, Dad liked them, so I think the best we would get is one pie with and one without.

After dinner, Mum got serious about the invitation list for my Eagle ceremony. We listed all the members of my Scout troop, family, friends, higher-level Scouters, and local politicians. It was also traditional to send an invitation to the President of the United States.

Of course, he would never attend, but you would get a nice form letter. This also went for the governor of Ohio and all the other county, state, and federal political offices that we cared to include. The more local the office, the more likely they would attend.

The only addition to our list that wasn't normal was an announcement and invitation to my godmother, now Elizabeth II, Queen of England. Of course, she wouldn't be there, but we hoped for a nice letter for my scrapbook. I remembered the thank you note I had received from the president. When I checked the address on it, it was different from the one given by the Scouts. We would use the one on the thank you note.

We included all the politicians who served us, including the governor, federal and state senators, and representatives. Also, the mayor of Bellefontaine. He might show up! As we were in the middle of this discussion, the phone rang.

It was our Scout Council executive. He asked for me. He had several questions to establish it was me in the newspaper story of the fire.

When I confirmed this, he told me, "It jumped out that you told them you knew to check the door for heat before opening and crediting your Scout training. We are going to put you in for a second Scout life-saving award."

"The one for using your Scouting skills in the car wreck is the Meritorious Action Award. The new one is the Honor Medal with Crossed Palms. It is for saving a life at great risk of your own. I got a call from the national office telling me to put you in for this.

When I told them your Eagle Court was coming up, I was ordered to do it on an expedited basis. Someone at Scout national headquarters has seen the photo and read the story," he ended.

When I related this to my parents, Dad laughed and said, "This is really good publicity for the Scouts; they will want to make the most out of it."

Well, that put me in my place. It was not all about me. That made me okay with the whole thing.

At bedtime, I started reading about Oscar, Peewee, Mother Thing, and Wormface. It was kind of juvenile but fun.

Tuesday started like any other day. The weather was halfway decent. It hadn't rained or snowed for a couple of days, and the sun had been out, so it was drying off. The temperature was in the mid-forties, so it was like a pre-spring day. After exercising, I was able to get out and run. I could tell how out of shape I was getting.

School went well. A few kids started calling me Fire Man, but it wasn't a big deal. I guess I was starting to get used to being the center of attention. I knew I was just another guy and nothing special. If they needed their heroes, so be it.

I knew a few kids over in Wapakoneta from Scout functions. They had met a local guy who was a real hero. He was a Korean

War combat pilot and was now a test pilot out at Edwards Air Force Base. They told me that from talking to him, they found that Neil Armstrong was the calmest, most understated guy they had ever met.

He acted just like a regular guy. I think a guy like that will be my model. He let his actions talk for him. No need to brag or be treated special. As if I would ever do anything as cool as to be a test pilot. Thinking of that reminded me that I could start working on my pilot's license next year.

At lunch, Tom Wilson told us he had heard from a friend in the office that there would be a school assembly on Friday. Tracy asked him why he had a friend in the office. He told her he spent so much time there that he talked to all the staff. Not my way of making friends. I wondered if he would get to know them in the booking center at the police station.

I mentioned that, and from there, the conversation went downhill as we all imagined the trouble Tom could get into. After having him appear before a war crimes tribunal for putting soap suds and green dye in the United Nations water fountains, we came to a stop. Tom acted as if the comments wounded him.

At least, I think that is why he held his hand over his heart as he fell off his chair. Of course, that brought Mr. Hurley over to check us out. I was getting to see that man too often.

After receiving a warning to settle down, Tom brought up a serious subject. Cheryl would be leaving soon. This assembly would be the last chance for this gang to steal Mr. Watkins's desk. That quieted things down nicely. I think we were all afraid to chicken out.

The next thing you know, we were solidifying our plans for the great heist. The two Toms would make certain that two of the windows would open, one for the desk and the other for the two in the room to come out. We all laughed that if we got caught, at least they couldn't make Cheryl stay for all the detention.

Chapter 9

A student from the office tracked me down as we were finishing lunch. Was I busted already? It was a guidance counselor, Mrs. Hawkins. She had been contacted by Warner Brothers Studio, at least the people who handled their tutoring program. They had been corresponding for several months.

What she had to say surprised the heck out of me.

"They are overly excited that you are going to be with them. We sent them samples of your work. They are always under pressure to show that they teach child actors. I think they see you as a showpiece. Since you will be having one-on-one tutoring, there will be no problem with them keeping you abreast of all your assignments and being able to finish up your school year on the set."

"The tutoring group claims if they had you for a year, they could complete your high school diploma. I thought they were bragging, but then they sent me the course syllabus and their tutor's credentials. If you worked at it, it could be done. However, that is if you spent a year. We will be happy if they can keep you up with your class.

"Having you ready for the end of the year would be a nice bonus for you, but I'm afraid that it would make the rest of the year boring. The State of Ohio still requires you to spend many days in the classroom," Mrs. Hawkins said.

"What if I tested out of the ninth grade while I was out there?" I asked.

"That would be different. You would have a certificate from the State of California, which the State of Ohio would recognize."

That is when I realized I had better slow down. This is one of those situations I had time to think about, so I should use it. The building wasn't on fire.

When I arrived home after school, Dad was waiting for me.

"Rick, I took your Civil War Colt to the gun shop. They examined it and test-fired it with a reduced load. It was fine, but you should never use a full powder load, no more than three-quarters of a load. Old steel can have impurities, and steel will stress crack with age. The cracks could be internal, so you would never know until the thing blew up in your hand."

"Dad, it sounds like I should only use it to complete the uniform and never load it."

"I would be most happy with that."

"I can't foresee any reason I would ever need it loaded."

Later in life, I would learn that you could seldom predict when you would need a weapon, and when you did, you needed it right there, right now, and ready to use.

Mrs. Hernandez showed up, and we talked about the latest news stories from Cuba. Castro's 26th of July Movement had overthrown Batista at the first of the year. Stories were now coming out of the aftermath. We were careful not to scare Mary, but it was ugly. The U.S. media was surprised that Castro was letting it be known that he was a Communist all along. I don't know where they were getting their information. We had known it for months.

After dinner, I talked to my parents about my visit with the guidance counselor. After discussion, we all agreed that I should go with the flow and take advantage of the opportunity as much as I could. In the worst case, I would return home current with my classwork. Best case, I would pass tests in California, finishing my freshman year.

During dinner, Mum and Dad informed us that they had hired a person to staff the office during the day. June Conroy will start tomorrow. She was in her early thirties, married with two children. She and her husband were new to the area from Columbus. He had just gotten a job as a supervisor out at DAB. Her previous work experience was as an office manager for a small real estate firm handling rental properties. She probably knew more about it than any of us.

Her hours would be 9:00 a.m. to 3:00 p.m. Monday through Friday and 9:00 a.m. till noon on Saturday. This allowed her to see her children off to school and be home when they returned. Mum had insisted her pay rate be the same as a man's. Dad would also keep the office open from 5:00 p.m. till 7:00 p.m. on Fridays for people who had to work.

I finished up my story that night. We had gone from travel within the solar system to interstellar and finally intergalactic. I had to look up the half-life of radium to know how long humans had to grow up. It looked like twenty-five thousand years or so. We would either have grown up or blown up by then.

The middle of the week arrived, and we started reviewing for semester exams. For me, this was more than boring. I could have taken the tests that day. To have to listen to a review was mind-numbing. I didn't even pretend in any of my classes.

I was two to three weeks ahead on everything. After this week, I will be almost six weeks ahead. That would mean I would've completed almost all the material I would miss while in Hollywood. I could do nothing out there and come back even with all my classes.

I hadn't any intention of that. I had decided to push it while I was out there and at least complete the school year. If the opportunity were presented, I would take the California final exams.

During lunch, the two Toms, we started calling them the Terrible Toms, let us know they had checked out the windows in Mr. Watkins's room and even oiled one with a squeak. I don't know where this will end up, but we most certainly would create a school legend. This was one I didn't want any credit for.

The rest of the afternoon flew by. They reviewed, and I worked. Miss Bales asked me after my last class how far along I was. She shook her head when I told her I was four weeks ahead.

"I know some schools in the east have what they call advanced placement classes. If you pass, some colleges will give you credit. Those would be perfect for you."

I took the time to explain to her about the tutoring situation with the studio. She told me I should push it as hard as I could. Her biggest concern would be that I got bored with school. That could be a big problem for everyone.

I should work at my own pace and get on with life. When she started teaching in the late 1930s, it was in a one-room schoolhouse in West Virginia. Since all the students were together, they could push as fast as they wanted.

She told me a surprising number of so-called normal students completed a year's work in half a school year if they were interested. The rules about graduation weren't as strict in those days. If they could pass their final exams, there wasn't a lot of concern about their grade progression. So, she was confident that if I wanted to push it, I could complete the ninth grade in California. That sounded good to me.

When I went home, we did the Spanish thing. It didn't seem like lessons anymore. We held a conversation. It just all happened to be in Spanish. Somewhere along the line, I realized that I was spending more time with my brothers and sister than most guys my age. I mean an hour a day with a four-year-old sister!

Chapter 10

After dinner, I cleaned up and put on my Scout uniform. Tonight, I was going to Springfield for the camporee planning meeting. Mr. Harris was punctual. On the way down, he wanted to talk about the fire. He wanted the details. How much smoke was coming out of the window when I first spotted the fire? How hot was the door? Did I have the palm of my whole hand flat or just touch it with my fingers?

I finally asked him why he wanted such fine detail. It turned out he was a volunteer fireman with the West Liberty Fire Department. He had never been in a multi-story office building fire and wondered how close his training was to reality. After I found that out, the trip was smooth as we talked our way to Springfield.

When we walked into the conference room, everyone stood and applauded me! I didn't know what to do, so I kind of waved and headed to the coffee pot. When in doubt, hide behind a cup of coffee!

The council Scout executive and council commissioner both pointedly shook my hand and told me that I was a fine representative of the movement.

I just thought I looked like a Christmas tree. The council commissioner had patches above his left shirt pocket. I had never paid attention to them before. There were four rows of three. They all looked like knots in different colors. Some of them even had several little metal badges with the Boy Scout or Cub Scout emblem on them.

He also had a leather necklace with four wooden beads on it. It was cool. I would have to see about getting one of those. Those with his red Philmont jacket and Smokey Bear hat with the First Class emblem made him as bright as any Christmas tree.

The meeting was brought to order. Mr. Tolson was there and gave an update on the Civil War re-enactors. It was going to be a full-blown encampment for them. They would have a full battery of four cannons present.

Enough Confederate re-enactors were coming so that they could do a mock skirmish. There would be enough black powder experts present that every boy in the camp would have an opportunity to fire a muzzleloader at least once.

It was mentioned that I would be the go-between the Scouts and the re-enactors. As Colonel Tolson put it, "Lieutenant Jackson will be our runner. While carrying out duties for the 6th Ohio Volunteers, he will be in the correct uniform."

One of the concerns presented was obtaining a high-ranking state or national figure to open the camporee. The governor, one of our two senators, and several of the more prominent representatives were all mentioned. I had a private thought but didn't mention it.

The rest of the meeting was on the logistics of having thousands of youths and adults together for an event. The planning included emergency services for broken bones. It was a given with a large group that there would be broken bones, maybe a snake bite or two.

Food poisoning was always a possibility with Boy Scouts. This meant a first aid station marked and transportation for any serious cases.

There would be a fire brigade for the inevitable campfire that got out of control. We needed to have a site map to find units and personnel in need. There would have to be a guide to lead each troop to its assigned spot. When it was time to leave, each camp would have to be checked out to ensure it was clean and everything removed, including Scouts.

The commissioner staff of unit, district, and council commissioners would aid the permanent camp staff as our "police" force. We would also have local sheriff's deputies on hand for any real problems.

Water, sanitation, and traffic control were concerns. Lost and found would be a major operation and would include lost Scouts. If someone's car wouldn't start, an arrangement was made with a local service station.

Inevitably, another person would set up their tent on an anthill; see notes on the first aid station. Religious services needed to be arranged for both Saturday and Sunday.

Multiple shooting ranges had to be developed as the current range wasn't large enough. The Ohio National Guard had agreed to bring in heavy equipment to put backstops in place and remove them later. This would count as their monthly weekend duty. We had to allocate them space to set up their equipment and camp. They would be responsible for their security. As if a bunch of Boy Scouts would want to climb over bulldozers and excavators!

A program for the Saturday night campfire had to be put in place. The camporee group took the easy way out on this. The Order of the Arrow would be asked to take care of the physical arrangements for the program.

A notice would be sent out to all units attending to submit skits they would like to perform. The program committee would pick and choose what skits were in what order. I had only been a Scout for four years and hadn't seen a new skit in the last two.

The 6th Ohio Volunteer Infantry agreed to take care of the daily flag-raising and lowering ceremony. They would also set up their mock battlefield and control access. Even without bullets, a close blast from a black powder rifle could cause severe burns.

We would have over ten thousand people in and out of camp that weekend. That was like an Army division commanded by a two-star general. Oh, what fun we were going to have!

On the way home, I told Mr. Harris I hadn't realized what work went into making a safe, successful camporee. He told me that if I thought that was something, go to the annual Scout show in

Columbus, where there would be thirty thousand people through on the weekend.

Or better yet, go to a National Jamboree. In 1957 they had over fifty thousand people at Valley Forge. There would be another special Jamboree next year at Colorado Springs to celebrate fifty years of Scouting. They expected even more for that.

That sounded like fun. Maybe I could make it to Colorado Springs.

When in bed, I read a short novel. It was pretty dark. A nice man lets his evil side emerge with destructive behavior. Utterson follows the mystery, and it comes to a head with the murder of Sir Danvers. When the good man can't reproduce the serum that keeps him sane, he commits suicide. Not a very cheerful book.

Chapter 11

Thursday was a nice sunny day, so I was able to run after my other exercises. Homeroom was the normal start of the school day routine. The only difference was the announcement of an assembly after lunch on Friday. The game was afoot!

At lunchtime, the gang talked the plans over. I think we were all afraid to chicken out. Cheryl was looking forward to it the most as she would be leaving the school next week. She was still friendly with me, but I noticed she didn't seem to be pining away from the prospect of moving on. To be fair, she'd had to do this many times, and I never had.

After school, I went home and typed up an essay in the basement. The other kids were playing Mr. Potato Head. They were getting very argumentative and loud. Mum came downstairs and issued a warning.

"Quiet down. I don't want to hear one more peep out of you!"

As she was going back upstairs, we all looked at each other. Wondering who would break first. It was Mary. With a grin, she went, "Peep."

It was in a clear soprano and loud.

We all laughed, but from upstairs came, "Richard Edward Jackson, one more sound out of you, and you have had it!"

Now that was unfair! I hadn't caused the first problem. I didn't peep, at least this time. Why was I getting the blame?

As I thought about life's total unfairness, I heard muffled laughter from upstairs. To add insult to injury, my saucy little sister stuck her tongue out at me. This was too much to bear. She was about to die from tickling. She saw her fate coming and ran up the stairs. It only saved her for a minute.

She tried to hide behind Mum, but that didn't work. I seized the little wretch and tickled her until I thought she was about to pee her pants. Only then did I let up. Mary didn't hesitate; she ran back downstairs, leaving me to face the wrath of Mum. Only there was no wrath.

She just said, "I trust you will always look out for your little sister."

"Of course, Mum."

"Orwell had it right, you know. People sleep peaceably in their beds at night only because rough men stand ready to do violence on their behalf. Mary is one of the good people. You will be one of the rough men."

Now, what do you say to that, especially when your mother tells you that? I said nothing.

She started to return, sticking S&H green stamps in books but stopped and added, "There is an article in the *TV Guide* that might interest you."

Now I seldom read anything in the TV guide. On occasion, I would look up when a game was on, but that was about it. I never read their articles.

She continued, "Read about Paul Grant."

I found the guide in its usual place in the family room. The article on Paul Grant and his hit TV show, *The Outlaw Kid*, told how the young star was going to have the second lead in an upcoming movie with John Wayne. They openly speculated how the difficult young man would get along with Mr. Wayne.

He had a reputation for being late for shoots, not knowing his lines, and being ill. I think that meant hungover. Then there were his hangers-on. Three or four other guys would accompany him everywhere. They thought they were God's gift to women. He and his gang sounded like a real pain. I guess I would have to work with him.

Dad got home shortly thereafter. He had stopped at the post office to pick up a package. It was from the engineers in Columbus working on the hairdryer. There was a complete set of drawings, a bill of material, the order of assembly, plus a prototype of the inner components assembled and fitted into a handmade casing. The casing was sheet metal. It gave a good idea of what the finished unit would look like.

They also included quotes for six plastic molds to manufacture complete housing. The molds wouldn't be production molds but could be relied upon to make at least a thousand parts. We went through everything in the package.

I ended up making two decisions with Dad's input. One was that I would resend everything to Mr. Christensen and ask that a Document Disclosure be filed with the patent office. That would protect my ideas for two years.

The second was to go ahead and approve the quotes. I would have to front a lot of money for it, but I believed in my hairdryer concept.

As Eddie put it, "It looks more like a ray gun than a hairdryer."

I was going to try it out in the morning after I wrapped the metal handle with some leather or cloth. I bet the metal housing would get hot. The plastic would be thicker and absorb the heat.

I typed up a letter authorizing the start of production on the prototype molds. Paul Samson, the ME, would be the one working with the plastic company. I should try to get over and see their facility in Worthington near Columbus, but I didn't know when I would be able to find the time before I left for California.

At dinner, we talked about San Toy. My parents had something going on Saturday, so they were not available. The following Saturday was my Eagle ceremony. Next week were semester exams. That meant I would only have to attend school to take the tests. This left me with all day Wednesday free. I brought that up, and Dad was all for it. He wanted to go to San Toy.

I had gotten a book from the library on acting. I didn't think I could learn acting in a few days by reading a book, but I could learn the terminology and differences. I spent my time before falling asleep reading about character acting vs. method acting.

I think I would have to be considered a character actor. I would be playing a teenage boy on a cattle drive. I think I had the teenage boy part down pretty well. I could ride a horse and, if needed, ride the cattle!

I also realized that it couldn't be that simple. I probably wouldn't have that many lines, but I would have to be believable when I delivered them. I would be able to memorize the words with no problem, but what about the required emotions? I had spent enough time out west in the rodeo that I had no trouble with the things involved, like horses and guns. It was the people interactions that concerned me.

There was also Paul Grant to consider. I doubted that we would become friends if he were really like the *TV Guide* had portrayed him. Remembering all the history I had read and the biases involved, I would try to keep an open mind. I know movies had been canceled because of a temperamental actor. I hoped that it didn't happen here.

Chapter 12

Friday was the big day. We were going to steal Mr. Watkins's desk from the classroom and have it in the center of the stage when the curtain opened. We had it planned out to the second. What could go wrong?

The morning seemed to drag on forever, yet as it got close to lunchtime, the clock then sped up. I saw various members of our gang in the hall as we changed classes. We all smiled and winked at each other. I guess we were keeping our nerve up.

We scarfed our lunches. We walked to Mr. Watkins's room. Cheryl took up her position by the staircase to intercept Mr. Watkins if he headed to his room. Tracy had headed to the auditorium. She would open the emergency door. It was double-wide, so we could get the desk in without a problem. Tom Watson and I went into the classroom to open the windows and pick up the desk.

I recruited Tom Pew yesterday to be our fourth guy. Tammy Woodstock hadn't been in school the last two days. Tracy called her house and found out she had the flu. So, it was three Toms and a Rick. There must be a song in there somewhere. Pew and Morton headed outside to take the desk as we let it down.

The desk was heavy, but we got it to tilt through the wide window. These windows were the old types that raised straight up, or we would never have been able to do it. We got the desk tilted out the window on its side, and then Tom Watson jumped out the other window. I finished tipping the desk over to the three Toms. When the desk was out the window, I closed both windows and exited the room through the door.

I saw Tom Humphreys talking to Mr. Watkins. Cheryl was still in position. I left through the end door of the building and went around so I could help the three guys. They almost had the desk to the auditorium door when it opened. We took it down the aisle.

Cheryl came in from the hall at that time. She was waving frantically as we pulled the curtains back to set the desk on the stage.

Her waves were too late. Waiting on the other side of the curtain were Mr. Watkins and our Principal, Mr. Gordon. Busted!

Mr. Gordon said, "You will have to hurry to get the desk back to its room before the assembly. Take the desk back, attend the assembly, and then report to the office."

As we lifted the desk to take it back, this time carrying it through the hall rather than trying to lift it back through the window, I asked Cheryl, "What happened?"

She was almost in tears as she replied, "Tom Humphries looked in the room and saw what you were doing. He went to talk to the teacher. I couldn't believe he would tell on us, so I didn't say anything."

"It was too late by that time anyway; we had the desk out the window, and there is no way we could've lifted it back."

That seemed to relieve her mind.

I sat through the assembly, which was an act put on by a hypnotist. I spent my time trying to think about what I could do to Tom Humphries to get even. Whatever it was, it would have to be in secret, at least anonymous, or he would just tell on us again. I didn't come up with anything immediately, but there would be retribution.

After the assembly, we trooped down to the school office. We all were a little nervous about what was waiting for us.

Mr. Morton took us into his office.

He looked directly at me and said, "This might have been a good time for the board of education. He wasn't talking about the school board because he was holding the school paddle when he said it."

Then he laughed a little.

"I will never admit it, but it is a shame we were waiting for you. Since every teacher's desk in school is identical, every teacher present would have been dreading returning to their classroom. They give me enough headaches as a group that I would have enjoyed it."

The other kids and I were smart enough to keep our mouths shut. Mr. Morton's desk was the same as all the others. He would have been wondering like everyone else.

"However, you were caught. Now I realize that Miss Hawthorne is moving after this week and that Mr. Jackson is leaving town next week. So, it wouldn't be fair for the others if you got off scot-free."

"So, everyone but Miss Hawthorne will spend every day after school next week doing our spring cleanup. You will report to Mr. Brown after school. He will provide you with gloves, rakes, and shovels. You will pick up all the winter debris on the school grounds.

"Miss Hawthorne, you get a pass. I don't want to communicate this to your new school. It doesn't merit that, and I don't want to start you off wrong with them."

Poor Cheryl was almost in tears again.

"It's not fair. I should be punished too!"

You could see Mr. Morton was becoming disconcerted. I put my arm around her and pulled her into a hug.

"Now, now we discussed this and saw this possible outcome. No worries."

I found I liked hugging her, and then it hit me that she was moving, I would probably never see her again. Damn it all to Hell!

We were excused to return to our classes, and our notes had been prepared. On the way back to class, I apologized to Tom Pew for dragging him into this. He told me he was glad to be part of the making of a school legend. Even though we had got caught, the story would be repeated for years.

Even though it had just happened, everyone in school knew about it by now, including all the teachers. Between classes, for the rest of the day, I was questioned by other students about the incident.

I just told them we had taken Mr. Watkins's desk out the classroom window to leave it on stage in the auditorium. We were caught and would have to clean the school grounds next week.

Somehow it became known that Tom Humphreys had squealed on us. When asked, he bragged about it. At least at first, then people started telling him how uncool he was. Before the afternoon was out, no one in school was talking to him. I heard that he would go up to people and try to talk. They would ignore him or even turn their backs. I guess shunning was the new school sport.

When I arrived home after school, I was glad to see both my parents were there. I told them I had a problem at school today. They wanted to know what, so I related the whole incident. I didn't name Tom Humphreys, just that someone told on us.

They heard me out, and Dad said, "I heard it was Tom Humphreys and that none of the students will talk to him now."

That took me aback. So much for keeping secrets from your parents.

"How did you hear about that?"

"You forget there are many phone calls in and out of the office each day, and the shop teachers sometimes have to go downtown to pick up parts. There is a mailman who stops there every day. There are deliveries to the cafeteria daily. You don't go to school in a vacuum."

Mum broke in, "I told you to act like a freshman. I didn't tell you to get caught doing it. Now, what lesson have you learned from this?"

"Don't do it?"

"Better planning. You should have realized other students would be in and out of that room. A couple of big guys at the door to act as minders would have kept people in line."

I don't understand my Mum.

Dad asked, "What is your punishment?"

I explained the trash detail. Both parents thought that fair and reasonable. What I didn't get was that Mum appeared to think the punishment should be for getting caught, not for the act itself.

I had to know.

"I don't understand. You haven't said, don't do that again even once."

"Rick, you are still young no matter how you act at times," Dad started. He continued, "It is like the Army. Officers are taught never to issue an order they know won't be obeyed. It does nothing but undermine their authority and make them appear weak. As a teenager, you are going to do dumb things in the future. It would be futile to tell you not to do dumb things."

It is nice to know that your parents have such a high opinion of you!

Chapter 13

As the conversation started to get repetitive, Mum brought out two letters for me.

The first was from the International Oil Rig and Drillers Union. It was a copy of a letter they had sent to the International Seamen's Union. One handy thing was it had the address of the Seamen's Union hiring hall in New York City, so that was one obstacle that had been overcome.

They relayed the information to the ISU that I was a member in good standing with the IORD and performed satisfactorily on all jobs I had been sent on.

That was an interesting way to word it. I had only been on one job for them, and it had only lasted for several weeks. I guess they take care of their members. I had only sent the letter to them on Monday and had a reply on Friday.

The second was from the patent attorney Mr. Christensen. He had a signed receipt from the patent office and an acknowledgment letter for the Document Disclosure letter we had submitted for the showerhead.

He had included seven copies of each document. I would keep one and send the others with my business proposal to the major manufacturers.

He had also reviewed and approved the letter I intended to send to the showerhead companies. It described the patent application that had been submitted, the sale design, and proposed license fees. We were in business!

All my problems forgotten, I headed to the basement. As part of my typing practice, I typed up letters to Delta, Moen, Pfister, Kohler, American Standard, and Detroit faucets. I then had our attorney, Mr. Burke, review and sign as corporate attorney.

I also signed as president of Jackson Engineering and Dad as chief executive officer. This way, my legal guardian had countersigned without telling the companies that it was a kid they were dealing with.

Each letter was addressed to the respective companies' heads of business development. We didn't even know if that title existed at any of them, but it would get the letters to the correct people.

I couldn't wait. Dad let me drive us down to the post office, where I mailed the letters with a return receipt requested. That way, we would have evidence that the company had received the information.

As Mr. Christensen had explained in his letter, we had to do that. Each company would turn the design over to their engineering group to see if they could achieve an adjustable showerhead without violating my patent. He didn't see how it was possible, but it was good business on their part to check out the possibilities.

Once they found out they couldn't get around the patent, they would then have a business decision to make. Was there a market for this device? What should they pay for this? In my letter, I had indicated that it wouldn't be an exclusive license.

That meant that one of their competitors might be selling the product. They would have to decide if they could afford to fall behind in the marketplace. The other thought was that having multiple licensees would strengthen my negotiating position with each of them.

I could walk away from any individual company if they were too far out of line on their offer.

Undoubtedly, the various companies would want to meet. Dad would be handling that. He would go to their offices if needed. If they came to Bellefontaine, Tom Donaldson had agreed that they could meet at his shop, and he would have all the parts that had been made on display.

It would be explained that they were the prototype shop and that Jackson Engineering worked out of our home address. I would probably be in California when this all occurred, so they may never know they had been dealing with a teenager.

After discussions with our attorneys and a phone call to Mr. King, Judy's dad and head of the Western Electric plant in Columbus, I decided to ask for an upfront fee of ten thousand dollars and ten percent of gross sales.

The upfront money was firm. The gross sales were negotiable, and Mr. King told me I should be happy with anything over five percent. The Donaldsons were satisfied with this. As minority partners in this project, if all six companies bought in, they would receive ten percent of the upfront money. This would give them each almost a year's salary, and though they had helped a lot, it was more than generous.

When it came time for Spanish, I pestered Mrs. Hernandez for some new words, like profit, loss, residuals, taxes, and any other capitalist term I could think of.

She laughed at me and said, "I don't think Senior Castro would like you."

I didn't think I liked him, so we were even.

I was too wound up for serious reading, so I reread *Tom Swift and his Motorcycle*. I could relate to my fellow inventor. Though I thought his life as portrayed was a little unrealistic.

Saturday morning started normally. That lasted until I came back from my run. The weather was okay. It was dull out, low overcast, and cold in the high twenties. I took my shower, drying my hair with my new hairdryer. I did manage to find some leather to wrap the handle from an old Scout project.

As I was eating, Mum told me, "After breakfast, go put on your best suit and tie."

"What for?" I inquired.

"You have enough going on, so we thought we would spring this on you. Today you will receive the keys to the City of Vincennes, Indiana. Warner Brothers will also film it as part of the television special they are making for the movie, *The Cowboys*."

"Like the rest of the nation, the studio saw the picture of you carrying the little girl out of the burning building. They called us and confirmed it was you. When they found out that Vincennes wanted to present the keys of the city, but time was limited, they arranged all of this."

"They have rented the Ohio National Guard Armory for the day. We are due there at ten o'clock, so go get dressed."

Talk about being blindsided! At least I didn't have time to get worked up over this. When we arrived at the armory, it was like a circus. The mayor of Vincennes and all of his family were there. Mary and Ruth ran to each other and hugged like long-lost friends. There was handshaking all around.

The movie crew had put a set in place. I looked like I was being presented the city keys in the mayor's office instead of the armory. It was like I pictured a movie set would be. The director, who was introduced as Juan Rodrigues, walked us through what we had to do for the presentation.

They had a scriptwriter work with the mayor on his speech. The mayor told me he would like them to help with his stump speech for his next campaign. These guys were good!

We did several walkthroughs of the presentation. Mayor Hobbs had practiced his speech until he had it down cold. The whole thing might have been done in one take if two certain little girls hadn't decided to go for a run right through the middle of the set as we were filming. I learned several new Spanish swear words.

Unfortunately for Mr. Rodrigues, so did Mary. She asked him what they meant, and she asked him in Spanish. I didn't know anyone with such a dark complexion could blush as deeply red as he did.

He stuttered and stammered until I bailed him out. Denny and Eddie were laughing too hard to be any help. The entire exchange had been in Spanish. Except for several people in the film crew, no one else knew what had been said.

I told him, "We speak a little Spanish in our house, so be careful of what you say around the children."

He gave a little bow, which was the end of that, or at least it appeared that way.

We proceeded to go through the presentation. On the side, Mum, Dad, and the Roses, Bill, and Melissa were talking like old friends. After the shoot, refreshments had been set up, so we all had coffee and donuts. While we were talking, I noticed that Mr. Rodrigues had Mary in various poses up on stage while still pictures and film were taken. It appears my little sister was auditioning for something!

I pointed this out to my parents, who promptly cornered Mr. Rodrigues. He explained that he thought she was cute as a button and that she might be considered for some child roles.

After a protracted discussion with Mum doing a lot of the talking, a blank release was filled out. It permitted the pictures and film to be shown to studio executives who might need a child actress. There was no commitment by any party to work or accept future work. This was all exploratory.

Mr. Rodrigues explained that while Mary was pretty in a childish way, what sold him was her Spanish.

"It's a very educated Spanish. Not a Castilian lisp, but still very high-class sounding. The difference between Mary's speech and the average Mexican is like the difference between British and American accents. She just comes off as high-class. If there is a need for an Anglo girl who speaks high-class Spanish, she would be a natural. Of course, the odds are that there will never be a need, but we are always looking for unique talents and people."

I thought about that in the context of character and method acting. Mary would be a character actress and wouldn't be acting the part. She was the part. She would just have to be able to deliver the lines. I would have to think about my movie role. I was to be a young cowboy. Maybe I should dress like one all the time on the set. That would help keep me in the cowboy character.

Next, I was cornered by George Weaver. He had to get an interview for the *Bellefontaine Examiner*. He told me that following my actions was becoming a regular part of his beat. We talked for a little while. I shared with him how I had been blindsided this morning. He asked how I took it.

"Well, it certainly was a surprise. It is like finding out you need to learn to swim because you have just been thrown into the deep end."

"Does this bother you?"

"I'm learning you had better be able to take a joke because life is full of them."

"Like having to clean up the school property?" he asked with his gap-toothed smile.

'I'm never going to live that down, am I?"

"Oh, maybe around 2010, but by then, you will be bragging to your grandchildren about it."

As a family, we had lunch at Isley's restaurant.

The afternoon was spent painting rooms at a new duplex Dad had just closed on.

Chapter 14

That night I continued to read about acting. It appeared that it was more work than I had ever imagined. The author made one point over and over that any acting project, whether a play, a movie, or a TV show, was a team effort. The actor is the audience's focal point, but the actor is only part of the equation.

It took the whole team to make it happen, and the actor should treat their fellow workers with respect. This made so much sense I didn't see why he even mentioned it once, much less kept repeating it. I had spent time on a movie set, but it was with real professionals like John Wayne. Maybe they weren't all like him.

Sunday was my last day to see Cheryl. I saw her in church, and we decided that we would say goodbye at the roadside rest near the radio station. It was halfway between our houses, and we would be alone but in a public setting. We didn't discuss why we wanted it to be public.

We met after lunch at the rest area. We sat at a picnic table and talked for a long while. There wasn't much for us to talk about anymore. We rehashed the great desk theft. She apologized again for not being there to help with the punishment.

Her parents were making her sweep out the house and wash the baseboards as her punishment. She would have been helping anyway, so it wasn't that bad. They wanted to leave the place spotless for the next occupant. At the level her dad was now, it was as much perception as reality. He would be getting his Star next week, and the family was looking forward to it.

I was finding out that it took all the family playing their part in the upper ranks to be successful. One bad move by a child could ruin the chances of a promotion. I just thought I had to behave myself!

Finally, we had no more to say. We kissed goodbye. It turned out to be more than I thought it would. It went from a kiss to passion.

We both drew back and looked at each other. Her eyes were as big as saucers.

I unsteadily said, "I think we had better stop."

She nodded yes, but then we clung to each other for the longest time. We kissed again and parted. I walked about fifty feet and turned to watch her walk away. She was looking back at me. We both waved and turned again. I think I turned quickly enough that she didn't see the tears.

Monday, there was light snow, the sort that wouldn't stick. I was able to run, but I can't say I enjoyed it. I prefer warmth and sunshine to snow and cold weather. I think college will be someplace warm. Even though we were Ohio State fans, it didn't mean I wanted to suffer through any more Ohio winters if I could avoid them.

Maybe I could do a movie in California every winter? This was a nice dream anyway.

This was the week of semester exams. I had most of mine on Monday and Tuesday, nothing on Wednesday, Latin on Thursday, and nothing on Friday. It would be an easy week for me. We will be going to San Toy, Ohio on Wednesday. I was anxious to see what a ghost town looked like. I had seen them in the movies, but never in real life. I bet it would be spooky.

My Eagle ceremony was on Saturday, and I had to pack for California on Sunday.

The first thing at breakfast Mum and Dad wanted to talk about was my trip to California. It was not as simple as I thought. I had to have a source of funds while I was in California.

Unbeknownst to me, the studio had been talking to Dad. My studio checks would be deposited in the Bank of America. It had been arranged with a branch near my apartment in Hollywood for me to be able to draw out two hundred dollars a week in cash.

This was news to me, an apartment in Hollywood! I had given no thought as to where I would live while filming. The studio had. I wouldn't be the first child actor they had used. As Mum called him, I would have a minder out there. He was Dick Wyman, the head stuntman for the movie.

He would have my power of attorney for any illness or medical emergency I might have while in California. My apartment would be next door to him. Part of his job was to ensure I got to work and back daily. He would be paid extra to ensure I received the support I needed and did what I was supposed to. There went my immediate thoughts of Hollywood parties and young starlets. From party animal to boring in sixty seconds!

When I thought about it, which I hadn't till now, I'm glad that people were watching out for me. I had never really lived on my own. My cooking skills were limited. My interest in laundry and house cleaning was non-existent, so I had given them no thought.

My test schedule for today was from 8:00 to 10:00 Algebra, 1:00 to 3:00 Biology. Tuesday was 10:00 to 12:00 English, 1:00 to 3:00 World History, and finally, Thursday was 10:00 to 12:00 for Latin. From past examinations, I knew that I would take no more than one and a half hours for each exam, and that would include going over everything twice.

Dad had been kind enough to write a note about my picking up trash for one hour after school every day. Since we wanted to go to San Toy on Wednesday, he offered my services from 10:00 to 12:00 today. Then 8:00 to 10:00 Tuesday, Thursday 1:00 to 3:00, and ending up with 8:00 to 12:00 on Friday.

I pointed out this was ten hours instead of the five the school required. He reminded me of the policy at our house, whatever punishment you got at school beyond detention, you got again at home.

There are times you argue with your parents, but this wasn't one of them. Though, from the smirk on Mum's face, I had to wonder if I was being punished for moving the desk or for getting caught.

When I took the note to the office, Mr. Gordon was called out to review its contents.

He smiled when he read it. "I love it when parents support us at school. It would be a nightmare to be a teacher if parents fought us instead. This is very acceptable, Mr. Jackson. See Mr. Brown after your first exam."

After my Algebra exam, I went to see Mr. Brown in the janitor's workshop. He was pleasant about everything. I was given a rake, shovel, wheelbarrow, and a pair of gloves and told to clear out under the bleachers by the football field. I was to start with the visitor's side. I would be doing good to get that done today.

I managed. It wasn't that bad, and I picked up one dollar and seventy-nine cents in change, so at ninety cents an hour, I would be making forty-five dollars a week if I did it full-time. I wonder if I could go from school to school with a bleacher cleaning service.

My aching back from working under the bleachers persuaded me to forget that. Also, people had been having sex under the bleachers from some trash I had to pick up. I wondered when they did this, certainly not during the game.

I saw the three Tom's at lunch. They all had similar receptions at home. None of them had their punishment extended at school but had extra chores assigned at home. We all agreed that it was unfair to have to do more than the school required. Tom Pew joined us at lunch for a change. He normally sat with his buddies in the shop class.

It made it easier for all of us since our table was the center of attention during lunch. Other kids came up and told us how insane, stupid, idiotic, and dumb we were and wished they had thought of it, except they wouldn't have gotten caught! I noticed Tom Humphries sitting by himself. He was still being shunned.

Humphries looked dejected. Those of us who were caught were being treated as heroes. He had worked within the technical rules and was a bum. I could see that wasn't fair, but I wasn't ready to forget and forgive. I had given up the idea of getting even. He was paying the price for his actions.

After school, we were still having our Spanish sessions. I showed my acting and film-making books to Mrs. Hernandez. She gave me the Spanish words for the technical terms used in filmmaking. I also asked about the terms cowboys used. I found out that *remuda*, *dinero*, *látigo*, and *vaqueros* were common Western terms that were Spanish words.

The only two I wasn't familiar with from my reading were remuda, which was the string of horses a cowboy would have on a trail drive. Latigo was part of the cinch and got its name from the latigo leather used. It was a particular brownish-red color.

I hand-wrote out a list of about fifty terms and then typed them up. This turned out to be our lesson for the day. We agreed to use the words tomorrow. Denny had a good idea that we could choose different technical books like ones on airplanes and learn specific terms for those. Eddie wanted to do cars. Mary was frustrated, so I ran upstairs and borrowed one of Mum's cookbooks.

I brought it back down and set it on the table between Mary and me without saying anything. It sat there as we continued talking.

All of a sudden, Mary exclaimed, "I want to learn Spanish for types of cooking!"

We all agreed this was an excellent idea and that we should do it later this week. Mrs. Hernandez winked at me.

She said, "Mary, I understand there are a lot of Mexican restaurants in California. You may have kept Rick from starving to death."

Mary liked this idea. She didn't want me to go hungry. She very solemnly said, "Rick is a growing boy. He needs to eat, or he will catch his death."

That night I started a book I had been meaning to read for a long time. It wasn't fiction but had been referred to many times in books I had read. It was an old Scottish book on the economy and how it affected countries. It was written several hundred years ago, and the language used was difficult, and the thoughts presented even harder. This would not be my usual hundreds of words a minute read.

The first section talked about how an economy couldn't grow unless there was a division of labor. The more labor was divided, the larger the economy. I had a hard time wrapping my head around this until I put it together that if one person could do everything they needed, there would be no economy. As soon as two people had different items the other wanted, an economy was born. There had to be a reason to trade.

As people became more specialized in what they produced, they had to live close to each other to obtain what they needed to live. When they lived close to each other, they had to have common rules on how to act. These became laws. There had to be makers and enforcers of laws. That is how cities and countries were born. I fell asleep on that thought.

Chapter 15

Tuesday was more exams and cleaning under the bleachers on the Bellefontaine side of the field. I only found ninety-eight cents there. The bleacher cleaning business was not going to happen, at least by me. While I was raking under the stands, I was thinking about my trip to Hollywood.

I would be flying from Dayton to Los Angeles on TWA. The studio had sent coach class tickets. I wondered if I could upgrade them to first class. There was so much more legroom in the front seats. The Constellation was a nice aircraft but rather cramped in the back.

I walked down to the AAA travel agency at lunchtime and explained my problem. They told me if I brought the tickets in and the additional eighty dollars to upgrade, I could do it if the space were available.

My exams were like yesterday, one step above boring. There wasn't one question I had any doubt about the answer to. Still, I went back over every question at least once to make certain I had read it correctly.

When I got home, Mum had something to show me. She had read the cover of a magazine in the grocery checkout line. One article caught her eye, so she bought it, which was highly unusual. On the cover were two pictures, Paul Grant and me.

"Dateline: Hollywood January 20, 1959

The Good Boy meets the Bad Boy.

In a *Movie Magazine* exclusive, we have inside information on the new John Wayne movie *The Cowboys*.

Working together will be the teenage heartthrob bad boy Paul Grant and teenage Eagle Scout Rick Jackson.

Speculation is running high on the set on how Grant and Jackson will relate. Will Grant corrupt the All-American Boy, or will Jackson redeem the brat?

Paul Grant, who is famous for his drinking and womanizing, has recently been suspected of using drugs. His famous temper tantrums and poor work habits have made him high maintenance on the set. Add this to a huge ego and the habit of bringing his hangers-on onto the set, and you have a problem for any director. If his show *The Outlaw Kid* weren't number one in its time slot, he would have been let go some time ago. However, the young ladies seem to love the bad boy.

When Grant was asked about Jackson, his only comment was, 'Who? Who cares?'

Contrasting is Rick Jackson, sports star, lifesaver, and bane of the bad guys. Jackson, a straight-A student, is the youth golf champion of the State of Ohio and the National Champion Youth Brahma Bull rider. He is an honorary member of the Texas Rangers for breaking up a gang of rustlers; he killed two murderous bank robbers in a botched bank robbery, and he's pulled people out of burning car wrecks. The world-famous picture of a young man carrying a young girl out of a burning building is Jackson at his finest.

The only blot on Jackson's record is that he was involved in a fight in Tijuana and had to bail Elvis Presley and Tab Hunter out of jail.

While not having the strong entertainment credentials that Paul Grant has, he appeared in *It Never Happened* with John Wayne and several *Spin and Marty* episodes on the *Mickey Mouse Club*. To a point, he can even sing, having reached the top ten playlists with 'Rock and Roll Cowboy', supported by the Beach Boys.

Strong credentials, but how will it come out when the good meets the bad—ugly?"

I didn't quite know how to react to the article.

I finally ended up saying, "It will be interesting."

"Yes, it will," replied Mum. "We called them Good Time Charlie's when I was young. Always up for fun, but they would run at the first sign of work or trouble."

"My best bet will be to go there and do my job and ignore the rest."

"Easier said than done, boyo. You will have to be careful. He will try to drag you down to his level or do you in."

"You don't think he would try to hurt me?"

"He wouldn't survive the experience. He would try to humiliate you. That would be his style."

"I wouldn't try to kill him!"

"No, but I would!" Mum replied.

I wonder about her.

"I don't see the big deal about me being in this movie. I haven't even been sent more than the outline script. So far, I've been told any dialog I have is so short and infrequent that there is no need for me to do any advance memorization. That sure doesn't sound like the good meets the bad."

"How many magazines would that sell?" asked Mum.

"Point taken," I replied.

At dinner, I asked about paying for an upgrade to first class. It was okay with my parents.

Dad joked, "You are one of those movie stars that Howard Hughes brags about flying on his airlines."

I laughed at that, "I'm looking forward to flying on a Constellation. I love the look of that tripletail."

Mum came out with, "That will be your second flight. When we came from England the second time in 1947, it was on a Pan Am Constellation."

"Oh, I don't remember that."

"You were only three. Why would you remember?"

We continued to talk about my trip. It seemed that Dick Wyman and his wife Janice had things pretty well planned out for me as far as housekeeping. A woman would come in to clean and do my laundry. It was up to me to cook or eat out every day but Sunday dinner. I would eat with the Wymans to keep them up to date on my week.

I would ride to the studio with Mr. Wyman every day. Dad told me he had asked the studio about getting me a California hardship driver's license so that I could go places on the weekend. They were going to look into it.

"If I get a license, I will need a car."

"If you do, let me know, and I will arrange for you to be able to withdraw the funds. Dick Wyman has already said he will help you find a car."

"What sort can I buy?"

"I would think in California you would want a convertible."

Mum added, "It has to be new; I don't want to have to worry about a used car breaking down."

"Would a Ford or Chevrolet be okay?"

"Exactly, either a Bel Air convertible or one of those new Thunderbirds," replied Dad.

"Those could get pricy, especially the Thunderbird."

"Rick, stop and think about how much money you have made, will be making, and what you have done for your family. Now do something nice for yourself."

This was from Mum, but Dad was nodding his head yes.

Denny asked, "Can I buy the car I want when I'm Rick's age?"

"Yep," said Dad. "Just earn the money."

You could see wheels start turning in Denny's head.

That night I read more of the book by the Scottish author. He explained that because waterways gave people and countries further reach, it exposed them to more diversity of trade opportunities. More customers and different products brought wealth into those near water nations like Italy, England, and Japan. This positively affected their policies worldwide.

Countries that weren't near open water, like Russia, would be at a disadvantage, and the lack would negatively dictate their policies. They would try to expand to water. This would lead them into wars that they normally would not have picked.

Russia took Ukraine to get to the Black Sea, but this was still far inland. This made them look at Afghanistan several times, which ended up costing them dearly.

I could see where being close to the shipping lanes could positively affect the wealth of a country and its people. The United States was connected by railroads, and now the interstate highways had both Pacific and Atlantic exposure year-round. No other country in the Americas or the world, for that fact, has used this advantage so well. We were taking full advantage of the Atlantic. I wondered about the Pacific in future years.

Chapter 16

Wednesday morning Dad and I got an early start to drive down to Morgan County, Ohio. It would take us almost five hours to get there. We left home at six-thirty, hoping to get there before lunch. Mum had packed us a lunch to save time.

We took Route 33 to Columbus and then to Broad Street, Route 40. We saw the new interstate highway between Kirkersville and Gratiot, but it wasn't open yet, so we stayed with 40 to Zanesville and went south on Route 60 to McConnelsville. From there, nameless back roads to a point out in the middle of a national forest.

At about twelve-thirty, we stopped at a small crossroads. Dad looked around,

"Here is where I grew up and our ancestors came from."

There was nothing there, just trees.

During the ride down, Dad had told me the story of San Toy.

The federal government had bought the entire area in 1935 and created a national forest. They had the WPA come in and tear down every building in the area. The town of San Toy, already derelict, was gone.

At the end of World War I, the government ended subsidies to keep marginal coal mines open. Peabody Coal had one of those mines at San Toy. Since it was no longer profitable, they ordered the mine superintendent to shut off the pumps and let the mine flood. This way, they could take the tax write-off.

The superintendent at the time was John Campsey. He was my grandfather Ross's uncle. This would make him my great-great-uncle. He went to the pump house and turned them off. He had armed guards with him because they were afraid of a riot among the workers. There was no riot. Everyone was packing and leaving.

San Toy had two sections. The main living area was for the two hundred employees and their families. Company-owned houses, the company store, a company-owned church building, and the jail were in the main area.

In what they called Over the Hill, which was on the other side of a nearby hill, were several bars and brothels. They had multiple bars and brothels so that various ethnic groups wouldn't have to mingle. This wasn't a black-white issue, more like English, Welsh, or any other European mixture that could be named.

The day the pumps were turned off, this all came to an end. Within hours no one was in that town or had lived there since. The buildings are long gone. You can see the remains of some foundations. The town property still belongs to Peabody Coal, so the federal government didn't come in to remove any evidence of occupation.

This crushed my dreams of a Western ghost town, as seen in the movies. This sounded more like a vacant field with bricks in it. The only building that still stands is the jail. It has only four walls and an inside division with four cells. The cells have bars on the windows, but the inside cell doors are gone. The walls are cast concrete, so they will stand for many years as mute evidence of this abandoned village.

We were looking for a box supposedly buried twenty-five feet northwest of the corner of the San Toy jailhouse. In his letter, Ross had said it was about four feet down.

We had brought shovels, picks, an ax, and a bow saw. It had been many years since the box was buried. There might be a tree on that spot now. If there was, we had to hope there wouldn't be a deep root system, or we would never get it out without dynamite, which would probably destroy the box.

We shouldered the gear and walked back into the woods about half a mile. As Dad had remembered, the town of San Toy lay before us. Or at least where it had been. Standing on a small hilltop, we looked down on an area of about fifty acres which had fewer trees than the rest of the area. You could see the pattern formed by the roads, both of them.

The town had been so small that there were only two intersecting roads. The roads had never been paved but formed using tailings from the mine. Nothing would grow on them, so the roads remained free of growth.

This would not always be as leaves and debris were covering sections, and weeds had sprouted where surrounding trees didn't shade them out. The trees were not as thick in the former town as in the rest of the area. My guess was within another fifty years, you would never know anything was here.

At the intersection of the former roads was the only building with portions standing, the old jail. The roof was long gone leaving the four walls. Dad pointed out what he remembered as a kid, the old mine face in the side of a hill.

The adit had railroad ties closing it off. He told me that further in, there was a cement plug. Explorers would die from drowning or methane gas if they got past all that. Not a place to go.

We walked over to the jail to survey the situation. Dad started laughing.

"Which way is north?"

It was so dark and gloomy from trees overhead that the sun would be no help. There was moss on all sides of everything I could see, including the jail walls.

"Be prepared," I responded as I pulled out my compass.

It was about the size of a dime. It was one of many World War II surplus items. It was intended for a flyer's survival kit. I had carried it in my pocket along with change for the last three years. This was the first time I needed it, but like a gun when you needed it, you needed it right now, ready to use.

We were lucky; there were no trees close to the area we had to dig. Within fifteen minutes, we had dug a trench five feet deep, twenty-five feet from the northwest corner. We were digging away from each other.

Dad's shovel clanged off something. It was a metal box. It looked like the boxes they used on stagecoaches for valuables. It wasn't that big, but it sure was sturdy.

It was closed with a hasp, but there was no lock, so Dad was able to lift the lid. The box itself would make a nice souvenir of the trip. Inside was an oilskin-wrapped package. After unwrapping several layers, there was an envelope. The envelope had a stamp that I recognized.

It was a twenty-five-cent stamp from the Columbian Exposition. It was worth some money, maybe fifty or sixty dollars, but certainly not a treasure within itself. The stamp was used, and the edges were torn, so the condition was poor at best. It might even be considered thin if removed.

The address on the letter was that of the old family farm. The postmark was almost illegible. It looked like Cal so it might have been sent from California.

When we returned home, a magnifying glass might help. Inside was a noticeably short letter. It was dated 1894. The stamp was issued in 1893 to celebrate the four hundredth anniversary of discovering the Americas, so that matched.

The letter, which was more of a note than a letter, was addressed to William Campsey Jackson, my great-grandfather.

It read, "As I promised your father, John Timms, here is the location of the deed. It is buried behind the tomb of the last governor."

That was it. No signature, no indication of who or what the last governor was being discussed.

We talked about it on the way home. If the letter came from California, then they were talking about a California governor, but the last one? Since they still have a governor, it wasn't that simple.

Was it the last governor after the letter was written? Dad was the one who thought of it.

"There was a last governor of California, the last Spanish governor!"

Now we had to find out who he was and where he was buried. It seemed almost too easy. Since I was flying out to California on Sunday, it would give me a weekend project out there.

But what was the deed for? If it were a land deed, it couldn't have just sat there all this time. Some entity, county or state would've taken it for taxes. So, odds were there was no value in this.

That didn't matter to Dad. It was a puzzle left by his father. The only thing he had inherited, so he wanted it solved. The fact that it was probably worthless wasn't the point.

I felt like I owed it to my dad to do whatever I could on this matter. I pledged to search out the last Spanish governor of California and try to find this deed. It looked like I was going to be a grave robber!

The whole family examined the letter under a magnifying glass when we returned home after nine o'clock that night. Well, everyone but Mary, who was sound asleep.

No one could make out more than Cal on the postmark. We only knew that it came from California sometime after 1893 and was addressed to my great-grandfather to keep a promise to my great-great-grandfather.

The deed was referred to as buried behind a tombstone. Why would it be hidden like that? Who was it hidden from? A mystery for certain. The real question was, was it a treasure hunt?

That night I read about money. It was enough to drive you crazy. Coins made of rare metal would be easier to carry around than ten hogs. I understood that. Coins made with a design on them to show who had minted them made sense. The design was proof, if you will, of the purity of the metal. Of course, you still had to worry about your fellow man clipping or milling the edges of the coins.

Then the government decided to debase its coinage by reducing the amount of rare metal in the coins. I could understand a citizen being responsible for knowing their coins. In the same way, they were responsible for knowing if the hogs they were using in trade were healthy or if the weight of the hog had been inflated by watering them well before the weighing. That all made sense.

It was when the paper was introduced that it became confusing. The old Scot tried to explain it to me. I must've read that section twenty times. I finally put it down because I realized I would never get to sleep reading this.

Chapter 17

Thursday, I had my Latin test and then picked up trash, this time around the tennis courts. I didn't find any change around the courts, but that made sense. There wasn't a refreshment stand near the courts. I did find some grungy tennis balls stuck in the bottom of the fence, but they went right into the trash.

I also learned that several students with poor grades had torn their papers up rather than taking them home. On several of the papers, I could read the names. They were names I recognized, but none of them were friends.

I decided to let well enough alone and pitched the scraps with the rest of the trash. Their grades would catch up with them in the end. It just made me feel stronger about what I was doing.

Later in the afternoon, Dad and I ran several errands. We stopped at the AAA travel agency and decided to upgrade my ticket to first class. We then stopped by the bank, where Dad bought me five hundred dollars worth of traveler's checks.

We then went over to Montgomery Wards and bought a large suitcase for my clothes. The ones we owned were good for a week's travel. I needed considerably more. Dad decided that the leather case made by Hartmann was the best.

It was pricey but the best quality. Then he bought a matching briefcase for me, which he said was a present from him and Mum.

When we got home, there was a letter from the International Seaman's Union. It contained a note and an application. The note said since I was in good standing with the IORD union, all I had to do was provide the information requested on the application and a money order for twenty-five dollars.

I filled out the application on my typewriter. Dad promised to pick up the money order tomorrow and mail it.

That night, I tried to read the paper money sections again and got more confused. Was it real money or not? I gave up on that and started to think about another issue that had come to mind. I had just joined my third union. Should I consider voting Democrat when I was old enough to vote? That is how I understood things worked.

But I was a businessman, and they voted Republican. Also, my godfather, a Republican, was the President of the United States. So, should I vote Republican?

Then, on the other hand, my godmother is the Queen of England. Should I be a Monarchist? I must have fallen asleep about then.

On Friday, I woke up from the craziest dream. Someone wanted to print paper money, and I kept saying, "Off with their heads!"

My head cleared after my exercises. It was clear enough for my morning run.

Arriving at school at 8 a.m., I went straight to Mr. Brown's hideaway as I had begun to think of it. Today he gave me a metal trash can that was mounted on a two-wheeled dolly. There was also a pair of gloves and a sawed-off broomstick handle with a nail. He told me to go two blocks in every direction from the school and clean up the trash dropped by my fellow students.

I filled the trash can up three times in four hours. I never realized what pigs we could be. This was a winter's accumulation but still a disgrace. I mentioned it to him when I was finished. He told me that it seemed to get worse every year.

Mr. Brown observed, "I don't know why that is, but since the war ended, it seems like parents are letting their kids get away with more all the time. The younger they are, the worse they are. Kids born before and during the war have been held to one standard, and those born afterward to another. I don't know where this is going, but it can't be good."

My parents seemed to treat all of us kids the same, so I don't know. However, it won't be pretty if these trash cans are a sign of future things.

When my time was up, Mr. Brown gave me the slip to take to the office. I read what he wrote, "Mr. Jackson spent all the required hours and did a particularly good job. Please don't hesitate to discipline him in the same manner in the future. I could use the help."

Some compliments you don't need!

I went down to Don's for a treat. I was tired of the school cafeteria. The food wasn't that bad. It was just boring. Please give me a hamburger and fries any day.

At Don's, it seemed like most of the school passed through during lunch. The number of kids who came up and wished me the best in California was surprising. One kid was sitting in the corner, and everyone was ignoring him. I thought about it for a minute and went to sit with Tom Humphrey.

"Tom, may I join you?"

"Sure. You are the first person who has spoken to me in a week."

"I know, and I must tell you I wasn't happy when you ratted on us. I can't begin to tell you how many evil thoughts I had for several days, but I think you've more than paid the price. Why did you do it anyway?"

"I wasn't thinking. I just wanted to get you in trouble. I didn't realize the problems it would cause me."

"So, you don't regret getting me and the others in trouble. Just that it caused you problems later."

"That's about it," he replied.

"Tom, you are a real SOB, but as they said about Patton, you are our SOB."

At that point, I shook his hand. He shook it back with a confused look on his face.

"Everyone in here sees us shaking hands, so they know it is okay to talk to you again."

"Thanks, I guess, but don't expect any breaks."

"I wouldn't expect any, Tom."

As I left, I thought, *what a loser in life. I hope he learns someday.*

I had my burger and fries. Several of the kids wanted my autograph, so they could say they knew me before I became a star. I kept a straight face as I told them they were too late. This gave everyone a good laugh.

When I got home, Mum had me go through all my clothes and decide what I wanted to take to California. I thought I would wait until Sunday morning to pack, but she wouldn't allow that. After going through everything, I began to understand. At her urging, I packed good clothes, shorts, and t-shirts.

She told me to plan on buying casual clothes out there. The California definition of casual might be different than Ohio's. As Mums do, she got her way, but I didn't see how they would be any different.

In Spanish class, I surprised Mrs. Hernandez with a small broach that Mum helped me pick out. It was in appreciation for teaching me Spanish. I could tell from how she received it that Mum had the right idea when she said I should give a thank you present. Maybe Mum does know some things after all.

That night I thought about paper money some more. I just didn't get it. The more I thought about it, the less real it seemed. It was okay when the bill said gold or silver certificate on it. Then you trade it in for an equal amount of gold or silver.

It was when the government printed more bills than they had metal to back them that it became confusing. In wartime, the government would rightly decide they needed more money, so they would just print it.

With more paper chasing the metal supply, wouldn't the value of metal go up? What if everyone wanted to cash in their paper for metal at the same time? I had read that some countries didn't even back up their paper money with precious metals.

They just declared the value of the paper, and that was that. Thank God the United States was on the gold standard, or our economy would end up like the South American banana republics. Here today and gone tomorrow.

Chapter 18

On Saturday morning, I was wide awake at the crack of dawn. Well, 7:51 a.m., to be precise. After all, it is winter. I knew the time because it was on the radio when I went down for breakfast. This was to be an exciting day. I would receive my Eagle Award from the Boy Scouts. Unlike many things that had happened to me in the last year, I felt like I had worked for and earned this.

The ceremony was at two o'clock at the Lutheran Church. That is where my Scout troop met. We had to be there by one o'clock to rehearse. The ceremony was fairly simple, but we still had to do a run-through. Mum had received the programs back from the printer, but I hadn't managed to see one yet. They were always somewhere else when I thought to ask about them. Today, they were all in possession of our Scoutmaster, Mr. Geist.

I wasn't nervous about the day. I just wanted to hurry up and have it happen. Time seemed to crawl. I went out in the garage and messed around with my electronics for the hairdryer. I didn't accomplish anything, but it did help pass the time. I was so desperate that I even cleaned my room. Mum caught me at this.

All she had to say was, "You poor boy."

After those encouraging words, I went to the kitchen for coffee. It was now all of 9:30. After another half hour of babbling about nothing, Dad sent me out for a run. It was drizzling, but Mum said, "You won't melt."

I asked her, "Will I catch my death?"

Her response was, "Better you out there than with us in here!"

I know they love me. Don't they?

I ran and walked for an hour. By the time I got home, I was soaked through but felt calmed down. A hot shower warmed me back up. I put on a clean pair of jeans and a flannel shirt. I wanted to keep my uniform creases sharp until the last minute.

Mary came to me with a request to help her set up her dollhouse. So, I went to the basement and moved the dollhouse miniature furniture. I now understand women and putting furniture in place. They practice it while young, the directing of men, that is, not the actual moving of furniture. I felt Mum's fine hand in this exercise. It did help pass the time.

Time does pass, even though it may be at the speed of a glacier. We had lunch at noon, and Denny and I wore our uniforms. Eddie wasn't interested in Scouting.

Denny is a Star Scout. Mary is too young to be a Girl Scout, but she can start as a Daisy next year.

The more expensive uniforms I had bought were worth the money. The fabric held their creases nicely and didn't show wrinkles. Denny looked sharp in his uniform, but it looked like he had been wearing it all day by the time we got out of the car. Eddie, like most eleven-year-olds, looked like he had been sleeping in his clothes for a week.

We did a walkthrough of the program. I finally got to see the formal printed program. Now I knew why it had been kept from me. There were all the normal events. Where it differed from other programs was the presentation of other awards. The Scouts presented awards in a Court of Honor. At an Eagle Court of Honor, they only presented the Eagle medal and badge. This Court had an exception.

There was a section on other awards. These were the lifesaving awards. Another item that set me back was the special guests. I had half expected our district and council Scout executives and commissioners, or at least some of them. The mayor of Bellefontaine would be present, which was again expected. The mayor of Vincennes was a pleasant surprise. I liked Mr. Hobbs.

Our local representative to the Ohio legislature and our U.S. representative were on the list to speak, and U.S. Senator Robert Taft. There would be a presentation from the White House by an aide to the president. The last presentation was from the Court of Saint James. I had no idea what that was.

To top it all off, a Warner Brothers camera crew was in the church's back. This day could go on forever.

All of a sudden, it was time. All the guests were seated. The church looked like Christmas Eve, standing room only. The Honor Guard led by my brother Denny presented the colors. We all stood for the pledge. Pastor Bowers gave the invocation.

I was led to the front by an Honor Guard of previous Eagles in our troop. One of those was Captain Bob Chapman in his Navy uniform. A graduate of the U.S. Naval Academy, he was home on leave and led me to the front. There were six Eagle Scouts present, and they all were successful people. It made me proud to be joining them.

Mr. Geist started the program by telling us that the Eagle Award was the highest award that could be earned in Scouting. He told its history and a description of what it meant. Candles were lit to show what the parts of the award stood for. The Eagle was a majestic symbol, the red in the ribbon for cheerfulness, the white for loyalty, the blue for courage, and the scroll symbolized service.

Our district commissioner gave the keynote address. Then the National Court of Honor was called to order. After that, my Scout Oath was reaffirmed. I was given the Eagle charge, the same marching orders all Scouts were given. Then my parents advanced, and Mum pinned my Eagle Award to my shirt.

After that were the other awards. The council Scout executive read the citations and presented these. I received an Honor Medal and an Honor Medal with Crossed Palms. These were pinned to my shirt. With my three medals, I would jingle while I walked. I thought of this while they were being pinned on. I wondered if Mum would take to calling me Jingles. At least my Arrow of Light from Cub Scouts was a patch rather than a medal.

After this, all the politicians had their say. They all said nice things, but you could tell they were giving canned speeches to keep in front of their constituents. The only one I felt who was sincere was Mr. Hobbs.

When the aide from the White House spoke, he was brief. He brought greetings and congratulations from the President of the United States, Dwight David Eisenhower. He also told us that my request for the president to attend the Springfield District Camporee had been placed on the president's schedule, and he would be there unless events dictated otherwise. That certainly started a stir in the room.

The aide also had a gift from the president. It was a campaign hat in its hat press. It had the largest First-Class emblem I had ever seen on the front. It must have been four inches tall. The aide pointed out that this was the president's hat from when he was a boy. Inside I would find his initials DDE. Wow!

The last presenter was the guy from the Court of Saint James, Sir Bartholomew Benton. On this auspicious occasion, he was here as a representative of my godmother Queen Elizabeth II. Yes, he talked that way. He also gave congratulations and presented a gift. It was a pretty ugly walking stick. Most U.S. Scouts used staff as tall as them. This was more like a cane.

When he announced that this stick had previously belonged to Lord Baden-Powell, I thought the professional Scouters were all going to have heart attacks on the spot.

When that was done, the colors were retrieved, and the ceremony was over. We went to the church basement for refreshments. The troop had arranged for the normal cookies and bug juice. Mum and Dad had provided a cake.

Well-wishers surrounded me. The president's aide introduced himself, and in turn, I introduced him to the commissioners and

Scout executives. There was no time for a conversation, but I knew there would be questions later.

Sir Bartholomew introduced himself. When I introduced him to Mum, he said, "Lady Margaret, I have heard a lot about you and your antics in the war." Lady? Antics?!!! What was that all about?

I will have some questions for her later! In the meantime, I examined the walking stick. It came with a nice storage case with Lord Baden-Powell engraved on a brass plate. There was even a picture inside with him holding it. There was also a letter from the queen to me stating this was a gift on the occasion of my earning the Eagle Award. There would be no doubting this provenance.

The politicians had all completed their handshaking and departed. By this time, the president's aide had concluded his talk with the professional Scouters. They all shook hands, and he departed. Mr. Stanton, the council Scout executive, and Mr. Harris, our district executive, joined me. They both wanted to know how I had gotten Eisenhower to agree to attend the camporee.

I thought about making up a story but settled with, "He is my godfather."

"What is your relationship with the Queen of England?"

"She is my godmother."

You could see the regret in the executives' eyes. So many fundraising opportunities were lost. They and every Scouter present asked to hold Baden-Powell's walking stick. Soon pictures were being taken of all.

As things quieted down, a familiar figure approached, Mr. Weaver of the *Bellefontaine Examiner*.

"Rick, every time I think I have seen it all, you come up with something else."

We talked about the day, and I explained my relationships. He wanted to know how I had come by such illustrious godparents. I sent him to my mother as if I were just an infant in arms. I would have loved to hear her answers, but other people kept coming up and congratulating me.

The day finally wound down, and we went home after helping clean up the mess that was made in the church basement. It wouldn't do for the Scouts to leave a mess!

At home, we all changed back to our regular clothes. I was impressed with my new uniform; it looked as good as when I put it on in the morning. I wondered how many more times I would wear it.

I removed the medals and placed them in their presentation cases. In each case was a fabric badge I could sew on my shirt. I wondered if I could talk Denny into doing it for me. His stitches weren't that bad.

When things settled down, I asked Mum about the lady remark and the antics during the war. She told me that Sir Bart habitually called all women lady and that her antics were riding with Elizabeth. Dad gave her a sharp look at these comments but held his peace.

Later, when I went to bed, I continued to read about how nations measured wealth but realized that it was like a giant con game that the normal person would never understand. We would have the illusion of understanding, just like we had the illusion that our paper money had value. We were like the people in the story. *The Emperor had no Clothes.* As long as the staff would buy what I needed or wanted, the emperor could walk around naked all he wanted. I think Miss Bales would have kittens at that mixed metaphor or worse, yet her kittens would be like tigers, then we would have a wild simile on hand.

Chapter 19

My flight was at noon on Sunday, so we left for Dayton at eight o'clock to be on time. Mum had finished my packing the night before. She did this because she said I would forget my head if it weren't screwed on. After she said this, Mary climbed onto my lap at the breakfast table.

She started feeling around my neck, and all of a sudden, she said, "Mum, I think he has a screw loose!"

That broke us all up. Mary beamed; I think that was the best joke she had ever tried.

We arrived at the airport with no problems on the way. After I checked my bags, the whole family escorted me to the gate. The boarding was on time, so I boarded with the first-class passengers after the proper hugs, kisses, handshakes, and admonitions to call and write.

As I showed my boarding pass, a photographer who I hadn't noticed took my picture. He asked me to pose again. I did, but I asked him what was going on.

He gave me his business card. As an independent, he had been contacted by the airline on their behalf and the studios to take shots of me boarding. He was pleasant about it, so I cooperated. I didn't realize it at the moment, but this attracted the attention of my fellow passengers.

As I got settled in my window seat in the second row, I started to understand why TWA was known as the Airline of the Stars. They made certain to get pictures of anyone in the business. That way, if I became famous, they would have pictures of me flying TWA. If I bombed out, they would never see the light of day. The studio wanted them for the TV story they were producing. This business certainly is complicated.

I looked everyone over as they boarded. There weren't many people flying on a Sunday. Still, the men all wore suits and ties like I did. There was only one woman passenger today. She and her husband were all dressed up. She had a lovely corsage on.

From listening to her short talk with the stewardess, I learned she and her husband were on their way to Hawaii to celebrate their fiftieth wedding anniversary. That was impressive. Not many couples lived that long.

We buckled in, and they gave the safety talk. They also informed the economy passengers they could buy two drinks during the flight. In first class, I found out they were free and had no limit. I'm not sure I understood the logic behind that. I would've given two free drinks in first and sold all you wanted in coach with no limits at all.

I found out during the flight that they should have first-class limits. The man, I won't call him the gentleman next to me, kept pounding the drinks back. He had drunk four of the small glass miniatures of whiskey before we landed in St. Louis to fuel up and change some passengers.

After we left Saint Louis, he had another. He decided that he was in love with our stewardess, grabbed her arm, and pulled her onto his lap. I had been dozing as there was nothing to see out the window at the moment. The commotion brought me up. I took him by his ear and twisted while lifting. Since he was buckled in, he couldn't go anywhere. That must have smarted.

This gave the flight attendant a chance to get up. She went to the front cabin and returned with the plane's captain. He invited the man to move to a seat in the back of the aircraft, or he could keep his seat and explain his actions to the police when we landed. He went to the back of the plane, and it was the last we saw of him.

The captain thanked me for my actions, and the stewardess was more profuse in her thanks. She wanted to know who I was as she knew my picture was taken as I boarded the aircraft. I explained that

I had a minor role in an upcoming John Wayne movie. I was treated like a king for the rest of the flight.

It was eight hours in transit to California, but with the time change, I arrived at 5:30 p.m. There had been a little headwind to slow us down. Mr. Wyman met me at the gate. He held a little sign that had Jackson on it. After retrieving my bags, Mr. Wyman took me to my new apartment. He suggested that I change into casual clothes, pointed out where he lived, and gave me a dinner invitation.

After changing, I went over and met Mr. Wyman's wife, Janice. They seemed like genuinely nice people. They were a little mismatched. He was taller and broader than me and looked as rugged as a mountain. She was a petite five foot two and looked like a little china doll. As dinner progressed, I realized that the china doll talked like a China sailor. Still, I liked both of them immediately.

Mr. Wyman explained he wasn't my babysitter but was available to help me learn the ropes. I had the impression from my parents he was to be my babysitter. This could be interesting.

I started yawning in the middle of dinner, so they invited me over for breakfast at six in the morning. I told them I might not be awake by then.

"Trust me, you will be awake," said Mr. Wyman.

I went back to my new apartment, unpacked enough to find my toothbrush, and went to bed.

I was confused when I woke up. It was dark out, but it read five o'clock when I looked at my watch. Then it hit me, the three-hour time change. Because of the time difference, I was awake exceedingly early.

Now Mr. Wyman's comment last night made a lot of sense. He said I wouldn't have to worry about oversleeping. Now I understood. It would probably take several days to turn my sleep around.

Since I was wide awake, I got up. The kitchen had a coffee pot but no coffee. I did my pushups and sit-ups, then put on clothes to go for a run. I also took some change in case I found a place open that sold coffee.

As I dressed and tried to wake up, I looked around at my new living quarters. It was a two-bedroom apartment. It was in excellent condition. I had worked on enough of our units with Dad to appreciate a well-maintained house interior.

The brownish shag carpet, which was wall to wall, in the new style, felt new. The walls were freshly painted all white. The only sign of repaired damage was where someone had used toothpaste to hide nail holes for pictures. The toothpaste shrinks after a while, leaving small dents in the wall. There weren't too many that I could see. This was normal for almost any type of rental unit.

The kitchen was open to the dining area, which in turn was open to the living area. The kitchen appliances were new and all white. The stove looked like it ran on gas. The countertops were a good grade of Formica. I opened the empty cabinets.

I would have to buy pots, pans, dishes, and tableware. That made me think of towels, sheets, pillowcases, lions, tigers, and Oh My! There was some serious shopping in my near future.

The furnishings were sparse in the rest of the apartment. The bedroom had a bed, an end table with a lamp, and that was it. There's an empty closet but no clothes hangers. At least there was a roll of toilet paper in the bathroom, and even it was getting down. I needed to start making a shopping list.

There was a small kitchen table with four chairs in the eating area. The living area had a pretty ratty-looking sofa and one matching chair, which meant it was just as ratty. There was a small TV sitting on a table with rabbit ears. The ears had been wrapped in tin foil.

I was so glad I had the money to fix this place. Even though I would only be here for about seven weeks, I needed some basics. While thinking of it, I checked the second bedroom out. Since it was empty, I wasn't certain it should be called a bedroom. I would buy a desk and chair for the typewriter I needed to buy. Then there was the typing paper, ribbons, lions, tigers, and Oh My! I had better start that list right now.

I dug a yellow legal pad out of my briefcase to start my list. I went to the kitchen table since it was the only place I could write. I then had to retrieve the lamp from the bedroom so I would have enough light to read by. There was a small chandelier over the kitchen table. It would work well as soon as I bought light bulbs.

The apartment was pretty nice. I just needed the furnishings.

I had on shorts, a t-shirt, and my running shoes. Making certain I had my wallet, house key, and some change, I went outside. It was still early, so the sun wasn't up. The area was lit up, so I could see that the apartments were two stories built around an inner courtyard that had a swimming pool.

There were four buildings, one on each side of the courtyard, but they weren't connected. To go from the second floor of one apartment to the second floor of another building, you would have to go down steps, walk to the next building, and go up another set of steps. I'm not sure I liked that design.

I walked out between the two buildings trying to find my way out of the complex so I could run on the streets. I found myself in a parking lot. It wasn't like any I had ever seen before. The parking spots were nose-in, all around the inner perimeter of the parking lot. On the outside, there were parking spaces with a roof over them.

There were no walls, just a metal roof set on poles. It was kind of neat, with no garage, but the roof would keep debris like bird poop off your car. Behind the parking spaces was a wall about eight feet tall, so I had to find the opening to the street.

It was on the other side of the parking lot. There was no gate, guard, or anything, so I went out to the street. Small stores were lining the block across the street from the apartments. One of them had lights on and appeared to be a diner. I would try that someday.

The sidewalks were ten feet or more wide, wider than anything I had ever seen in Bellefontaine. I started on an easy run down my side of the street. Gradually picking up speed, I went north for what felt like several miles. I crossed the street and made my way back. It felt good to be running. It was warm out, maybe in the mid-seventies, which was much better than Ohio.

Chapter 20

I returned to the apartment, which I had yet to start thinking of as home, and showered. I had brought my metal hairdryer, so there was no chance I would catch my death. I think I was going to like this California weather! I was at Wyman's door at six as requested.

Janice and Dick Wyman were maybe in their early thirties. I'm an extremely poor judge of ages. They made an attractive couple. They made it clear they were Dick and Janice, not Mr. and Mrs. Wyman. Any Dick and Jane jokes were made at my peril.

As we ate bacon and eggs along with coffee, Mr. Wyman told me what to expect for the day.

"The first day on set is always a real mess as things get organized. A cast meeting is first. There will be refreshments there, so there is no chance of your starving to death."

I think he told me that because I had practically inhaled my breakfast. After my morning workout and run, I was hungry!

He chuckled when I explained my morning routine.

"We will have to run together. I also put in five miles this morning. Where did you run?"

"I went north for several miles and back."

"Most of this area is safe. I would have been concerned if you told me you went south. I run on the school track around the block. They have a half-mile oval; it is easier on the feet, and there are no traffic concerns."

"I will join you tomorrow if that is okay."

"It is. I'm supposed to watch over you, but I'm not certain what all that means. I've never done this before. You don't look like you will need a babysitter if Janice and I go out in the evening."

"Uh, can I select the sitter?"

Janice spoke up, "Absolutely not!"

"Just kidding," I mumbled.

"Sure," she said with a smile. "I was fifteen once."

Dick moved the conversation forward.

"You will meet with your dialog coach, tutors, studio representative, and stunt team."

"I understand the tutors. What does a dialog coach or a studio rep do, and why will I need a stunt team?"

"The dialog coach will work with you memorizing and delivering your lines. The studio rep will be your contact for any problems you may have. The stunt team will evaluate your need for stand-ins."

"Dialog coaching is a relief. I have been concerned about my lines. I already have a question for the studio rep, and I think I will be able to do most of my stunts."

"What is your question for the studio rep?" Dick asked.

"Would it be possible for me to get a hardship driver's license here in California?"

"That question has already been raised, and the studio is looking into it. I suspect the answer is yes. As you can imagine, the studio has a lot of pull. Be sure to bring it up if your rep doesn't. The stunt team will want to ensure you can ride a horse and know common sense procedures around large animals like cattle."

"You don't know much of my history, Dick?"

"Not really. I was given a chance to pick up some extra money and grabbed it."

"I'm the reigning National Champion Bull rider in the Junior Division."

"That will make things a lot easier for all of us! From that, is it safe to say you can ride a horse? What about handling weapons?"

"Yeah, I can do that," I replied dryly. "You need to catch up on my biography."

"Rick, save us some time, and please answer the question."

"Dick, I can ride a horse with no problem. I only fell off once, as planned in another movie with John Wayne. As far as guns, I'm an honorary Texas Ranger for helping capture a band of cattle rustlers, and I have killed two men in a bank robbery. Is that enough of an answer?"

I didn't like getting grilled. It must be the teenager in me.

Dick looked at me for a minute as though he was deciding whether or not to believe me.

"Yep, that is more of an answer than I ever expected. I don't think you would be stupid enough to lie about things like that."

"You can check it out easily enough."

"Please don't be offended, but I will."

"None taken. I understand you have to know what you are working with."

Janice swatted at her husband, "I told you you should have found out more about Rick before taking on the project."

That lightened the mood, which had taken a serious turn. I wonder where it would have gone if I had started talking about the FBI and Russian saboteurs.

"Janice, I need to go shopping. Can you recommend somewhere?"

"There is a Kresge at the mall. They will have everything you need. By the way, I need the sheets and pillows that were on your bed. They are just a loan until you buy what you need."

"I know I have to buy quite a few things; I will just add those to my list. Are you available this evening?"

"Hmm, watch TV or go shopping? Yes, I'm available."

I looked at Dick, "You are welcome to join us, and I will buy dinner."

"That sounds like a deal."

"One last question. Dad told me banking arrangements have been made for me."

"We ended up with Wells Fargo. They have a branch around the corner."

That was cool, as I thought of stagecoaches and the Old West.

"Will I need to stop by before I get paid?"

"No, and that is another question! Now let's head out to the studio."

We got into his Jeep, a World War II surplus, and drove the ten minutes to the studio. Whenever movies were discussed, I thought of Hollywood. The Warner Brothers studios were a hundred-and-ten-acre compound in Burbank.

Mr. Wyman had a badge to let us past security. The first stop we made was at the studio security office. They had my name on a list and had a studio identity card waiting for me. I had to wear it on a lanyard around my neck when coming and going. I would leave it with my regular clothes when on the set.

After that, we went to a small building which had a large meeting room. We weren't the first to arrive but were still a little early. There was a coffee pot set up and a display of donuts, so we headed over there. I had decided that I would try to blend in and not be noticeable until I knew my way around.

The room was set up with tables and chairs forming a horseshoe. Dick picked out our seats. He chose the ones closest to the refreshment table and the exit door.

"When the coffee runs through, you can leave without a commotion, or if the meeting runs long, you can escape for a while."

I filed this strategy away and will be using it in the future.

As we settled in, Mr. Wayne came in, so I stood up again to shake his hand as he worked his way around the room. He seemed to know everyone and was very professional in his greetings, except for me. He took one look at me and let out a roar.

"Welcome, Pilgrim! I hope you brought bail money for everybody!" "

So much for blending in.

"I think I have enough unless you kill someone, then we might have to take out a loan or run for it."

Mr. Wayne thought that was funny. Everyone else sort of chuckled. Since he was laughing, they were laughing, but they didn't get the joke.

I looked around for the other child actors. There weren't any. I then realized four fresh-faced young men in their twenties were the other child actors. I was the kid on the set. I walked over to them, intending to introduce myself, but they turned to ignore me.

About that time, someone said, "Please take your seats."

A gentleman in a three-piece suit made an announcement. "It is starting time, so would everyone please take a seat?"

We all sat down, Mr. Wayne on one side, Mr. Wyman on the other, and me. Mr. Wayne leaned over to Dick.

"I see you are teaching him about being closest to the coffee pot and exit."

Dick just winked back. I felt like I had just joined a club or something.

The man up front introduced himself as Saul Goldman, the producer of this film. With him was Ronald Dodge, the director. I thought there would be a little speech about how this was going to be a great movie and things like that. Instead, it was right to work, or at least that was the intention.

Mr. Goldman looked around and stated, "I see everyone is here but our second lead, Paul Grant. Does anyone know where he is?"

No one appeared to know anything. There was a whispered conference between the producer and director.

"We will wait one-half hour more; he is probably held up in traffic."

"Or he is still dead drunk," Mr. Wayne murmured.

While we were waiting, a man in a business suit came up and introduced himself as Don Pearson.

"I am your contact with the studio," he began. "I understand you need a hardship driver's license."

"I do. There is no way for me to get around without bumming a ride from everyone."

"Okay, you can run over to the DMV after we are done here. It is all arranged. They just need your signature. Is there anything else you need right now?"

He was very brusque, and I didn't think he was interested in me.

"Not at the moment. I will let you know if I do."

He handed me his business card and started to turn away, then stopped. "You can drive, can't you?"

"Yes, I can."

"Good, that helps a lot," he said as he turned and left.

"Welcome to our world, kid," said Dick Wyman.

"Yeah, it can get really weird at times," added John Wayne.

Sitting there, I thought, you guys aren't kidding about that. What is weirdest is that I'm here.

Everyone was up and milling about with coffee and donuts. It was obvious they knew or knew of each other from various movie projects. After the half-hour, the producer called us to order again. This time it started right. The day's first order was handing out scripts, then a shooting schedule.

He told us to hold the scripts till later. We had to go over the shooting schedule first so we knew when and where we needed to be. I hadn't thought about it, but every actor wouldn't be required to be on the set ready to go every minute of the day.

We were all scheduled for our scenes. Some days, we may not even have to be on the set. There were even multiple shooting sets for indoor and outdoor scenes.

The kicker was that shooting schedules needed revising every day as they changed so frequently. So, you had a one-day notice as to when, where, and if you were needed.

We had finished page one of the shooting schedule when Paul Grant showed up. He made an entrance. Some entry, he could barely stand up. There was no doubt that he was hungover. If one of his gang hadn't been helping him, he wouldn't have made it to the table.

His buddy set him in a chair, where Grant promptly fell asleep. The producer and director looked like they had just swallowed lemons. This wasn't a good start.

Strangely, Mr. Wayne seemed pleased about something. I gave him a look. I had practiced for several hours in front of a mirror. I could raise one eyebrow at a time. It was like asking a question without saying a word. He shook his head and didn't answer.

We spent an hour going over the schedule. My part was a supporting role. There was no scene in which I would be the center of attention. All my interactions were to give the stars an audience to play to.

After the meeting was finished, we all filed out. Paul Grant was still sleeping in his chair. The two guys that had come with him were also sleeping in chairs against the wall. We left them all where they were. These guys needed Mr. Hurley's attention!

Mr. Wyman then took me to another building. Someone had a sense of humor at Warner Brothers.

Dick said, "Here is the studio school."

It was a one-room schoolhouse.

When I expressed that thought, he replied, "Actually, some days you will have to be in a period costume because they will be using it as a set."

"If they have ink wells, can I put the girls' pigtails in them?"

"Sure, and you can throw spitballs and play mumbly peg on the playground or roll your hoop."

"I'm going to like this school."

When we went inside, it was like any other schoolroom with modern desks, lighting, blackboards, and pull-down national and world maps. The Zaner-Bloser alphabet series was posted above the blackboard with both small and capital letters.

There were pictures of George Washington and Abraham Lincoln. There was an American flag on a stand. There were hooks for our coats near the door.

Two people, a man and a woman, were waiting for us. Mr. Danson and Miss Sperry were to be my tutors. Miss Sperry would be doing most of my teaching while Mr. Danson was a supervisor for the company that provided the tutoring service for the studio. He would also help monitor tests. They explained to me that right now, I was the only person on the lot of my age and grade so it would be one one-on-one.

They had reviewed my shooting schedule and had it arranged for me to take a series of tests that the State of California approved of to see where I stood academically. They would use my Bellefontaine lessons as a starting point but would move me forward or backward, as indicated by those tests.

Mr. Danson explained, "We see students from every educational background you can imagine. Those backgrounds are not all equal. Also, all students aren't equal in their intelligence or how they apply themselves. Unfortunately, we see too many through here that think because they are in the movies, they don't have to learn anything else."

He went on to add, "Rick, we've high hopes for you. Your grades from Bellefontaine are extremely high, and the curriculum used is a particularly good one. The studios are always under pressure from the State School Board to prove that their academic programs are as good as the public ones. Your results should help vindicate our program."

No pressure there!

"After placement is confirmed, we will provide any other textbooks you need. I have an example of your work. Do you type all your essays and reports?"

"I do."

"Then we will get a typewriter in here for your use. What make and model are you used to?"

"I have an IBM Executive Model B at home."

"That is a nice machine. Do you know that there is now a model C?"

"Yes, I was able to get a good price on model B because of inventory clearance."

"We will buy a model C for the classroom. It won't feel that different from your B."

"Then that is what I will buy for my apartment."

"I didn't think you would be out here long enough to justify that."

"Probably not time-wise, but I tend to keep busy so I will need it."

We agreed I would be back after lunch tomorrow to start my placement testing.

Chapter 21

Dick Wyman took me over to the studio café for a quick lunch. He talked me into trying something called a taco. It was so good I went back for another one.

Afterward, we went to the DMV to get my driver's license. He had me drive his Jeep. I had never used a stick on the floor, only the column, but the feel of the clutch was the same, so I caught on pretty quickly. The hardest part for me was remembering to use the hand signals.

I would remember right and left turns but had to think to hold my hand down to show that I was slowing and stopping. It made me appreciate the newer cars with built-in turn signals.

We made it there without any wrecks, and Dick didn't look too nervous. We had been given a name, Mr. Dawson. He turned out to be a cheerful-looking person about fifty years old. He was expecting us. He sat me down at a table and handed me the written test.

"Take this, so we know you know the rules of the road."

It wasn't a problem as I had studied them in Ohio when Dad was teaching me how to drive. I'm glad I had since Mr. Pearson hadn't said anything about this.

There was one other thing Mr. Pearson hadn't bothered to tell me about. After I handed my test in with a score of ninety percent, Mr. Dawson showed me a book where twenty miles per hour was the speed limit in unposted residential zones. After that, he asked, "What vehicle are you using for your driving test?"

Dick never paused, "He will be using my Jeep."

We went out to the Jeep.

Mr. Dawson said, "I haven't been in one of these for many years. It doesn't bring back any fond memories."

A great way to start a driving test I hadn't been warned about.

The first thing I did was adjust the driver's seat. Dick and I were close enough in height I didn't have to do that, but I wanted to demonstrate that I knew it might have to be done. Then I adjusted the rearview mirror. There were no side mirrors like our car at home.

While exiting the parking lot, I mentioned that today was the first day I had driven a vehicle without automatic turn signals, so I had to think about using my hands.

Mr. Dawson chuckled, "Try doing it with a BAR in your lap."

We drove around for close to fifteen minutes, with Mr. Dawson giving me turning directions. He even had me out on Highway 101 mixed in with speeding traffic. Going fifty miles an hour in an open Jeep is a thrill ride. We returned to the DMV, where I parallel parked. The parking gods must have been with me that day. It did help that the Jeep was shorter and that I had a good view behind me.

While we had been driving, Mr. Dawson asked me why I needed a hardship driver's license. I explained that my parents were at our home in Ohio while I was in a movie at Warner Brothers. I needed a way to get around because in LA, if you couldn't drive, you couldn't get anywhere.

He laughed at that and told me it was getting more like that every day. There were now so many cars; if I looked south to the city in the basin, I would see a brown haze. They were calling that smog. It was from car exhaust fumes.

He told me he didn't know how they could fix it, but it would hurt people's health in the long term. As it worsened, there were days when you couldn't see the mountains. We went back inside where he typed out my new driver's license.

We were done with work for the day, and it was only two o'clock. I did comment to Dick that it was a good thing I already knew how to drive.

Dick welcomed me to the world of studio support. "It depends on who your support person is. Obviously, as a supporting actor and brand new, you don't rate very highly."

"I guess not, but since it came out okay, I now know to be careful in my dealings with Mr. Pearson."

"As they get to know you and appreciate your work, you will get better support. Of course, that could take years."

"All I need to do is survive the next seven weeks. To do that, I need stuff for my apartment. When are we going shopping?"

"The sooner, the better. Let's go pick up Janice and get it done."

It didn't take Janice exceptionally long to get ready to go shopping. The S.S. Kresge store was at a mall about two miles away. We piled in Janice's 55 Chevy and rode over.

They had grocery carts to carry your merchandise. I didn't think we needed one. Little did I know. Janice first asked if I had enough money on me. When I told her three hundred dollars, she said, "That's a start."

We filled up a cart with kitchenware. There were dish towels and cloths, potholders, a starter set of pots and pans, four place settings of tableware and silverware, a spatula, and a cutlery set. I thought Janice would flip over some Corning Ware baking dishes. They were white with a blue design on them that she called *Cornflower*.

She informed me this was the latest in thermal shock dishware. These dishes would last forever. They even had drop resistance. It would take work to destroy these. You could take it from the oven to cold water, and it wouldn't crack. I don't think I would care to try that, but I did pick up a set.

Dick and I kidded her that future archeologists would dig up these dishes from our toilets. They would be the only sign of our civilization. Janice didn't think this was funny. When Dick and I discussed the possible religious significance of cornflowers in blue, she huffed away to get another cart to fill. Dick had to push the full one.

We went to the bedding area next. Two sets of sheets, pillows, pillowcases, and several blankets. Towels, washcloths, lions, and tigers. Oh My! I didn't think it would end. I got to push this cart as Janice retrieved another.

She insisted I needed a broom, whisk broom, mop and bucket, a small radio, TV dinner trays, and a vacuum cleaner. We now had three carts full. We headed for the checkout. One hundred and fifty-six dollars later, we loaded the stuff in the trunk of the Chevy.

Dick and I started to get in the car when Janice said, "Where do you guys think you are going? We aren't done yet. He needs rods and drapes."

Dick tried a weak, "But we don't know the measurements."

"I have those," replied Janice.

A warning doesn't even try to stop a woman in full shopping mode. I have made this trip seem quick. It was anything but. Janice had comparison-priced every item we bought. She insisted I give my opinion on color and design even if I couldn't have cared less.

I thought buying the kitchen and bedding items was painful. Drapes are another whole level of pain. Nothing at Kresge met her approval. I was bullied into agreeing with her. We went to another store in the mall and finally found them at a third store. After we bought them, it was after six o'clock.

We stopped at Danny's Coffee Shop. Dick was known there, so the evening manager came over to talk to us. He told Dick that their name would change to Denny's Coffee Shop later in the year because of confusion with another LA shop.

They were also exploring the possibilities of expanding their menu. Donuts and coffee wouldn't make dinner, so after we rested a little from the horrible shopping trip, we went to a steak house across the road.

We returned to my apartment and unloaded everything. Janice told me I could still use her sheets tonight, but please wash and return them tomorrow. That is when I realized that while we had bought cleaning implements, we hadn't bought any cleaning supplies. That and the single roll of toilet paper made me realize that I would be shopping tomorrow.

Dick and Janice left, and I spent the rest of the evening unwrapping purchases and finding places to store them. At ten o'clock, I fell into bed exhausted. That is when I figured out it was now 1 a.m. in Ohio and that I had been running all day long. That was my last thought until six the next morning.

I did my morning duties in the bathroom, performed my exercises, and was just finished dressing for my run when Dick pounded on my door. Most people knock on doors, and Dick pounds. You would always know it was him or the police. Come to think of it, I had pounded on a door not that long ago, but the building had been on fire.

We walked over to the high school track, did some stretching exercises, and then took off. We worked up to our regular paces. Our strides were close in length, so we stayed within ten feet of each other on one circuit of the track. I had been on the inside our first trip around.

Dick moved over to the inside, and we stayed pretty even for the rest of our laps. We didn't talk at all while running, but it was still pleasant to have someone else there. After walking a cool-down lap, we headed back to our respective apartments.

We talked about the day and the week ahead as we walked back. I mentioned buying a car. He told me that he had been asked to help. Dick asked what kind of car I was thinking of. I told him a 1958 Thunderbird convertible.

He whistled and said, "It must be nice to have parents who can afford that."

He didn't say it in a meaningful manner; he meant it must be nice. I laughed and reminded him of what I was doing.

"Oh, yeah. Then it must be nice making that sort of money at your age."

I asked him if he could tell me what he was making as the head stuntman in this movie.

Now he laughed and replied, "It is nice to be me!"

We talked about the car for a couple of minutes and our schedules for the coming week and decided to put off the purchase until early next week. That would only leave me stuck for one weekend. Since I would probably need the downtime by then, it was no big deal.

I did have the grace to blush internally when I had that thought. Fifteen years old with a driver's license and getting a brand-new convertible. Most teen boys would give their left nut for this. Well, maybe not a nut. We had plenty of imaginary uses for them.

I showered and put on jeans, a Western shirt, and my hat and boots, which certainly put me in character. Then I went over to Dick and Janice's place. She had fixed a smaller breakfast for us today. It was oatmeal from a round box, but it sure looked and tasted like porridge to me.

After breakfast, we left for the studio today; the guard at the front waved us through when he saw we both had badges around our necks. I went to my assigned room, where I was to meet my voice coach.

Chapter 22

My coach was a twenty-some-year-old named Vince Jacobs. Vince told me he had studied at the University of California for dramatic acting. He was considered to have a wonderful voice, but the camera didn't like him. I didn't know cameras had emotions, so I questioned this statement. He explained that some of the best-looking people in the world didn't look right on camera.

For example, Vice President Richard Nixon was very presentable in person but looked like a thief on camera. He could have played villains but never a good guy. I thought that a pity since if he was vice president, he must be a man of honor.

Vince explained that he would work with me on naturally presenting my lines. The background of the story had my family bringing me with them from Ohio, so I had no accent to worry about. All I had to do was say the lines like a real person.

I had no more than two consecutive sentences in the entire script, so I figured it would be easy.

He had a Grundig tape recorder which he started. He then read a line from the script to which I had to respond. I had the script open and read the sentence. He then played it back. From its stilted sound, it was obvious that I was reading the line. He had me repeat the line five times, then try it without the script. It took me several more tries, and I was finally able to say the line naturally.

He played my line back, and it sounded very natural. Then he played his and my lines back. It sounded like two different conversations were going on. While the lines were both clear, they didn't come across as though we were communicating with each other.

Vince pointed out that the line presented to me came across as a challenge, and while the words I used were the right ones, they came across as accepting an invitation to a tea party.

Mr. Andersen, played by John Wayne, says, "Are you up to this boy? It is long and hard. There will be no running home to Mama."

My reply is, "Yes, sir, I am up to this."

Not a whole lot to say. Even when I said the sentence naturally on the recording, it was still flat, as if I was disinterested. Vince said the same line but had a rising inflection at the end. The neutral sentence now came off as returning the challenge with a little resentment thrown in.

I tried it that way several times. The last time on the recording, it sounded like it was supposed to. Vince came out in an extremely high-toned British accent.

"By Jove, I think he's got it."

In the same accent, I returned, "Thank you, me Lord, it is appreciated."

This stopped him dead in his tracks.

"Where did you learn to do that accent?"

"Me mum; she is British."

"Can you do any others?"

"Not really, unless you count my Spanish accent."

We continued in Spanish. "You speak Spanish?"

"Some. I have been learning it this school year."

"Who taught you?"

"A neighbor lady, Mrs. Hernandez, from Cuba, has been teaching me and my brothers and sister. She is originally from Spain, so I don't know what the accent is."

"It sounds as though Mrs. Hernandez is highly educated."

"Do the scriptwriters know you speak Spanish or can do an English accent as if you were from Mayfair?"

"No, and where is Mayfair?"

"When you hear English royalty speak, their accent is described as a Mayfair accent. It is an expensive part of London."

"Oh, I didn't know that, but now you say it, it is mentioned in Pygmalion."

"Did your mother come from London?"

"Close by, Essex."

"Essex is not considered close by to Mayfair. I wonder where she got her accent."

I thought about telling him who my godmother was but decided it wouldn't make a difference and would come off as bragging. Vince dropped the Spanish and told me that I had a fairly good command of the language. He also said that I should somehow let the writers know of my other accents as they might need them someday. Actors always had to be planting seeds for the next job.

We continued with my lines now. I would memorize them to speak naturally and then work on the inflection. After a while, it began to flow. I would read and understand the intent of a scene, then structure the strength and tone of my reply based on the scene.

We did this till lunchtime and then adjourned to the cafeteria for lunch. I tried a burrito for lunch. It was pretty spicy, but I thought I could learn to like them. My first bite was funny, though. I thought my mouth was on fire. Vince had been waiting for it. He laughed as I gulped a Coke.

"You Easterners aren't used to this. It won't take long, and you will be putting Tabasco sauce on everything."

He then had to show me what Tabasco sauce was. He poured a drop on my burrito, and I was gulping Coke again.

After lunch, I went over to the schoolhouse where Miss Sperry was waiting for me. She immediately started me on the tests. The first one was math. Towards the end of the test, I was running into problems that I hadn't seen before. Since they were solved by using formulas, I used the knowledge I had, and the solutions cross-checked, so I think I did okay. It also told me what I had to do tonight.

I asked her what days each subject's exams would be given. This did not breach any exam protocol, so she told me Latin tomorrow, English on Thursday, Biology on Friday, and World History the following Monday. Fortunately, in my suitcase were my textbooks from school. Since the tests were based on the whole year, I would have to at least look at the entire book. I had no illusions that I would learn everything, but anything was better than nothing.

That took me up to four o'clock. Dick Wyman was working until six, so I had several hours to kill. I wandered about and looked at the various buildings and sets that were not in use and open.

I was in one mansion, well, mansion false front, when I noticed plumbing fixtures in a fancy bathroom. It looked like a scene had been shot here. What I noticed was that the fixtures looked more like artwork than bathroom faucets. I thought the rich lived differently than we do.

From there, I walked over to where the stuntmen were headquartered. It was a barn-like structure that did include a stable with horses but also had some weird stuff like giant trampolines. I saw a group of guys lifting weights in the corner of the yard. When I sauntered over to practice being in character, a couple of them smirked at me but didn't say anything.

After a while, one of them did ask, "You look pretty fit; do you work out?"

"I do pushups and sit-ups daily and run five miles whenever possible."

"Work with weights at all?"

"No. I don't own any and don't know how to use them."

"How long are you going to be here?"

"Six weeks is on the schedule."

The next thing I knew, I had a ten-pound weight in my hand and was being shown how to do curls. I was asked my name, and a blank form was filled out. In the next hour, I learned about ten different exercises I could do with the weights. They had me record my starting weights and the number of repetitions or reps I could do, as they called them.

I had finished the last ones when Dick showed up. He looked around.

"Well, it didn't take you guys long to find a new acolyte. Rick, these guys will have you worshipping at the altar of bodybuilding if you let them. Nothing wrong with looking good, but don't take it to extremes."

Gee, I was only lifting weights. It's not like going to church! As we started to leave, the guy who started me out said, "See you tomorrow, Brother Rick."

I was concerned, which must have shown on my face because they all started to roar with laughter.

Dick, Janice, and I grabbed a burger and went to a supermarket. One cart was loaded with cleaning and laundry supplies, the other with food.

The foods were basic, teenage boy basic. This included hot dogs, hamburgers, milk, bread, butter, strawberry jam, peanut butter, mustard, and ketchup. For some reason, Janice also insisted on salt and pepper. Oh, yeah, and lots of toilet paper.

We were home before seven. They had a meeting, and I had an appointment with a Latin textbook. My Latin teacher in Bellefontaine, Miss Audie, had taught the four conjugations and six tenses: present, perfect, imperfect, pluperfect, future, and future perfect during our first semester.

Her intention was then to have us learn additional vocabulary and practice the use of the tenses for the second semester. This worked to my advantage because the textbook spread them out over the year. My real lack would be vocabulary. I also remembered something Tom Watson had mentioned at lunch one day.

The final exams in Latin by State Board of Education regulations had an essay portion which counted as twenty-five percent of the grade. Tom had explained there was a trick to doing well on this portion.

The idea behind the essay was to gauge how well you had learned the Latin language. It was not a test of your ability to write a reasoned response. It was a test of your language comprehension skills. So, they weren't looking for a strong response. They were looking for a well-written response.

The trick was to plan a general response and then spin their question to fit your response which you had written out in advance. You couldn't make a copy, but if you wrote it down and made sure the language was correct, then rewrote it on the test, you would do well.

The example Tom gave was a question.

"What were the ethics of the early Roman Republic?"

He answered that the average Roman was a very hard-working, ethical person and supported this with a description of working life on a farm. Any question that he was asked, he would turn to the working life on a farm.

This took a lot of the pressure off the last question of the exam and gave me more time for the rest of it. I figured it probably didn't change much from state to state, so I spent two hours constructing a grammatically correct answer. Now I had to hope that there was an essay on tomorrow's exam.

After all that work, I made myself a jam sandwich. It also made me realize that the next time I was near Kresge, I needed a toaster. I also needed to buy some furniture, office supplies, and a typewriter. I started a list. Setting up housekeeping was expensive!

I managed to stay up until eleven o'clock. As I was falling asleep, I realized I hadn't let my parents know I had arrived and was okay! I could be in trouble. I also needed to add phone service to my list.

Chapter 23

When Dick and I went running in the morning, I related my failure to call home and asked if I could use his telephone. He laughed.

"Your Dad won the pool."

"What pool?"

"About how long it would take you to remember to call home. Your Mom, Dad, Janice, and I all had bets going on how long it would take you. Your Mom thought it would be right after you landed, Janice and I divided up yesterday, and your Dad got from today on out."

"Ouch. I'm going to be in trouble."

"Not really, I let them know you arrived that night, and Janice talked to them last night. You will never be allowed to forget it, but I don't think you will be in trouble. They realize this is one heck of a life change for you."

It was early in California but midmorning in Ohio, so I called home from Dick's. When I called, Mum answered the phone. When I said this is Ricky, she replied, "Ricky, who?"

I was toast. She gave me a hard time for a little while, then got serious about my trip and how I was getting on. We talked for half an hour.

This would be an expensive call. We agreed that I would call once a week on Sunday to get the cheapest rate. I would send a weekly letter with more details so the whole family could keep up with me. Dad wasn't available, but I got to say a quick "Hi" to Denny, Eddie, and Mary. Mary wanted to know if I had gone to Disneyland yet. I promised her I would buy her a present when I did go.

After the call, I gave Janice twenty dollars for the call and told her I would pay whatever extra appeared on their phone bill. After breakfast, Dick and I headed out to the studio. This morning was to be the first scene that I would be in. I had to go to the costume department and then make-up.

The people in costume looked at me and asked if I knew I didn't have to provide my costumes. They then proceeded to have me change into my costume. The Levi jeans they had me wear had buttons on the front instead of a zipper. That was so odd.

The shirt was plain brown or what they called butternut; it had no collar. I wore suspenders instead of a belt. The boots were battered and plain looking, but they fit well and were amazingly comfortable. I wasn't wearing a hat in this scene.

From there, I went to makeup. The studio had me skip my haircuts for the last two weeks. The first thing the makeup people did was give me a haircut. It looked like they had placed a bowl over my head and trimmed around it. When I mentioned this, I was thanked for recognizing the effect they were trying to achieve.

They touched up my face with some stuff they said would cut down on shadows so that I wouldn't look like a corpse. Other than that, there wasn't much to it. The lady doing it told me for some movies, they would have to spend two or three hours in makeup for a two-minute scene.

The scene being shot today was all of us boys hearing a speech from John Wayne about how we were too young for a cattle drive. I had no lines. I just had to pretend I was listening and then look disappointed.

I arrived on the set five minutes early. It was interesting to see the various prop people, cameramen, soundmen, and others doing their preparation. Mr. Wayne was there but didn't look like he was in a good mood, so I only nodded to him. He nodded back, and that was it.

Everyone was there but Paul Grant. Starting time came and went. The director wasn't happy. Since Wayne and Grant had dialog, they needed him for the scene. A runner was sent to Grant's trailer.

That is how I found out that real stars had a trailer to retreat to during the time they weren't working. The runner came back and told the director there was no one at the trailer.

We waited till lunchtime, which was the end of the filming sequence for the day. We were all excused for lunch and told to be back here in the same place at the same time tomorrow. I heard the director talking to an assistant. I won't repeat what was said. It wasn't nice.

After lunch, the schoolhouse and Latin test were next, so I headed there. I was allowed up to three hours for the test. I took the whole time. I was incredibly lucky the essay question was on the test. It was about the life of the average Roman. I wrote about the life of the average Roman farmer as that was what most Romans were. At least, that is what I said. I would have no idea if it was true or not. Of course, I wrote out my prepared two-hundred-word essay with that introduction.

There were some vocabulary words that I didn't know, but between English and Spanish, I had several good guesses. I hoped my test results would be good enough to show that I had completed one semester of Latin.

After the test, I was glad to go to the stunt area and work out with weights. It was restful after concentrating all afternoon. I recorded my weights and number of reps on my sheet on a clipboard kept in the barn. I had a fifteen-minute wait for Dick Wyman. We headed back to the apartments right away.

During the drive, I told him about my morning and Paul Grant's no-show.

"That is not good. On the first day of shooting the movie is behind schedule. If it gets too bad, they will abandon the movie."

On the way, I saw an office supply store. I asked Dick if we could stop in. He was okay with it as long as it wasn't more than forty-five minutes.

I was able to buy a Model C IBM typewriter along with all the supplies. They even had office furniture, so I bought a desk, chair, credenza, and bookcase. They agreed to deliver the furniture on Saturday morning. Since it was guys shopping, we were out of there in half an hour.

Getting home, I set the typewriter up on the kitchen table. I realized that I could have skipped the office furniture completely, but I was glad I hadn't. It was neat to have my own office.

I tested the typewriter by starting a letter home to the entire family and making personal comments. I told my brothers I would be buying a weight set for us to use at home. For Mum and Mary, there was a paragraph on going through makeup. I told Dad about the specialized fixtures I saw on sets of wealthy homes and wondered if there was anything we could do.

I skipped dinner with Dick and Janice that night. I felt that I had imposed enough. Instead, I went to a little restaurant across the street. I quickly learned that no English was spoken here, at least any that I could hear. It was seat yourself, so I went to the counter.

The waitress looked at me and asked in good English what I would like. I ordered the meatloaf, mashed potatoes, and gravy with corn. It was great. The Hispanic crowd looked like a working-class, blue-collar group. I didn't feel uncomfortable around them. They seemed like decent, hard-working men.

One of the guys teased my waitress about her serving the good-looking gringo. This was all in Spanish, but I was amazed that I understood every word. She told him that if she didn't have a handsome husband at home, she would rather be with a good-looking gringo than a poor excuse of a man like him. Everyone laughed. So did I. That got me some looks.

The waitress asked me in Spanish if I spoke the language. I told her a little. We chatted in Spanish for a while. Finally, she asked me where I had learned Spanish. I explained the whole deal to her. She nodded her head.

"You have a very educated accent. You sound like a professor from Spain would. Be careful not to take up the local accent. Yours will stand you well if you can keep it."

After returning to my apartment, I opened my English textbook. The second semester concentrated on reading comprehension. There were short stories in my text, these had to be read and questions answered at the end of the story. This was my strong suit, and I would have normally overkilled it with an essay on every question.

This time I settled for reading the story and making certain I knew the answer to the question. I would do okay if they used the same stories in California as they did in Ohio. If they used different ones, I had a problem. I read that most states bought the same books as the state of Texas, as they purchased more than any other state, so prices were kept down. I hoped this was true here.

I studied until eleven o'clock, then turned out the lights. As I was trying to go to sleep, I thought about meeting some girls, maybe at the swimming pool on Saturday if it was warm enough.

Chapter 24

Thursday morning, I was up at six a.m., and already, a routine was developing. I met Dick as he was coming out of his apartment. We did our run. It felt good as my stamina was coming back. I wasn't huffing and puffing at the end as I had been from the winter layoff. I wished I could run all year round.

At the studio, Paul Grant made an appearance. He showed why he did well on his TV show, delivering his lines in one take. After the shoot, Mr. Wayne complimented Grant on his performance.

Grant told him, "Old man, some of us have it, and some don't."

Mr. Wayne replied, "I wouldn't make a habit of calling me that, son."

Several of the movie's writers were on the set to observe. I noticed one nudge the other.

After lunch, I went to my one-room schoolhouse. As the only current student, I was getting possessive. I lucked out on the test. California and Ohio were currently using the same textbooks, so the questions were about the short stories I had read.

They also threw in some general questions that were no-brainers, like what did Sherlock Holmes do when he was high on cocaine? That was easy. He shot the letter V in the walls of his room. The V was for Victoria. I wondered how hard it would be to shoot E's for Elizabeth.

I felt fairly good about that test. My workout went well, and I was able to increase the number of reps by five. Dick Wyman also had me saddle a horse and ride around the lot to prove that I knew what I was doing.

I swear my horse fell asleep moving. That is until we turned towards the barn. Then he took off at a gallop. He also cut the corner at a shed so close I had to duck so the eaves wouldn't take my head off.

For that little trick, I rode the horse around that shed ten times and made him stay away from the corner. I then took him out away and turned towards the barn. The horse must have learned its lesson because while it did move fast, it gave me clearance on the corner.

After I rubbed the horse down, Dick told me, "You know your way around a horse."

I think from him that was high praise.

I ate at the same little diner. This time going with what I thought was Mexican but was told it was Tex-Mex food. It was great, and I developed a liking for spicy foods. Mum never cooked like this.

I returned to my apartment and started on Biology. There were no tricks here, you knew it, or you didn't, and there was new material introduced the whole year. I picked several systems to try to understand how they worked. If I had to list specific details of each system, such as the names of the major nodes of the nervous system, I was done. I would be doing all I could to pass seventy-five percent of the material on the test if they distributed the questions evenly.

Before falling asleep, I thought about girls again. This was getting to be a problem. I had to meet someone.

Friday was the same, get up, exercise, run, and go to the studio. Go to costume, go to makeup. Go to set, wait for Paul Grant, and wait for Paul Grant. This time the director didn't rant and rave. However, he was in serious conversation with the producer and all of the assistants. Mr. Wayne was also involved in the conversation. None of them seemed happy.

The Biology test was as I feared. They wanted specifics that I didn't know. I felt like I had bombed it. I needed the workout after that.

I decided to worry about World History on Saturday and Sunday and spent Friday evening watching my little TV. I did add to my letter home.

Saturday morning, they delivered my office furniture early. I set everything up and added some more to my weekly letter. Later, I walked to the mall to buy some new underwear.

Walking towards the mall, I found a public library. I stopped there and was able to obtain a library card using my new driver's license. I browsed for a while, checked out several books, and then headed to the mall. After that shopping, I returned to the apartment. I now had to go to the bank.

At the apartment, I dropped off the books and picked up letters from my father and our attorney. They identified me as being able to draw from the checking account that had been opened by mail.

At the bank, I went to a window, where they, in turn, sent me to see an officer of the bank. After I shared the letters and my driver's license, the officer, Mr. Sloan, went to a cabinet and withdrew a file.

After reviewing it, he commented, "This is highly unusual, but all is in order. May I ask what brings you to California?"

I explained about the movie. All of a sudden, he was okay with everything. This branch had a lot of movie industry experience and a good understanding of their specific needs. He ordered me personalized checks for future use. In the meantime, he asked me how much I needed.

I told him that I would be taking fifty dollars a week out of living expenses but that I would be buying a car this coming week and would need close to three thousand dollars.

This led to a discussion of what sort of car I was buying. When I told him a '58 Thunderbird, he about drooled on his tie. Turned out he was a Ford man. I think I had a friend for life. This week, I filled out a counter check for my money, and he had one of the tellers cash it.

I had tacos for lunch at a little stand. This food was growing on me.

I spent the afternoon studying. After six o'clock, I knocked on Dick's door and made a call home. Everything was fine for them and me. I gave an update on the movie and setting up my apartment. Denny wanted to know if I had been swimming yet. I told him I would be doing that tomorrow.

I sat and talked with Dick for a while when I hung up. Janice was at a card club with friends. We discussed the upcoming week and decided that Monday would be a good time to start looking for a car.

He also shared that the producer of the film was beginning to feel like having Paul Grant in it was a big mistake. They were hoping that they could get him to the studio on time on Monday, ready to work. It costs a lot of money to have crews sitting around. Too many days like this past week, and they might be unable to finish the movie.

I returned to my apartment and started one of my library books. It was a Western with everything you could ask for, a gunman, a pretty girl, a masked rider, rustlers, and gunfights. I was glad to see Jane and Lassiter fall in love. Bern and Bess escaping to the East made sense. I don't see how you could live forever in a sealed-off canyon, even if it were an earthly paradise. Other than that part of the story, it was a fun read.

Sunday morning was like the other days of the week, except after my run with Dick, I had nothing to do. I had packed a swimsuit from home, so I went down to the pool. It was in the mid-seventies, but I was the only one there. I swam a few laps in the chilly water and then stretched out on a pool lounge chair.

I had been there long enough to turn over when a female voice stated, "You're not from California, are you?"

Wondering how she would know that, I looked up to a lovely vision. She met the requirements of a Beach Boy surfer girl. Since she was wearing a frock, I doubted she would be swimming today. Unfortunately, she looked to be in her mid-twenties.

"I'm from Ohio, but how did you know I wasn't from California?"

"Californians don't swim in unheated pools in January."

"Oh," was my brilliant return.

She laughed and walked away. That was so much for my dream of meeting a pretty girl by the pool. Dreams crushed, I returned to my room, cleaned up, and walked the two miles to the mall. I ended up buying some golf shirts at Kresge. At least I called them golf shirts. The salesman called them polo shirts. Polo was considered a higher-class sport than golf.

I had lunch at a nondescript restaurant on the way home. I decided not to eat there again. The place didn't look that clean, and I didn't want food poisoning. When I got home, I cracked my World History book and started memorizing names, dates, and places. I didn't spend much time on the whys, which were what I enjoyed. I was studying for the test.

I had hotdogs for dinner and then watched some TV. For the first time, I started to feel lonely. I added more to my letter home.

Chapter 25

It started as a normal Monday. I dropped my letter home in a mailbox at the studio entrance. When I arrived at my voice lesson, things took a strange turn. There was shooting going on, but I wasn't in it today, so I had to work on my lines for my next speaking part. It was to be a four-hour session.

Halfway through, two gentlemen came into the room. I thought I recognized one of them from his distinctive mustache, but I said nothing since no one had introduced him.

The other guy, one of the writers, said.

"He was a no-show. We are looking at Plan B."

I wasn't sure what that was all about, but I figured Grant was the no-show. Vince Jacobs gave me a thicker group of papers.

"Read these in your posh accent."

I cleared my throat and started. Each page had a different flavor. I had to be happy, sad, angry, really angry, tired, and insulted, to name a few of the emotions that had to be demonstrated. The entire time I had to keep the accent. The further into the reading, the easier it was. This was something I had done for days on end at home if I wanted to tease Mum a little.

In the end, the unnamed gentleman spoke up.

"He has the accent; you must work on his delivery."

He then asked me.

"Was your Mum's maiden name Newman?"

From his accent, I knew who he was.

"Yes, it is, Mr. Niven."

"You look a lot like her. I thought I recognized your last name. I knew your Mum during the war and met your father several times. We were all jealous of him, you know. We couldn't figure out why she picked a Yank. Tell them I said hello."

"I will, sir," I said as he left with the writer.

"What was that all about, Vince?"

"I think Plan B might be a change in your role in the movie if Grant doesn't come around."

"But why do they want an accent?"

"That part I don't understand."

I had lunch at the cafeteria with several of the stuntmen. I thought I would be hanging out with the other child actors. I mentioned that, and the stuntmen laughed.

"They play the part of children. The youngest is at least twenty-five. They just look young. They show up when they are needed for a scene."

"What about their coaching sessions?"

I then had to explain my sessions on learning how to deliver my lines.

"Someone likes you, kid. That is not normal. Actors are professionals who take care of themselves. If they need a coach, they hire their own."

I suspect I owed a thank you to Mr. Wayne.

After lunch, I went for my World History exam. It was easier than I thought it would be. I had picked the right people, places, and dates to memorize over the weekend. Of all my tests, biology had given me the most trouble.

I finished the exam by three-thirty, so I headed over to the stunt area to start my workout. When I arrived, I saw something remarkably interesting going on. The stuntmen had the trampoline set up and were practicing falling off a roof. Of course, I had to watch that. It didn't take long, and I had a short course on how to fall off a roof.

It was really fun. One of the stuntmen told me he had seen me be dragged behind that horse in the movie *It Never Happened.* He told me that it looked so real. He wanted to know who the stuntman was. I told him I had done it.

He wanted to know how the shot was set up, how many takes it took, and other details. I finally broke down and told the truth that it was an accident caught by the cameras.

He thought that was a hoot and had to tell everyone in listening distance. I figured I would hear jokes about falling off a horse for a week or so.

I had finished my lifting routine when Dick showed up. Of course, he was asked if he knew about me falling off a horse in *It Never Happened*. Dick hadn't, so it was related all over again. He loved it. His comment was, "And a star was born."

On the ride back to the apartment, I told him about the morning's events and this mysterious Plan B. His response surprised me.

"Rick, do you have an agent?"

"No," I replied.

"It is time you had one. Right now, you are swimming with sharks."

"I don't know anyone or how to contact one."

"Would you trust me to recommend one?"

"Sure, if I could interview him before signing anything."

"That is a sensible attitude. You should also call your parents tonight and let them know what might be going on."

"Who is the agent?"

"John Baxter. He is an old pro in this business. He represents me."

"Sounds like I should meet him."

"I think you should, I owe John a lot, and I know he is going through some tough times right now."

"Such as?"

"He has a granddaughter with leukemia, and her treatments are costing a fortune. They seem to be working, but he needs every cent he can get."

"I will talk to him; how can I contact him?"

"I will call and have him meet with us as soon as possible. I think you are going to need an agent real soon.

"There is something else, Rick. We planned to go car shopping later. Do you think it is wise with everything going on to put a new car in the mix?"

Dang, I hate this adult stuff!

"Yeah, you're probably right. Let's put it off till next week."

When I called home, Mum answered, and I explained my apparent need for an agent. I explained everything I knew and then retold it all to Dad. In turn, Dad talked to Dick and then me again. He told me to go ahead and speak to an agent but not to sign anything without talking to him first. This made complete sense to me.

As I was about to hang up, I remembered to tell them that Mr. Niven had told them hello. Mother thought that was nice. She told that to Dad. I heard him in the background.

"Tell that Limey bast—," Mum interrupted and told me we would talk later.

Janice reminded Dick that it was eight o'clock, and neither of us had eaten dinner. She made us some toasted cheese. They were the best I ever had. She used whole wheat bread with real cheddar cheese instead of Kraft American cheese slices and put salsa on them. Wow! Better than Wonder Bread any day of the week.

For the first night in a week, I didn't have any studying to do. I spent the evening in front of the TV with a Coke, potato chips, and a new item from the grocery. While Janice and I were buying groceries, a pretty young lady had me try something new. It was a dip for potato chips. The French onion flavor was perfect with the chips and Coke.

That night I had too much going around in my head about next week and my new car, possible changes in the movie, where I could visit in my new car, and then there were thoughts about girls and my new car. I wondered if there would be girls in the movie changes. That raised the possibility of girls in the movie riding to cool places in my new car. I had so much to consider!

Chapter 26

I love California! I met Dick, and we went for our run. Last night they told me it was snowing in Ohio. Here I was, running in sunshine and seventy degrees. It was perfect. On our way to the studio, he told me he had already spoken to Mr. Baxter, and we were having dinner with him.

Dick also told me, "Enjoy your dinner tonight. If he becomes your agent, he will never buy again. It will be your money no matter who picks up the check."

I'm not certain how I felt about that.

I heard a voice as I walked over to the set where our shoot was taking place.

"Hey partner, hold up."

It was Mr. Wayne, and he was calling me. He caught me in two strides.

"I sort of brought you into this business by the side door. By any chance, do you have an agent?

"Not yet. I'm having dinner with Mr. John Baxter this evening."

"I see the rumor mill is working simply fine. John is a good man. He is in a bit of a bind right now; he needs money desperately, which might send him in a bad direction."

"What do you mean?"

"He is supporting an extremely sick granddaughter and needs a lot of money. If you sign with him, he will try to get every dime he can for you from the studio."

"What's wrong with that?"

"It could wreck the budget, and the project wouldn't get off the ground. If he does get the higher amount, he will also want the highest percentage from you that he can get, so he, in turn, will receive enough money to take care of his problems. I can't blame him for trying to take care of the family, but he might end up losing it all if he goes overboard."

Mr. Wayne continued, "This is a small town business-wise. Everyone hears everything. If John messes this up, he will destroy any chance of making the money he needs for his family."

"That sounds like a mess. Could you give me some real numbers, so I have a perspective on this?"

Mr. Wayne stopped in the middle of the street. We were in the middle of a turn-of-the-century housing development. He led me over to the steps of a Victorian mansion and sat down.

"We will be late for the start," I said.

"Oh, I think they will wait for us."

I felt really stupid for saying that. Of course, they would wait for the star!

"Here's the deal. We think Paul Grant is trying to get out of his contract. The word is that he has been offered the lead role in a comedy with Doris Day.

"It would give him a lead role and break him out of the Western mold. In a way, I can't blame him for wanting to do it, but I do blame him if he welshes on a deal."

"It was talked about you taking on his role. You have the size needed. All the other guys are older than you, but they play younger kids.

"Odd when you think about it; the older guys can only play young parts, and the young guy can play an older guy. I'm getting a headache just thinking about it.

"Then your speech coach told a writer about your ability to do a good British accent. The writer told the production group. David Niven was on the set, so we roped him into listening to you. He says you can maintain the accent under all conditions. That would fit in perfectly with another project I have had in mind for some time."

"What's that?"

"I will get into that later when we see how it is going to work out with Grant. In the meantime, here are the numbers. You could ask for two hundred and fifty to five hundred thousand for a lead role. Baxter will ask you for five to ten percent as his fee. His problems are solved if he can stick us for five hundred thousand and get ten percent from you. Unfortunately, we could never agree to the higher amount."

"You keep saying 'we' about the project and the money. Is this your project?"

"I had better learn to watch my tongue around you, youngster. Yes, I would be putting a lot into the project. That way, I would have major points in the movie."

"What are points?"

"One point is one percent of the profit."

"What would it be reasonable for me to get?"

Mr. Wayne looked at me sharply. "Are we negotiating?"

"Not yet, then I will get tough."

I hoped the way I smiled told him I was kidding. He let it go, so it must be okay.

"Realistically, three hundred thousand would work and possibly points."

"My dad told me that when I had time to think before acting, I should. There are times you can't, but now I have a little time to think about this."

Mr. Wayne stood up, slapped the dust off his pants with his Stetson, and we moved on. Yes, I slapped the dust off with my Resistol; we must have looked like a pair.

This time we were the late ones on set. I was rushed through costuming and makeup. Part of costuming was putting on a gun and holster. A studio armorer presented these. He was responsible for all weapons on the set.

He had me double-check that the barrel of the single-action Colt .45 was clear so there would be no squib shots. He also showed me the color markings he put on blanks and how there was no bullet, just a wad holding the black powder in. He explained the powder was a three-quarter load.

This resulted in lots of smoke, flame, and noise, but there wasn't a projectile. He cautioned me that you could kill someone with at two feet the wadding, a piece of cardboard. At four feet, you could blind them. Beyond that, there could be burns, but they would live. Over ten feet and there was no effect at all.

I pulled the Colt out to examine it. One thing I noticed right away was the weight.

"I own a pair of Colts, and this one seems lighter."

"This weapon will only fire blanks, so a lighter frame and barrel work. This cuts the cost down. They seem to walk off the set after every picture, so we have to watch our budget."

"I see," I replied.

I also thought about the pair of real .45s that came from the set of *It Never Happened*. Oh well, too late now.

Chapter 27

When I went over to the shooting area, Paul Grant was in position. He made a snide remark about the new kids not being able to show up for work on time. I was about to say something when I decided to ignore him. I couldn't change how he thought, so fight the battles that mattered. This one didn't.

In this scene, we were at the end of the cattle drive and whooping it up in town. That was a little strange because we hadn't even started the drive yet, but that is how they did things. I and several others would be firing our pistols on cue into the air.

We did a walk-through and were ready to film. Mr. Wayne wasn't in this scene, but he was watching on the sidelines to my right.

As we were getting into position, I heard someone say, "What the heck!"

I looked to my left and saw a coyote standing in the street.

The coyote had a problem, a real problem. It was foaming at the mouth.

Someone yelled, "Rabies!"

That started the stampede. Everyone started running past me as quickly as they could.

The coyote saw everyone running and took off after them. That left him coming straight at me. I drew my pistol, and time seemed to slow down, and my vision tunneled in on the coyote.

He was coming straight at me and was starting to leap. I fired when he was in midair. The armorer was correct. It was loud, the flame did shoot out the barrel, and there was a cloud of smoke. I hit the coyote in the throat, and it knocked him down.

He was down but not out, so I cocked the pistol and shot it in its ear from one foot. That ended the coyote.

To put it mildly, there was pandemonium on the set. The director told us all to go home. Studio security took custody of the coyote and my weapon.

Did they think I was going to shoot someone? I found out later it was to prove there were only blanks in the pistol. There had been some nasty accidents over the years.

Paul Grant was the one who caused all the real commotion. He stormed off the set, saying that he had been promised security and that the studio was now in violation of his contract, so he was done.

Several people came up to me and thanked me for what I had done. Mr. Wayne had an odd comment.

"David Niven said your mother has a lot of grit; I see you have it too."

"He said he knew her in the war."

"You could put it that way."

You could see Mr. Wayne almost jerk himself like a running dog that had reached the end of its rope. I wonder what he had been going to say.

Los Angeles County Animal Control appeared on the scene and wanted statements from everyone. When they heard that I was the one who tangled with the critter, they examined me closely for any sign of bites. Of course, there weren't any. They took the coyote with them to have it tested for rabies, but it sure looked classic to me.

John Wayne approached me again with the director and producer in tow.

"Rick, am I to understand that if this movie is canceled, you would be willing to work with us on another one?"

"Yes, sir, I would."

"It looks like the time isn't right for *The Cowboys*. We will make the movie someday, but it doesn't look like now. You are not old enough to play the lead, and it would take too much to bring someone else in. We will have legal battles with Grant and might have to pay him over this incident today, which ruins our budget."

"If we could have you lead in another movie at a lower price, we could use the assets we have and still make a profitable movie."

'Sir, I'm having dinner with a prospective agent. I will talk to you tomorrow."

"That sounds good, partner."

It was late enough I went to lunch by myself. While eating, at least twenty people came up to me about the coyote. They all wanted to know how I had been able to stand there calmly while it charged.

I thought that said something about the movie industry. They played the parts of heroes but couldn't understand how someone could face up to a problem in real life.

One person was very persistent in their questioning. They wanted to know where I was in relation to Mr. Wayne. He was on the side, away from the coyote. When it was over, he was next to me.

"So, John Wayne charged into the trouble."

"I guess so. I hadn't thought about it."

"Where was Paul Grant when the coyote was sighted?"

"His place in that scene was next to me."

"Where was he after you shot the coyote?"

"I don't know. He must have left the set because he came back on to yell at the producer."

"So, you stood your ground, John Wayne charged into trouble, and Paul Grant ran?"

"That's what it looked like."

"What do you think of Grant for running?"

"I don't think anything of Paul Grant. He does what he has to, and I do what I have to."

I began to get uneasy about all these questions, so I gave nothing answers and excused myself to go to class.

Both Mr. Danson and Miss Sperry were waiting for me at the schoolhouse. They had the results from my exams. They were incredibly pleased. From my scores, if I took the California end-of-the-year exams, I would pass everything but Biology, and that was close. They felt with three weeks of concentrated study. I could easily pass the test.

I asked, "What about grades? How does that work? From what you are telling me, this is a pass-fail exercise. I could pass, but then I would have no grades for the year. Right now, I am carrying an A average. If I pass the tests, I will get credit for the ninth grade, but there will be no way to tell if I did it with A's, B's, or C's."

"You are correct, Rick. That is why we would also start you on the SAT exam series. Grades have meaning if you are trying to get into college. I have never heard of a factory job application wanting to know your grades, only if you graduated," Mr. Danson told me.

"The universities and colleges rely on the SAT scores more than grades. The SAT is a standard test where high school grades are all over the place across the country. What is an A in one school may be only a B in another," chimed in Miss Sperry.

That made sense to me. I knew that grading in Bellefontaine varied from teacher to teacher. Heck, every kid in school knew that you didn't get near Miss Bale's class if you wanted an easy A in English. She insisted you know the subject.

"So, passing the state requirements and then doing well on the SATs will be the same as having high grades?"

I had reached that conclusion but wanted them to reaffirm it. They did, so we proceeded to the next steps.

"Rick, what we think is needed is a concentration in Biology for the next three weeks plus some review work in the others," Mr. Danson told me, then added, "It wouldn't hurt to expand your Latin vocabulary to include the rest of the year."

A sudden wild thought hit me.

"Can I sit for an exam I have never had the coursework for?"

Miss Sperry replied, "Yes, you can. What are you thinking of?"

"Do you speak Spanish?"

It turned out neither of them could. However, Miss Sperry walked out the door and yelled that she needed someone who was bilingual in Spanish and English. Two stagehands came over. She told them to see if I could speak Spanish.

The two stagehands and I talked about the coyote incident this morning. They both thought I had *cojones* for standing there while the coyote charged. I told them it wasn't bravery; it was the fact that I couldn't run fast! They both thought that was funny.

After several minutes of this, Mr. Danson interrupted.

"From the way you guys are carrying on, I gather he speaks Spanish?"

"Yes, he does. He comes across as very educated."

"Well, then we will test you on it tomorrow, and if you do well, you can sit for the California final."

This gave me a lot of food for thought. How much could I test out of? There was no lesson plan for the day, so I was excused. It was only two o'clock, so I had plenty of time to do my workout.

That gave me time to think. I sat on the steps of a courthouse and thought about my options for the possible new movie. The way I saw it, three needs needed to be addressed. Mine, John Baxter's, and John Wayne's, and all of those needs had short- and long-term requirements.

In the short term, John Baxter needed a lot of money. If he got it, it would hurt me in the long term. John Wayne needed to spend less money. This would hurt John Baxter and help me. No matter how much I was paid, it would be considerably more than I was making now. Even the money I was making now was whipped cream on top of my sundae.

So, I had to come up with a plan that helped Mr. Baxter and Mr. Wayne achieve their goals. Something that would financially hurt me in the short term but could set a solid foundation for the future. Then I had a thought about how I could even improve my short-term problem.

Chapter 28

I went to the studio office and arranged to use a phone in private to call my parents. They checked to see what movie I was working on so they could bill the phone call to that budget. The lady who took care of this was businesslike and helpful.

She also wanted to know about the rabid coyote. She had heard that it had bitten two people before I shot it. That was news to me. I later learned that didn't happen.

I talked to Mum and Dad and explained what I was facing and my possible solution. They both agreed that it might just work and that long term, I would be a big winner in goodwill and probably money. I thanked the ladies in the studio office and headed over to the stunt area.

Today they were roping a post. The guys showed me the basics, and I got to practice for a while. I was also given a free roping gear run so that I could practice on my own. The point was made that I wasn't to jump off any roofs unattended, but if I want to shoot any coyotes, feel free.

After working with the lariat for a while, I started to get the feel of it. I soon became proficient at roping a fence post while standing. I'm sure roping a moving cow on horseback wouldn't be much harder. In my dreams!

I did all my weightlifting with some of the stuntmen. We took turns spotting each other. As usual, I desperately needed a shower when we were finished.

Dick was on time, so I had plenty of time to clean up. I took a quick shower and changed into grey slacks and a light blue golf shirt, or call it a polo shirt if you want to be Hollywood glamorous. A dark blue blazer with gold buttons and a black belt made me look spiffy with a preppy look. I still wore my boots. They were too comfortable to give up.

Our reservations were at the Hollywood Brown Derby which was a cool building built in the shape of a hat. Inside were cartoon drawings of famous actors and actresses.

Mr. Baxter arrived almost at the same time. We had to wait less than a minute. Dick introduced us, and we were seated. Mr. Baxter appeared to be in his sixties with silver-white hair. I had heard men with hair like that called Silver Foxes. He had a tanned face that had some lines, but not as many as you would have thought. There were none of those burst blood vessels in his cheeks or nose like my Uncle Wally had from drinking.

He wore a dark blue pinstriped suit with a red tie. His tie clip had a diamond in it. I don't know what brand his watch was, but it appeared expensive. Every inch of him screamed here is a successful man. I also knew he was a desperate man.

We made small talk all through dinner. He asked questions about Bellefontaine, school, and my life but avoided business. We all turned down dessert. I think Dick, Janice, Mr. Baxter, and I wanted to get to the real reason we were there.

Mr. Baxter opened with, "I hear you are looking for an agent."

"When Dick Wyman and John Wayne tell you to get an agent, you would be a fool not to listen."

"I'm prepared to represent you on certain conditions. I understand they are putting *The Cowboys* on hold and want to star in another vehicle. You can make a lot of money doing this. I think we can get you half a million dollars. For that small fortune, I would want ten percent."

It was nice to know that Mr. Wyman and Mr. Wayne were being straight with me. It made my next statement easier.

"I believe in having all the cards on the table. You need fifty thousand dollars for your granddaughter's medical bills. That is how you came up with my price and your fee. John Wayne needs to keep my price under three hundred thousand dollars.

"Here is my proposal. I pay you fifty thousand dollars to negotiate for me as a one-time deal for this movie. That way, your problems are solved. We also sign a standard agent contract for future work where you receive five percent. That way, my longer-term monies are maximized. As my earning potential grows, you will still come out ahead."

I had everyone's attention. "I would like you to negotiate for two hundred thousand dollars...."

I let it wait for a beat and then added, "plus one point."

Mr. Baxter looked at Dick and asked, "What sort of monster have you set loose on Hollywood? That is brilliant."

He looked at me and stated, "You are playing the long game, creating markers all over the place and setting the precedent that you will ask for points in every movie you are in."

Dick asked, "Rick, how did you come up with this?" "

"I had time to think today. I had just learned what points meant in the movie business. If you believe in the people you work with, why not share the risks and rewards? I knew both Mr. Baxter and Mr. Wayne had a problem and that I was in the middle, so I thought about how to make it a win for all of us."

Mr. Baxter leaned over the table and offered his hand.

"I will be proud to be your agent. I knew that getting the money I needed would destroy me in this business, but I didn't see any way out. I regret I don't have a granddaughter the right age for you."

Now that was embarrassing!

The floodgates of cheerful conversation were opened. Luckily, I remembered the name of the law firm that had reviewed my original Warner Brothers contract. Mr. Baxter would have his agreement in their hands tomorrow.

I would call home again, keep my parents up to date, and ask them to contact the law firm on my behalf. A power of attorney held by Dick would let him sign the contract on my behalf if I countersigned it.

After all, we decided that dessert was a good idea, so we indulged. Dick found out that Mr. Baxter hadn't heard about the coyote incident. He asked all sorts of questions. He was most interested in who talked to me about the incident.

He gave a small grimace when I named the last person who questioned me and how they concentrated on where people were and what they did.

"It will be in the papers tomorrow. The kid stands, and Paul Grant runs. The kid has a poor opinion of Grant."

"I didn't say that!"

"Did you say you didn't think much of Grant?"

"Well, yes, but I meant that I had so many things on my mind at that point, he wasn't one of them."

After I gave that reply, I remembered everything I had learned about historical reporting in my essays.

"Uh, oh. I'm in for it."

"A little bit. Since you are the hero of this, you will get away with it. I wouldn't recommend ever asking Paul Grant for help, though."

After that, we went our separate ways. On the way out, Mr. Baxter introduced me to Mr. Cobb. He told him he would be seeing a lot of me in the future. I shook hands with him, and we left. While waiting for the valet to bring our car around, I made a little joke.

"It must be tough being named after a salad."

This received way more laughter than I thought it would.

Chapter 29

Before running in the morning, I called from Wyman's and talked to my parents. I told them things went exactly as we had talked about yesterday. Mr. Baxter will be dropping off a contract at our Hollywood lawyers today. Dad said he would make the call to let them know about it and that Dick held a valid power of attorney.

As Dick and I were running, I thought about all the attorneys in my life. It was getting crazy. There was our family attorney, my patent attorney, and now my entertainment attorney. Thank God our family seldom had divorces.

When I stopped at the front gate, there was a note waiting for me to report to room 107, building 3. The buildings were marked well enough that I could find building three without asking one of the tour guides leading groups around.

John Wayne, Producer Saul Goldman, and Director Ron Dodge were waiting for me. There were also two writers whom I hadn't met. They were introduced as Dusty Rhodes and Jim Turner.

Mr. Wayne began.

"I talked to both Dick Wyman and John Baxter this morning. They both told me that you had agreed with John to take care of his problems and meet my goals. They didn't want to give me details until you signed a contract with John. I will be extremely interested in seeing how you appear to have achieved the impossible.

"In the meantime, we want to discuss a movie with you. As of today, Paul Grant has told the studio that they have broken his contract by not providing the security required. He claims the studio should have had safeguards in place against rabid coyotes and trained personnel rather than an irresponsible teenage boy who could have gotten him killed."

I liked that I was irresponsible because I stood between him and danger. Would that have made me responsible if I let it attack him?

Mr. Wayne continued, "That puts *The Cowboys* on hold for the foreseeable future. While we will all be paid as we haven't violated our contracts, we are effectively out of work. The studio will have to take the loss. That gives us a unique opportunity."

"We can rent everything in place for another Western, which will reduce the studio's losses. At the same time, we don't have to pay the upfront costs of bringing everything together. We will use the sets that are already in place on the lot. We will not have to pay for any of the filming already done, but from it, we know how everyone should look."

"The current cast will stay in place. The only addition will be a young lady to play my daughter and to be your love interest. We will use someone from Central Casting rather than an established star."

"Sir, you appear to have given this some thought."

Mr. Wayne made a gesture to include the others, "We have worked as a team for many movies. For us, time is money. We could make a little money drawing this movie paycheck or a lot of money by producing and selling our movie."

"Part of the deal with the studio would be that we give up our paychecks from *The Cowboys* and draw our money from *Sir Nicklaus*. All the other actors won't see a change and yours will go up so that shouldn't be a problem. You and I are the only people who are needed, me for the drawing power and you for the ability to play an English cowboy."

"An English cowboy?"

"Dusty, give Rick an outline of the story. The boys wrote this several years ago, and we have been holding it as an ace in the hole if we had to fill in with a B movie. I hate to admit it, but with me as the only name in the movie, it will be rated as a B."

"Rick, the story opens in 1889 England. Sir Nicklaus, an eighteen-year-old, has just been sent down or, as we would call it, expelled from Eton. Sir Nicklaus, son of and heir to the 6th Earl of Grays, had smuggled a goat into the dons' or dean's lounge."

"By itself, no big deal, except the lounge was set up to entertain visiting Queen Victoria. While her tea was being served, the goat made its presence known. Her Majesty was not amused. Unfortunately, Sir Nicklaus, called Nick by his friends, is seen leaving the premises. His father, the Earl, is also not amused."

"During the first scene interview, Nick is informed that he is being sent to the earl's younger brother James Braxton in the Wyoming territory. The Honorable James Braxton has established a successful cattle ranch of twenty thousand acres. There Nick will hopefully learn what it takes to be a successful adult."

Dusty continues, "The earl doesn't know that he is sending his only heir into the middle of the Johnson County Range War.

"Nick's Uncle James, played by John Wayne, is determined to stay out of the war; thus, he pleases neither side. He has a larger-than-normal number of ranch hands who all can handle their weapons. He doesn't hunt for trouble but is ready when it comes to him.

"When Nick arrives at the ranch, he goes through a learning curve with some humor. He proves that it isn't a good idea to try to rope with an English saddle. It has no saddle horn to tie the rope off. He is pulled off his horse as he tries to halt the cow.

"Then he probably will take a bath in a horse trough when he smarts off to his Uncle James. We see him go from an English dandy with no goals to a serious young man who aims for excellence wherever life may take him.

"There is a love interest in the ranch foremen's daughter Anna, who turns out to have been educated at, as Nick puts it, a quaint colonial college called Yale.

"Nick is tested in the movie several times. The first is a run-in with The Hole in the Wall gang while in town. Life becomes serious as he kills a man in a gunfight.

"Nick's major test comes when Uncle James and his wife go to Cheyenne for the second anniversary of Wyoming as a state. James had been instrumental in obtaining statehood. While they are away, Wolcott's Regulators attack the ranch from two directions.

"The bulk of the ranch hands protect the herd from being taken while Nick leads the defense of the main ranch. After a prolonged gunfight, the Regulators withdraw, and the ranch is saved.

"At the end of the movie, Anna and Rick pledge their love as he returns to England to attend Sandhurst Military College.

"The last bit of the film will scroll that Colonel Lord Braxton 7th Earl of Grays, VC, GC, KG, GCB, GCVO was killed in the battle of the Somme, 21 March 1918. He is survived by his wife of thirty-three years, Anna, son James the 8th Earl of Grays, and three other children."

"Why are all the honors and final history displayed at the end?"

"Three reasons, Rick: it shows that Nicklaus went on to a full and eventful life, it gives plenty of room for action sequels, and it gives closure to the story if there is no sequel."

Mr. Wayne added, "The TV special the studio has been making to introduce you still works and can be used to promote *Sir Nicklaus*. You know you will be the big winner in this. You are now a lead actor."

"I have to do the job first."

"We have faith, Rick. Hey, I hear you are buying a new T-Bird."

"That's right. Want to take a ride after I get it?"

"Sure, if we find the time," Wayne responded.

How cool would that be, me driving down Hollywood Boulevard, top-down with John Wayne! We never did find the time, but it was a nice thought.

Ron Dodge asked us if we had seen today's newspaper. We hadn't. He told us it had the story about the rabid coyote and how Paul Grant had run from the set while I killed it and John Wayne was running to the danger. It went on to quote me as saying I didn't think much of Grant.

Mr. Wayne wanted to know what I said. When I told him, he responded, don't worry about it. They always twist things. Regarding the person who asked all the questions and then sold the information to the newspaper, it is a time-honored tradition in movieland.

"Wait a couple of days and see what Hedda Hopper, Louella Parsons, and Jack Parr have to say. I suspect Parr's *Tonight Show* will have several jokes about Grant. When you are done here, check with the office; there are probably several requests for interviews. Before   you   talk   to   anyone, see————————————————————————————————me and I will have Will Jamison, my publicist, help you come up with responses."

Mr. Wayne continued, "You should be aware that cameras were running. The studio had the whole event from three angles so that pictures will be released to the paper and a clip added to the TV feature. At the rate you are going, it won't be on TV. It will be a full feature-length movie!"

We adjourned, and I did stop at the office where they did have twenty-five of those pink "while you were out" call slips. They were with various media requesting interviews.

Chapter 30

I checked with the receptionist, and Will Jamison was on site in a suite of offices reserved for Mr. Wayne. Taking a chance, I walked over, and I got lucky. He was in and had time. John Wayne had forewarned him, so he knew what was going on.

Mr. Jamison was a lot younger than I thought he would be. He was in his mid-thirties. He was dressed casually in a golf shirt and dress slacks. He was well-built and looked like he could shoot a good round of golf. That reminded me I had to get some clubs and a course to play.

His advice was pretty much common sense. I did what I had to do. What other people did and how they reacted was their business. As far as Mr. Grant, I was too busy to think anything about him or anyone else. A charging rabid coyote can cause you to focus.

"All that is true, you know," I told him.

"I know, along with any other combat veteran, you don't worry about the small things at that moment. Surviving is enough."

"At least I could take action," I said as I thought of Bill Samson waiting for that landing craft door to open on Normandy Beach.

"Yeah, I hated the waiting. It gave you too much time to think." Mr. Jamison continued, "How close did that coyote get anyway?"

"It was in the air when I shot, so I suppose a couple of feet and closing. I didn't have to move when it hit the ground to stick the pistol in its ear."

"That's what you want to tell people. Before the story is done, it will have left fang marks on your neck."

"I think I will wait for my grandkids before I let it get that close."

He helped me go through all the call slips and decide which ones to return. We finally settled on Jack Parr, who probably wanted me on his show. I had to talk to both Hedda Hopper and Louella Parsons or neither one as they had a feud going, and if you talked to one and not the other, it would cause bad feelings. Walter Winchell was to be avoided like the plague as he was pure poison.

As he went down the list, I realized that everyone who had stories in print would be able to twist things as they wanted. The only place I had a real chance of getting my side out was on TV. Even that could be edited, but I had the best chance there. Besides, I liked the idea of being seen in Bellefontaine by my friends.

I explained my reasoning, and Will agreed. He thought I could get away with it this time, but I would have to face the press someday.

After lunch, I went to my schoolhouse. To my surprise, half a dozen kids and several chaperones were there. A new movie had started filming. They all looked like fourth-graders, so I would have nothing in common with them. Both Miss Sperry and Mr. Danson were there. When he saw me, Mr. Danson came over.

"Rick, as you can see, we have more students. Let's step outside where we won't disrupt them."

"Sure," I said as we stepped outside.

"Rick, this is a little embarrassing. We didn't know we were getting these kids till yesterday morning. A film schedule changed overnight."

"I can relate to that."

"Yeah, I guess you can. Anyway, we told you how we could handle anything in that one room. However, little kids need close teaching and supervision. Miss Sperry will have to do that. We have come up with a plan B for you."

"What is it?"

"Your tutoring will be at Hollywood High by their Biology teacher. It actually will work out because you do need some lab time. Dissecting earthworms, a frog, and any other creature they have lying around."

"How long will I have to go there?"

"The teacher, Miss Powell, has reviewed your exam results and feels that she can have you ready for the California competency tests in three weeks if you apply yourself. I can tell you I have had one busy morning setting this up."

"When do I have to be there, and where are they? Besides Hollywood High, I mean."

He gave me the address and a letter to take to the school office. The school had to sign off for me to have my tutoring there. They were used to working with actors and actresses. Most of the student's parents were connected to the industry in one way or another.

"That sounds like it will work. Thanks for your effort."

While saying this, I shook his hand.

"You're welcome, Rick. I'm glad you are taking this well. We have set you up in another room for the Spanish test. After that, you are free for the rest of the day."

After taking the Spanish test, which seemed extremely easy, I headed over to my home away from home, the stunt area. They were dueling with Civil War sabers today, so I was extremely interested. As usual, they had me in the mix when I showed interest. There were four of us in a line with an instructor facing us. He showed us the positions and basic moves.

After we had the basic moves down, he started calling them out by name. We would have to go from one to the other. He kept calling them faster and faster. I felt like my arm was going to fall off from the weight of the sword, and I was sweating like a pig. I also realized that I was the only one still moving. The others had stopped and been watching me.

"Rick, that was the darnedest swordplay I have ever seen. Once you know the moves, you do them by reflex. I have never seen anyone do them so fast. If you can do this every day for the next couple of weeks, we could have you do swordfight scenes. You have the reflexes and coordination. What you're lacking is the muscle memory, so you can act without thinking, and the strength."

"Strength?" I inquired.

"Try holding that sword straight out for two minutes."

"Oh, that will take work."

"Until you can do it for ten minutes, you can't win a fight. Most real sword fights are over in seconds, but you have to be prepared for an equal match."

"You act like I need to be able to fight with the sword."

"All stuntmen can. It's the actors who can't. Which do you want to be?"

"Could I have one to take home to practice holding out when I do my morning exercises?"

"Sure, we will sign that one out to you."

So, now I was going to be a swordsman.

He started me up again on the moves; of course, I had forgotten the names associated with most of the moves. Some moves I had forgotten already.

"Don't worry, Rick. That is normal for a beginner."

I had time to look closely at the sword when we were done. It was a replica of a Civil War army officer's sword from its markings.

He asked me, "Ever seen one like this?"

"I own one that is original."

I then told him I was a second lieutenant in the 6th Ohio Volunteer Infantry, a Civil War reenactment unit. They thought that was cool. I didn't tell them I had just joined.

I lifted weights. I hadn't been at it that many days, but I could feel a difference.

Dick was seeing an attorney on my behalf, so I took a taxi home. When I got back to the apartment, there was a note on the door. It was from Dick. Dad had a call from our entertainment lawyer, Mr. Spiller, who had reviewed the agent's contract. The contract was a standard contract with a five percent fee. The only thing not standard was the one-time fifty thousand dollars for the first movie.

Mr. Spiller thought that the upfront payout was a good idea. By paying a large sum upfront, I could potentially save a lot of money over the years. Of course, I would have lost big time if I had never made another movie. He recommended we sign the contract.

We could have Dick Wyman sign using a power of attorney. It had originally been intended for medical treatment and minor contract modifications. This was a new contract, but nothing precluded him from signing on my behalf. Dick indicated in his note that we would both meet at the lawyer's office in the morning before going to the studio for the signing.

There was a note from Janice that she had called the phone company and that I would have a working phone of my own by the end of the week. I think that was a hint. It had been a busy day; I didn't even think about reading.

Chapter 31

After the morning routine on Thursday, Dick and I went to the law office. They were ready for us and seemed to be nice people. Later, when I found out that they had made one hundred dollars for reviewing the contract. I felt they should have been nicer.

Mr. Baxter was there and anxious to get the deal signed and start negotiating. I took him aside in the parking lot and told him on the way out, "From the way Mr. Wayne was talking, I think maybe we should ask for two points."

Mr. Baxter laughed and said, "No, we will ask for five, hope for three but settle for two."

When I arrived at the studio, they immediately started coaching me on Sir Nicklaus's lines. John Wayne sat in for a while to confirm that I could do the accent. He must've been satisfied because he quietly left.

After lunch, Mr. Danson took me over to Hollywood High. After checking in at the office and confirming that everything was still on track, he took me to Miss Powell's classroom. It was a free period for her, so we were able to talk.

I liked her and was convinced she would help me. She was the first black teacher that I had met, so it was going to be interesting. She was a happy, outgoing person. If she is like that all the time, Biology will be fun.

We agreed that I would come back at one o'clock next Monday and stay till three. Mr. Danson took me back to the studio, where I spent the time with the stuntmen. I practiced roping on the ground. I was hoping to graduate to a horse one of these days.

After that, I went through the sword exercises. I had a list of the moves. If I saw the name, I could go through the correct motions. I started to do them slowly and sped up each round.

My arm was starting to get tired, so I switched to lifts. These seemed to help the tiredness. It must be stretching the muscles in the other direction or something.

When I got home, I found that the telephone installers had been and gone. Janice had come over to let them in. I called Mum and Dad and talked to them for a long time. A lot had happened. They thought I had been handling things well.

Dad had some big news. We had our first inquiry on the adjustable shower fixture. Detroit Faucets wanted to meet with Dad to see about a license.

I reread a book that night, a Western about Cullen Baker. The author had him as a good guy. The actual historical record shows a different story. The theme of the story is that a man should have good friends in life. While the story wasn't close to being accurate, it makes a fine tale.

Friday there was a light rain, the first rain I had seen in California. After my exercises with my new addition of holding my sword out straight, I managed two minutes before my arm began to quiver.

Dick and I still ran. When we got to the studio, they had me go to costuming and makeup. They had me try on several outfits for a young English nobleman. They fit so that they would be used in the movie. They already had my Western clothes from the other movie.

After that, we did walkthroughs of several scenes so we wouldn't waste time learning in front of the camera. Fortunately for me, the longest speech in the movie was given by Sir Nicklaus' father after he had been sent down. My responses would be, "Yes, sir; no, sir; and as you say, sir."

It was your standard teenage boy chewing out.

My dad had given me a few in the last couple of years, so I knew how to play that part. I could play resentful of being unfairly put upon. Of course, from a distance, they didn't seem so unfair at all.

There was no school for me today though I had cheated and brought my Latin book with me to add to my Latin vocabulary. I wanted to close out ninth grade before I went back to Ohio.

At three o'clock, I headed over to the stunt area. Lately, I had become one of the guys. They called on me if someone needed a spotter for weights or a partner to practice a stunt move. It was fun.

I did the sword thing and weightlifting. I was able to add five pounds to my heavy lift.

It was almost five o'clock, and I thought Dick Wyman would be here soon. He was, but he had John Wayne in tow. Mr. Wayne started, "Rick, I thought you would like to know we have a deal hammered out with Baxter. Dick has signed for you as the holder of a power of attorney. John will be providing you with copies.

"I want you to know you have done a fine thing. Taking care of John Baxter's money problems and keeping our expenses in line is a smart move. Word will get out that people can work with you. That means a lot in this world. Too many of your fellow actors are plain greedy. Speaking of greedy, that SOB Baxter tried for five points, but I held him off at three."

I tried to look unhappy, but I'm not that good of an actor. Mr. Wayne took one look at me.

"Oh, hell, I could have got it down to two."

Then he started laughing.

I think Dick Wyman was more up about it than I was on the way home. I invited him and Janice out to dinner, my treat, but they had other plans. So, it ended up a quiet evening with hot dogs and a pint of Alta Dena ice cream in front of the TV. I was tired, so I didn't read.

Saturday was another day in sunny southern California. Man, it rained and rained. I watched a lot of TV, studied Latin, and read up on Biology. I did get so bored that I called Bellefontaine. Everyone was fine. Dad had heard from two more showerhead manufacturers; they were extremely interested.

I talked to my brothers and sister for a long time. They insisted on using Spanish, so I even got some practice in. I found out that Denny was dating a girl, and he wanted some big brother advice and didn't want Mum and Dad to hear.

I explained what French kissing was and told him he was too young. I had only one chance to do it with a girl my age, so why should he get to start so young?

Sunday, I finished up my letter while the rain still came down. It seemed like a waste of paper as I had talked to them at home three times this week, but I kept my word.

I did buy a Sunday paper from the dispenser on the corner. There were pictures of me standing my ground against the coyote in the entertainment section. They even had a shot of the coyote in midair as I fired. It was a cool shot. They made a big deal about Paul Grant running away and now suing for the lack of security. It didn't cast him in a good light.

There was a lot of TV watched. I did my regular and sword exercises and, later that night, read about a man who lived in an Iron Castle.

Chapter 32

At the studio Monday morning, we had a kick-off meeting for Sir Nick. We would be working differently in this movie. We would be on set ten to twelve hours a day. My schooling would be worked in between my shots, the same with workout and coaching time. The day would start in costume and makeup at 6 a.m., and we would hope to be done by 6 p.m. at the latest.

The daughter of the ranch foreman who would be my love interest was coming from Central Casting. Five young ladies were auditioning for the part, one each day this week. They would arrive at eleven o'clock to read lines for the camera. Then they would accompany me to lunch to see how we got along.

I was shown the girls' pictures. I had no doubt which one it would be. There was Cheryl's twin. It was scary how much she looked like my Cheryl with dark hair and big eyes.

The meeting lasted till eleven as all the details of this movie were worked out. We would have to do several shots on location. For some scenes that needed to be done in the country, instead of a set, there was a ranch in Colorado we would be going to. It was called Easterly Ranch.

Mr. Wayne looked over at me. "It's a small world, Rick. It's Clint's place. When we did *It Never Happened*, we got talking, and we had a scout go check the place out. The countryside matches Johnson County, Wyoming."

I did wonder why we didn't go up the road to Johnson County, but who am I to understand the movie business?

The first young lady was too nervous and flubbed her lines badly. She was so upset her mother, who was accompanying her, took her home before lunch. It was a shame.

After watching the failed audition, I went to makeup and costuming. As usual, the scenes were being shot in logistical order rather than in the linear story form of the movie.

Today was working on the scene where Sir Nick ropes a calf and finds out that his English saddle won't work. English saddles don't have saddle horns to tie the rope off. A calf fighting the weight of a horse is one thing. The strength of the human arm is another.

The hardest part of the scene was holding onto the rope long enough to show the strain but letting it go before my arm was ripped off. For the first three takes, I let go too early. No one gave me a hard time about it. I held on too long on the fourth attempt and was pulled right off my horse. I was extremely fortunate that I wasn't hurt.

That caused a hold-up in production. They discussed having a stuntman performing what they first thought was a simple scene. While this discussion was going on, I had a thought. Why not use a breakaway rope? Take a normal lariat and splice in a section with lower tensile strength. Have the strength that puts some strain on the rider but breaks before they are pulled off the horse.

I brought that up to the prop man handling the lariats. He thought for a few minutes and said, come with me. Since they were still arguing about how to handle the scene, I wouldn't be needed.

I told the assistant director I was going to a workshop with a prop man. He had no problem since he could retrieve me with a runner if needed.

My trip to the workshop was my first but would be far from my last. It was better than I envisioned Disneyland to be. They could make or jury-rig anything. While I wasn't a hands-on mechanic, I did love to see how my ideas could be brought to life.

The prop man, Raul Rodrigues, told me, "We are always concerned about tensile strength, but in the other direction, we don't want it to break. I think we have some string that is rated at one hundred and fifty pounds. We used it for items that weigh fifty pounds or less."

He found the string in short order. He cut ten strips, each five feet long.

"Why so many?" I inquired.

"Retakes," was his one-word reply.

The only problem was its diameter was less than the lariat. I asked, "Do you have any fabric-covered wiring?"

"It is somewhere around here."

He led me directly to it. Raul certainly knew the inventory.

We found a section that was close to the same diameter as the lariat. Raul stripped the cloth off the wire. He cut a section and pulled the wiring out of the cloth. He peeled the cloth back a couple of inches, then he put the bare wire in a vise and pulled the cloth right off. He repeated this ten times.

After threading the string through the cloth, he cut ten lariats and spliced the string to the lariat. As a Boy Scout in good standing, I was interested in how he did that so the string wouldn't pull off the lariat. We then headed over to the paint shop, where they did a quick and dirty match and painted the cloth. It wouldn't stand up to close examination, but it would do.

Raul explained, "If this were a big-budget movie, we would have had weeks to do this and would've dyed the cloth to a perfect match."

By this time, we had been gone an hour, so I figured the scene would've been shot by now, and our efforts wasted.

I was wrong; when we got back, they were still arguing. I learned this happened a lot. Instead of shooting the scene as written, they were now trying to rewrite it. Why, I don't know. Maybe some writers can't let things go.

Anyway, Raul and I talked to one of the animal wranglers, and they let a calf loose after I was mounted. I chased it down and, of course, missed it with my first attempt. On my second throw, I nailed it, and the string hidden in the rope broke perfectly.

The director was watching as he was getting upset with the arguing. He asked how we did that.

I replied, "Raul made a breakaway lariat. It will work perfectly every time. We have nine more of them. You will just have to edit out the rope breaking."

"That's no problem," he responded.

At that, he hurried the crew back to work. As people were setting up one more time, Raul spoke up, "Señor Rick, the way you told the director, he will think it was my idea."

I answered in Spanish. "It doesn't matter who gets the credit. We are a team making a movie. Let's get the job done, friend."

Raul beamed in reply.

"Did you go to school in Spain?" he asked.

"Spain came to me," I told him.

That began a good working relationship with the crew. Raul shared his experience with the other members, and word got around that I was a team player, not a stuck-up star. It is amazing how much easier things go when people like helping you.

It only took two more takes, and the director was satisfied. He told me that it was a really good shot, showing me almost being pulled off my horse but letting go before I got into trouble. It was exactly what he wanted to portray.

He also said, "I'm going to arrange a small bonus for Raul. He bailed us out."

"Good idea," I replied.

Chapter 33

We broke for lunch, then I went to the schoolhouse to meet Mr. Danson. He informed me that I had passed the Spanish exam and then took me over to Hollywood High. After checking in at the office, we headed for the Biology Lab.

Miss Powell was ready for me. There was also another student there, a nice-looking girl my age. She was taller than average, with light brown hair and brown eyes.

I would say all her features were average, but when put together, she had a nice look. As she got older, I could see she would look extremely high-class. Dignified is the word I was looking for.

Miss Powell introduced me to Nina Monroe.

Nina very quickly said, "No relation to Marilyn."

"Of course not. She is Hollywood. You are Paris."

Where that came from, I had no idea, but it worked. Nina lit up. Miss Powell told Mr. Danson, "We are going to have to watch this one."

Nina was to be my teammate in the lab exercise. She had been out with whooping cough and missed Biology's lab portion. This was one of her study hall periods.

Nina asked if I was the actor in the paper who was feuding with Paul Grant. I told her I didn't know I had a feud going. Miss Powell broke in and told us it was time to get to work. I decided I liked the inside of machines better than the inside of frogs.

I had done the study portion of the lesson, so I knew the names and where to look for things, but it still took a while to figure out what I was looking at.

I'm sorry that Nina was all girl on frog innards. She wanted no part of them. She held up her end by taking notes and drawing diagrams. That worked out very well as her writing was so much neater than mine, and we had to turn the notes in. I'm afraid the typewriter had ruined my handwriting. Use it or lose it!

We worked most of the lab period while Miss Powell graded papers. If we had any questions, we were to ask for help, but she preferred we sort things out for ourselves. While Nina and I cut up poor late Mr. Froggie, who would no longer go a-courtin', we talked a little about our backgrounds.

She loved the line about Paris and couldn't wait to repeat it to her friends. Too soon, the session was over, and it was back to the studio.

I told Mr. Danson I was going out with Mr. Wyman to look for a new car this evening. He was pleased to hear that. I could drive myself to class.

Back at the studio, I headed to the stunt area. After my sword work and lifting, I sat and listened to a bull session while waiting for Dick Wyman to show up. They were talking about parachuting as a sport. World War II surplus parachutes were available for a couple of bucks each.

There was a small airline company out at Bakersfield that had modified an aircraft so that it was easy to jump out of. They were talking about buying chutes at an Army-Navy surplus store and trying it. It sounded like fun. I asked them to keep me posted on when they were going to try it.

Dick showed up and asked about my day. I updated him as we pulled out of the studio.

He then said, "Now let's talk about the important stuff like a new car."

"I'm holding out for the '58 Thunderbird convertible in red."

"You can afford that?"

"I'm fifteen years old, single, working in the movies. Yes, I can afford that," I said smugly.

"Well, if you are going to be snotty about it, I can drop you off at your apartment."

"Hey, wait, I'm sorry. I do have the money, and my parents have approved. It is from the money I earned before this movie ever came up."

Dick knew most of my history. I filled him in on the rewards from the bank robbery, capturing the rustlers, and how I had helped set my parents up in a successful business. I didn't say anything about gold sitting in a safe deposit box. That was my ace in the hole.

"So, the movie money is all gravy. Good for you, kid. I guess you have earned whatever car you want."

As we finished the conversation, I realized we had pulled into a Ford dealership. He had never intended to take me home.

"You got me, Dick."

"I have noticed that teenage boys need that occasionally to keep them straight."

When we went into the showroom, there it was, sitting on a rotating pedestal, my dream car. The 1958 Ford Thunderbird convertible in red was beautiful. The sticker said it was an eight-cylinder with 352 cubic inches and a four-barrel carburetor.

A salesman came over and said, "She is a beauty, isn't she?"

Dick had stepped back, so I replied, "Yes, she is."

When I replied, the salesman looked disappointed for some reason. He introduced himself and shook hands with Dick and me. He asked which one of us was buying a car today. When I told him it was me, he told me, "Now you have seen your dream car. What can you afford?"

For some reason, Dick was now sniggering.

"This is the car I want, and I can afford it."

The salesman looked at Dick for help. By this time, Dick was holding his mouth shut and getting red in the face. Some help he was.

"Mr. Daniels," I said to the car salesman, "I really can afford this car. It is going to be an outright purchase. May I take it for a test drive?"

Even I could see the poor salesman was torn. Luckily, my ever-so-helpful mentor was back under control by this time.

He told Mr. Daniels, "Rick can afford the car. I'm his mentor from Warner Brothers. He is working with John Wayne on a movie currently."

At the same time, he handed Mr. Daniels a business card. Those were the magic words.

Mr. Daniels recovered his composure which he had just lost and suggested we take the car out for a test drive. He asked to see my driver's license.

When he saw my birthdate, he muttered, "Movie stars."

The car was a dream. I would've done nothing but drive it around all day, but Dick and Mr. Daniels convinced me that we had to eat dinner sometime tonight.

We went back to the dealership, and the fun began. Mr. Daniels wrote the deal up at sticker price. I looked at him, raising one eyebrow as I did.

At the same time, I asked, "What numbers are in the Blue Book?"

From there, we went back and forth enough that Mr. Daniels had his manager come over. That was a good sign. I would have been paying too much if the salesman didn't have to ask for the boss. I had looked up the names of several Ford dealerships in anticipation of this moment.

"Dick, didn't the studio recommend Claremont Ford?"

"They did, but this one is closer to your apartment, so I thought it would be easier to get it serviced here."

"Well, this isn't working. Let's go to Claremont."

As I was saying this, I was standing up.

"You're the boss."

That got the price to a reasonable amount. After signing all the paperwork with Dick countersigning as a holder of my power of attorney, I showed them Mr. Sloan's card from Wells Fargo.

"I will have a certified check drawn up for this full amount and drop it off tomorrow afternoon after you have the car prepped for delivery."

The manager whined enough about a deposit that I pulled out the cash in my wallet and gave him two hundred dollars as a down payment.

He was going to start whinging some more but suddenly shut up. If he kept it up, I think he saw the deal going down the drain. During all of the negotiation, Dick had made very few comments and those in response to direct questions from me.

When we left for home, he asked me where I had learned to deal like that.

"I talked with my Uncle Wally before I left home. I knew I was going to buy a car."

"Your uncle must be some wheeler-dealer."

"Knowing Wally, he would have talked them into giving him an unaccompanied test drive and kept it for the whole seven weeks. He would've taken it back with a bill for all the gas he had used."

It wasn't that late when we returned to Dick's apartment. It would be eleven o'clock in Ohio. I called Mum. After convincing her everything was all right, I told her about the car purchase. She wasn't that impressed. It could have waited until next Sunday.

That night I read about a slave boy who got lucky when Baslim bought him. He was educated in the skills he needed to survive. After Baslim was captured and executed, the boy escaped on the starship Sisu. He ended up being identified as the heir to a spaceship-building company.

The company was involved in the slave trade. He ends up taking over the company and getting the pretty girl. I found it to be pretty unbelievable. The guy having one piece of luck after another was hard to swallow. A good read but an unreal plot.

Chapter 34

I set the alarm for four-thirty on Tuesday morning. That enabled me to do my morning workout and run while making it to the studio on time. The first thing I did at costuming was grab my first coffee of the day. I was awake and ready to go when I was out of makeup.

We were walking through our scene by seven o'clock and had film by eleven. I spent about half of the time watching other people do their jobs. I had brought schoolbooks with me, so I used the time well. I was determined to do as well as possible on the state final exams, even though they were pass-fail.

The girl at the eleven o'clock audition was the Cheryl look alike. She was flawless in her performance. We had lunch together. After lunch, I was asked for my opinion.

My response was, "In one of the few Sunday school classes I attended, they told us not to say anything if we couldn't say anything good. I shouldn't even acknowledge this girl's existence. She is the most egotistical whiney brat I have ever met."

John Wayne came back with, "Okay, now tell us what you think."

"I'm not allowed to use that sort of language."

"Scratch that one off the list then," Mr. Wayne replied.

Mr. Danson took me over to Hollywood High after lunch for my lab session. Nina was there already. The bells rang to change class. I noticed that several girls made a point of looking into our classroom. I wonder what that was about.

We played with poor old Mr. Froggie some more. This time we hooked a battery up to the nerves in his leg. That was amazing. Maybe he can go a courtin' some more. Nina was fun to be with; she could joke about what we were doing. I was still the hands-on one while she took the notes.

She couldn't understand how I could touch the frog. I told her about how my dad and I would gig frogs from a flat-bottomed boat with tridents. The frog legs were delicious! She wasn't impressed. I decided not to tell her about walking a trap line in the winter. Dad would get fifty cents a muskrat pelt. We needed the money that badly.

Mr. Danson took me back to the studio and dropped me off at the stunt area. I did my sword drill and weightlifting. The guys who had talked about parachuting weren't around. After doing my exercises, I still had time, so I worked on my roping. One of the wranglers was kind enough to saddle a horse and take care of him when I was done.

When I thanked him, he said, "You took care of Raul. We'll take care of you.

When I finished roping, Dick still wasn't there, so I waited. Time seemed to stand still, but finally, Dick showed up. We headed out to the Wells Fargo bank and picked up a cashier's check. The car dealer had called the amount in for the car as promised.

When we pulled up to the dealership, the T-Bird was all ready to go. I handed over the check. Dick signed another million or so papers. Then they handed me the keys and the title in my name. It was really strange the State of California wouldn't let me buy a car, but I could own one. It didn't matter now; I had the pink slip.

The dealer insisted on several pictures of me taking delivery of the car. I asked him why. He told me it was in case I became famous. He also told me he had heard about some excitement at the studio, a rabid coyote. He wanted to know if I had seen it.

"I did," was my answer.

Somebody asked a question right then, so he couldn't follow up.

When I slipped behind the wheel of my new car, I felt like the King of the Road. This car was the coolest thing on the road, from the white leather upholstery to the white wall tires. The Corvette was nice. This was better.

My salesman showed me how to put the top down and presented me with a pair of sunglasses. That was nice of him, especially after how I had beaten him up on the deal.

When I thanked him, he responded, "The best thanks you can give me is to direct other people who want to buy a car towards me."

At that, he handed me business cards to put in the glove box. That seemed like a reasonable request.

So, with the top down, and sunglasses on, I drove my new T-Bird off the lot. No doubt about it, I'm hot stuff. That feeling stayed with me for half the trip home. At the traffic light, a 32 Ford hotrod pulled up beside me. The driver asked me if I wanted to race for pinks.

Now I'm many things, but I'm not that stupid. I laughed and told him, "You would eat me alive. I know a dragster when I see it."

He waved and took off when the light changed. I don't know what he had under the hood, but he would've cleaned my clock. The car had a picture of a guy with his fingers in his ears. Under it was "Sounds by Rocket".

That made me realize I had a nice car, but I was not the King of the Road after all. It was a good thing that I learned that lesson early. The police had Sounds by Rocket pulled over. I thought about waving as I drove by, but that would have been tacky.

When I returned to the apartment complex, it took me a minute to figure out which parking space was mine. They had a complicated system. They put your apartment number on your parking space. I parked the car and started to walk away. I stopped and thought, you're not in Bellefontaine, Ohio anymore. I went back and raised the ragtop and, after further thought, pulled the keys.

The keys were always in the car at home, but this was a big city, and things might be different. I had watched enough *Dragnet* and *Highway Patrol* to know that things were different.

In bed, I quickly fell asleep. It had been one heckuva day.

In the morning, I drove myself to the studio. First, I had to stop at the studio office and sign for a studio parking sticker for my windshield and assigned parking space.

I was assigned to the far reaches as a low man on the actor's totem pole. I laughingly thought that I could drive to work and get my morning run from the car to the backlots.

The girl at eleven o'clock today was good in her performance, and lunch was okay, but there was no spark between us. Ron Dodge agreed that while she would work, there was no extra spark. Also, her mother kept breaking into our attempts to talk as though she was trying out for the part. We had two more to look at.

When I was finished, I realized I didn't have to wait for Dick anymore. I had my wheels. Of course, I had the top down for the ride home. I took a quick shower and changed out of my jeans and Western shirt into slacks and a golf shirt. I was going for the preppy look.

I spent the late afternoon and evening driving around. I ate at an A&W Root Beer stand. It was cool. The carhops were on roller skates. I loved those frosty mugs they used to serve the root beer.

The carhops kept skating over to me. I first thought it was the car. Then me. I finally realized the Warner Brothers parking sticker on the windshield was attracting them.

I drove down Highway 101 as far as Santa Monica. I didn't have time to go out on the pier, but I made a mental note to do that one day.

In the evening, I read a good time travel story. Andrew Harlan had been tasked with creating a time loop where the group that recruited him would be brought into being. It gave me a headache to think about it.

It was neat thinking that a 1932 advertisement would show a mushroom cloud. I liked the idea of getting power from using the sun's power when it went nova. The concept of the hidden centuries was also neat.

Chapter 35

It was a little easier to get up at four-thirty on Thursday, but not much. When I finished running and had my shower, I decided that I might live. It was still easier to get coffee at the studio than make it at home or pick it up on the way.

The morning's acting was just like a job, with many hurry-up and wait moments. No one my age was on the set, so I hung out with the production crew. Mr. Wayne seemed to be conducting business if he wasn't on the set.

After lunch, he always disappeared, so I never had a chance to talk to him. The other actors weren't rude to me but weren't interested in socializing.

This left me the crew to talk to. It did give me a chance to learn a lot about the technical end of the business. Since I helped Raul with the breakaway lariat, they always had time for my questions.

They even brought a few of their technical problems to me to see if I could help. I was able to help in small ways, but nothing earth-shattering. It must have been enough because they treated me as a member of the team.

That meant my horses were always saddled first, my lighting exactly right, and my sound checks adjusted till they were perfect. It seemed to me like one professional courtesy was being returned for another. I couldn't understand why others didn't work in this manner.

The actor who played the ranch foreman, Lee Somerset, acted like he was above everyone. He wouldn't extend himself in any way to make it easier for others. If he had been a king, the peasants would've had torches and pitchforks.

My eleven o'clock date, as I thought of her, was it. She was perfect in her lines and presentation. At lunch, it was like we had known each other forever. Her mother, who had accompanied her, sat back and let us talk, unlike the girl's mother on Tuesday.

Her real name is Alice Shellenbacher. Her stage name is Ellen Shelly. She was originally from Texas, but her accent was incredibly soft and almost nonexistent. It suggested the West but could be understood very clearly.

She grew up in a small farm community and attended a local high school. She now lived in what they called the Valley across the mountains from LA. That was the only reason she could audition for parts. While she wanted to be in movies, it wouldn't be the end of the world if she didn't get selected for the part.

Our backgrounds were close enough that we clicked. After a while, I realized that we had been talking and goofing around and had forgotten all about her mother and our director sitting there. I turned to Ron and raised my eyebrow.

He said, "I will cancel the Friday, girl."

For some reason, the way he said it made me think of one of Mum's nursery rhymes. It partly went, "Thursday's child has a long way to go; Friday's child is full of woe." I had read several versions, but this is the one I remembered.

School was cool. Well, it didn't rhyme, but it was fun. Nina and I got along very well. Today we stretched out some worms to dissect. I did the worm thing while she kept notes and drew our diagrams. There was a pattern here. But I knew her time was coming. I had cheated. I have read the course material for next week.

After our session was done, she accompanied me to my car. I had told her about my new purchase, and she wanted to see it. She didn't come across as a gold digger or a user like some of the girls in Bellefontaine, but I was still a little leery. She oohed and aahed as I showed her the various features. I offered to take her for a ride, but she had to get back for her next class.

Back at the lot, I went through my sword routine as usual. I could now hold two swords out straight for five minutes at a time, one in each hand. I was now doing two sessions a day, once at the studio and once at the apartment with two swords I had checked out and taken home.

My weightlifting was starting to show some results. My body was beginning to look "cut," as some of the guys called it. There was a definition of my muscle groups. I was finishing up my routine earlier and earlier each day. I didn't even have to wait for Dick anymore but felt that I shouldn't get in the habit of leaving the studio in case something came up.

One of the guys saw me starting to sit down.

"Oh no, you don't. It is time for you to start your boxing lessons."

What! He took me over to a gym that served as a set that required a boxing ring and was a real gym for training boxers. He introduced me to Don Palmer, the studio trainer, and walked away. As he left, I realized I didn't even know his name.

Mr. Palmer explained to me that to do a boxing scene, first, you had to know how to box. Since there was a fight scene in my movie and I was an English student, it would be assumed that I had been trained in formal boxing at school.

I didn't know if that was how it was done in England in 1890, but very few people in the audience would know the real facts. Besides, it would be fun to know how to box.

They had clothes in every size, so I put on some shorts and canvas shoes. They didn't put me in a ring. They introduced me to a punching bag. Actually, there were two bags, a heavy bag and a speed bag. They gave me some light gloves and had me spend fifteen minutes with each after some basic instruction.

Mr. Palmer stopped me and told me to be back at the same time tomorrow unless I was in a scene. Everything now revolved around the shooting schedule.

Since it was now six o'clock, I went over to the set and found everyone had left. They were done for the day, and so was I. I drove home, showered, changed clothes, and took off in my new car. I drove pretty aimlessly around the Burbank area just to learn it. I spotted a small restaurant that I thought I would try for dinner. I wasn't there exceptionally long.

It was self-seating, so I selected one. The ashtray hadn't been emptied all day. Stuck under the booth top was a ton of chewing gum. The deal-breaker was the four strips of flypaper hanging from the ceiling. They were loaded with dead flies. I decided that I didn't want ptomaine poisoning and left.

I did find a drive-in called In-N-Out; it was fairly good. I wasn't used to fountain drinks instead of out of the bottle, but the Coke was okay.

Later I tried to read my biology book instead of fiction. Reading a biology textbook in bed put me to sleep quickly.

The guard had a message when I arrived at the studio gate Friday morning. They wanted me in the front office. Mr. Pearson, my studio contact, and Will Jamison, Mr. Wayne's publicist, were both waiting for me. Mr. Pearson informed me that Jack Paar wanted me on the *Tonight Show* this afternoon.

That was how I learned that the *Tonight Show* was taped in the afternoon and replayed later. The studio wanted me there, and Mr. Pearson reminded me it was in my contract. I told him I had no problem appearing but didn't know what to say. Mr. Jamison piped in.

"That is why I am here. John asked me to help prep you."

That was a relief. The prepping turned out to be "don't pick your nose;" a lot of people will be watching; and be careful of what you say; a lot of people will be watching. He was extremely helpful in suggesting how to dress and to watch my posture on set. When in the green room, which wasn't green, watch what I said and did as it was taped.

If I had coffee in the green room, don't use sugar or cream if in the little packets as they would create a mess on my clothes. I should go to the bathroom before going to the green room and before going on the air. Most of all, tell the truth and don't try to make jokes. That was Jack Paar's job.

We covered the most likely questions centered on my relationship with Paul Grant.

"I don't have a relationship. We were on the set together but didn't communicate off-screen."

Another question was how I felt about him running from the coyote.

"I don't know that he ran. I was focused on the rabid coyote."

He did run. How do you feel about that?

"We all do what we have to do. I don't know if his weapon was loaded. I won't presume to judge him when I don't know all the facts."

Mr. Jamison thought I would be okay if I stuck to those answers.

After makeup and costume, I went to the set. Today's scene was my uncle throwing me into a horse trough. I swear John Wayne enjoyed it too much. There were six retakes. That meant I had to dry off, change clothes, have my makeup retouched, and my hair dried six times.

I wish I had my handheld drier there; it would have been faster, and I wouldn't have looked so stupid with the little bag over my head. Of course, Mr. Wayne didn't have to do any of that. I had fantasies of revenge. Sure, I was going to throw John Wayne in a horse trough. Not in this lifetime!

Ellen Shelly was there to observe. She didn't have any scenes today. Her mother accompanied her, and they stayed by themselves. I tried to talk to them in between setups, but they were standoffish today, so I left them alone. This was new to them, and they might be nervous.

They did sit with me at lunch. Then it became clear. Ellen was afraid that she was mine since I was a lead, both on and off. I assured her that was anything but the case.

Would I like her company, sure; I was a fifteen-year-old boy a long way from home and a little lonely. She let me know that she was nineteen and had a boyfriend. They were almost engaged.

I raised one eyebrow at that statement.

"Almost engaged?"

She told me that they would be soon. She just hadn't told him yet.

Why men think they have a chance, I don't know. Anyway, that cleared the air with us, and Ellen, her Mother Jean, and I got along fine for the rest of the film production. We were never close friends but always cordial with each other.

School was fun again. Nina found out that we had to work with a pig's heart. We both had to open and close the heart valves. She was so grossed out it was wonderful! Hey, I'm still a freshman. We are gross by definition.

After school, I went back to the studio, where Mr. Pearson had a car and driver waiting for us. We went straight down to the theater. This event was unusual in several ways. First of all, the show was normally done in New York City. The second was they normally had more intellectual people appear, very seldom would they have a mere actor like me.

He was in California because they were experimenting with color videotape. Previously everything had been in black and white. Their concern wasn't the technical issues of color taping or color TV. It was having makeup people available who worked with color filming. I think they wanted an excuse to get out of New York for a change of pace.

I remembered to go to the bathroom and didn't pick my nose on the air or in the green room. Since I was waiting with no company but Mr. Pearson, I had this almost irresistible urge to pick my nose but fought it off.

Things went well on the air at first. Mr. Paar made me feel amazingly comfortable. He talked to me like an adult. Then he asked the predicted questions, and I gave the preplanned answers.

Then he hit me with, "Earlier today in an interview, Paul Grant described you as a thug who has killed people. While he is a professional actor with a bad boy image, he said you are just bad."

My defense is that I'm fifteen for what I said in reply.

"Mr. Grant says he has a bad boy image. He has a bad actor image."

"By bad actor image, do you mean he doesn't act well or that he treats people badly?"

"Yes."

The timing was perfect. Before anything else could be said, the show cut away for a break. During the break, I left the set. My interview had only been for the time slot before the break, so I was done.

Mr. Pearson was a happy camper. My response would up the stakes in the "feud". I didn't think there was a feud or wanted one, but he thought it would give the movie publicity, which was the name of the game.

When we got back to the studio, I called home to let Mum and Dad know that I would be on the *Tonight Show* later today. She wanted to know how it went. I told her it was fine but got a little dicey at the end. I didn't give her any more details which frustrated her, but I told her to wait. It was worth it.

They called back later and were supportive. No one was going to call their son a thug. Dad said I should punch him in the nose. Mum said she had access to Baratol if I was serious. I had no idea what that was, but it sounded dangerous. I fell asleep, wondering what the next few days would bring.

Chapter 36

I found out how the next few days would go the next morning when I left the apartment to run at five o'clock. A reporter was waiting at my front door. That interview was easy to handle. I just started running and didn't stop. When I returned home, there were five of them at the door. I gave up.

I told them, "Come on in. One of you put the coffee on while I take a shower."

There were three men and two women. It was one of the guys who made the coffee.

Needless to say, I rushed through my shower and dried my hair using my prototype hairdryer. The women were curious about the noise from the bathroom when I came out, so I showed it to them. They about freaked when they realized what it was and that I had patents applied for.

At this point, I had decided not to fight it. Be honest and see where it went. It went well when they realized they didn't have to badger me to get answers. They all gave me a business card that showed they were for real. Well, one might argue about the tabloid that was represented.

Two of them had done some homework. They had read up on my previous achievements, however notable they were. The guy from the tabloid was incredibly open. He needed something that was either scandalous or newsworthy in a blow-your-mind kind of way.

I replied, "Well, I don't think my godmother will be happy about all of this."

I then went to my desk and pulled out my Eagle Scout presentation letter from the queen. Before I showed it to him, I asked the others if they could give him some lead time on this part of the story. You could tell they weren't enthusiastic about it, but as one of them said, "I've never seen such openness before. You know this could do you in."

"I know, but I will be hounded until all this comes out. I figure the sooner it does, the sooner things will settle down."

"You're wrong. This is going to make you more newsworthy than ever. Others will chase you to the ends of the earth."

"If I give you guys access, will you advise me on how to handle things? I realize that it won't be perfect, but I am a novice at this."

"Sure, and I'm the Queen of England," said one of the women.

This set the man from the tabloid giggling. Yes, giggling.

He said, "This is too good not to share."

Then he handed her the card Queen Elizabeth had sent me.

"Oh my god," the woman shrieked. "Yes, I will work with you."

She was the first, but all five agreed to answer questions and give me advice if I would take their calls.

Sitting at my kitchen table, drinking coffee, they each came up with their story. The tabloid would have the most depth, which helped him because his deadline was further out. The others wanted something that day. It was kind of cool when they borrowed my typewriter and started editing each other's stories. I was sworn to secrecy, for if their bosses found out, there would be trouble.

As one of the women put it, "They will wonder who I was sleeping with to get such clean copy."

When I laughed, she blushed, "Oh lord, you're just a kid. I forgot!"

They all agreed that Grant would have something not nice to say in reply to my performance on the *Tonight Show*. They agreed my timing was impeccable. They all took it as inside information when I shared that it was more by accident than by plan.

One of the women looked thoughtful. She asked me, "If Elizabeth is your godmother, who is your godfather?"

My answer almost brought the roof down. I made a point of telling the whole story then of how Mum was with Elizabeth in World War II as a helper on the ambulance and how things snowballed. I had never met either Her Majesty or the president and didn't think it would be fair to imply a connection that wasn't there.

My press corps didn't want to let it go that easy. They played with the story and twisted it slightly so that it appeared Paul Grant had no idea that he was dealing with the heads of state of two powerful nations. There was nothing untrue, but I would hate to be Grant when he read it.

They advised me to stay away from everyone for the rest of the day, and maybe take a drive down the Pacific highway. That way, they could beat the competition with their stories. The lady from *Variety* and the man from the *Los Angeles Examiner* both had early deadlines, so they wanted to get right on it.

I took their advice and made a day of it, driving south. I made it clear to Malibu for a late lunch on the beach on the veranda of an old hotel. It was nice. No one recognized me, but I realized that wouldn't last.

The next morning, I picked up the *Los Angeles Examiner* on the way back from my run. When I got home, a TV crew was set up outside of my apartment. They didn't see me approach, so I knocked on Wyman's door. Dick and Janice thought it was all fun and games. I was getting publicity; that was the name of the game in Hollywood.

I read the paper while Janice was fixing bacon and eggs. If the other reporters treated me like this one, I had it made. If you could read the whole article without throwing up, you would find that I was handsome, a brilliant inventor, a savior of women and children, a professional actor, golfer, and bull rider, and that I had connections with the most powerful people in the world.

I admired the fact that the reporter didn't step on the tabloid expose. I shared it all with Dick and Janice.

They looked at each other and went, "Wow."

Janice brought up an interesting point, "As long as you live in that apartment, they will be at your door. You're going to have to buy a house soon."

"I will only be here for five or six more weeks," I replied.

Dick went, "Dream on. You would have to be the worst actor in the world before you wouldn't get jobs with your resume."

We sat and talked for a while, and then I had a thought. I called George Weaver at his home number and gave him the whole story. One had to take care of those who had been there initially. He had heard about the *Tonight Show* and was wondering how he could get ahold of me. I didn't tell him about the arrangement with the other reporters.

Janice kept an eye out, and when the TV truck and reporters got tired of waiting, I made a dash to my apartment for a quick shower and shave. I then called home and updated Mum and Dad. Dad advised me to keep it low. Mum told me that she had a Sterling that might be useful. I had no idea how sterling silver would be of use in this situation, so I ignored her comment.

I took my longest drive to date, going out to Cucamonga of Jack Benny's fame. It was forty miles from Burbank, so it took me most of the day to get there and back, with stops for lunch and dinner.

Lunch was interesting because two young ladies in the next booth were arguing the merits of Paul Grant and Ricky Jackson. They agreed that Grant was being a jerk but that he still was dreamy. I was too young, but they wouldn't kick me out of bed for eating crackers.

That came under the heading of too much information, so I left there as quickly as I could.

When I returned to my apartment, I was unlocking my door when I was grabbed from behind.

Someone said, "Paul says hello."

They then proceeded to knock me around. They didn't do real damage other than bruised ribs. They left my face alone. I would have appreciated their artistry if it weren't me on the receiving end.

It was a shame I wasn't further along in my boxing lessons. I decided I was going to get profoundly serious about self-defense. Also, buying a gated house looked better and better. I would like to say they ran away from me. The fact is, after pounding on my ribs, they strolled away.

After one final kick in the ribs, one of them said to the other, "Boots, he's not so tough after all."

I was panting hard and in pain. I made it to my bathroom, took four aspirin, and went to bed.

As I lay there, I thought about calling the police but wouldn't even have a description of my attackers. I didn't even know for certain they were from Paul Grant though they probably were.

Chapter 37

When I woke Monday, I was a mass of bruises, all on my chest and back. It hurt to move. I took some more aspirin and tried to do my workout but couldn't do it. Instead, I took a long hot shower. I called Dick Wyman and asked him to come over. We needed to talk.

I left my shirt off so he could see the problem when he showed up.

I explained what happened, "Two guys ambushed me at the door as I was unlocking it.

They said, "Hello from Paul Grant," then kicked the crap out of me.

He wanted to know if I had called the police.

"And tell them what? That two unknowns assaulted me?"

"You need to get this on record. Have you called your parents?"

"Not yet."

Dick used my phone and called my house. Mum answered, and he gave her the details. She asked to speak to me. When I told her that I was okay except for being sore all over, she told me to take it easy for the day. I had expected her to be upset; instead, she was very cold and factual about the whole event.

She then asked to speak to Dick again. They talked for a while. He recommended that I rent or buy a house in a gated community that would give me some protection.

When he hung up, he told me, "Your Mom has asked Janice and me to help you find a new place to live."

"Okay, I understand that I do need security right now."

Dick asked me what my plans were for the day. "Right now, I'm going to see if I can run some of this off. I don't want to tighten up any more than I am."

So, we did our morning run at the high school. I made the distance in about twice the time. But it did feel better the more

I went. At home, I was able to do pushups. But the sit-ups were beyond me.

Fortunately, my scenes didn't include any action. We did our walkthroughs. I was spending less time with my voice coach all the time. I was getting better at delivering lines. I wasn't ready for Shakespeare, but I could do a conversation on film in a normal manner.

I had to take more aspirin halfway through the morning. Ellen and her mother noticed I winced several times. I told them I had a little problem with a horse. This happened regularly on set, so it was no big deal.

After lunch, I went over to Hollywood High. This was my second week of lab work there. One more, and I would be on a full-time shooting schedule.

Nina and I had fun in the lab. There was nothing gooey to cut up. We just had to organize our notes and prepare a presentation on how nervous systems worked. She told me that she had shared my "from Paris" remark with her girlfriends. That was why so many girls had looked last Friday. They thought I was romantic.

This was high praise from a critical audience. These kids had been living with movie lines all their life. Later I found out that one of the girls shared the whole line with her father, a writer, and it made it into a movie.

Nina wanted to know my plans for the weekend. When I told her I didn't have any, she asked me if I wanted to join a group surfing down by the Santa Monica pier.

"Sure, that sounds like fun, though I haven't ever surfed. I had a problem with a stunt, and I'm stiff and bruised, but think I will be okay by the weekend."

"You will enjoy it. I will borrow one of my dad's lighter boards for you. I think we have a wet suit that will fit you. I think half the actors and stuntmen in Hollywood are bruised at one time or the other."

After class, I returned to the studio and checked up on the shooting, which was proceeding on schedule. I went to the stunt area and did my sword exercises. I found that I couldn't do the moves but could hold the swords out with both hands. The weights were about half and half. Some I could do, some I couldn't.

I went over to the boxing area and talked to the trainer, Mr. Palmer. I told him I was assaulted last night. I didn't bring Grant's name into it. After looking at my bruises, he told me that I had been worked over by professionals, with lots of bruises but no permanent damage. He agreed that I should skip practice today and try again tomorrow.

I was feeling pretty tired by then, so I went back to my apartment earlier than usual. I picked up an *LA Examiner* from the box on the corner. Since it was a nice sunny day, I took a Coke down by the pool and read the paper.

The Entertainment news section had a quote from Paul Grant. When asked about my comments on Jack Paar's show, he replied, "That punk will get what's coming to him one of these days soon."

The paper continued that he was in New York for a fashion show where a new line of teen clothes in his name was being debuted. They made a big deal about the show this evening, which was apparently at one of the better fashion houses. They gave all the details of when and where if people would want to go. The fashion house name meant nothing to me.

I think maybe that day Grant referred to had already arrived. I tried to think of something I could do but couldn't think of anything legal. Anything illegal would cause me more problems than it was worth. I would have to suck it up until a chance presented itself.

I fixed dinner at home and spent the evening studying. By ten o'clock, I was very tired and went to sleep without reading.

Tuesday was better, but I was still stiff and sore. I was able to do all my pushups and half my sit-ups. By the time I finished my run, I had loosened up enough that I knew I would get through the day okay. Sore, but okay.

I checked out my body in the mirror after my shower. As expected, it was ugly. The bruises had started to change color. By tomorrow, I will be in Technicolor. I think I've been in show business too long already.

When we ran, Dick questioned me about how I felt. The fact that I could do the run must have reassured him. He still thought I should file a police report, but I didn't think that was a good idea for some reason.

I didn't want to create a link to Paul Grant and violence. It wasn't logical, but Mum had always told me that I should pay attention to those feelings if I felt strongly about something.

At the studio, I was cornered by Mr. Wayne. He asked me how I was doing. I wasn't surprised that he knew what had happened.

"Dick told me you didn't want to file a police report," he started.

"Mr. Wayne, I couldn't describe my assailants other than the fact someone beat me up professionally. What do I have to go on? Besides, I don't want to build this up in the press because it might encourage other copycats if it wasn't Grant and his people."

"Well, you have a point there. What do you intend to do?"

"I don't know right now, but I will think of something if I can be certain it was Grant and company. I don't get mad. I get even."

"I like to get mad and even," he said with his trademark grin.

We both laughed and went to work. Considering everything, the scenes went well. Ellen and I clicked on the screen. Our romance in the movie was to form a deep attachment that wouldn't be concluded in this movie.

To her, at first I was a brat, then not a brat, then a friend, and then more than a friend. In the movie, my progression was similar, but we changed our view of the other unevenly to keep some tension in the relationship. In other words, it was your standard Hollywood movie romance.

The real Ellen and I were friendly on the set but didn't go out of our way to be with each other. The age difference worked against us, and strange as it seemed, she held me in a little awe. If I had let her, she would've called me Mr. Jackson.

I received a note around ten o'clock to call my dad at home. That was alarming. I had talked to them not that long ago. I hurried over to the office in a break between scenes.

Dad answered the phone and let me know that Mum was on her way to England. Her mum had taken extremely ill. He was short on details of how ill. Mum had received the call while he was out.

She had called him at the office and had hired a cab to take her to the Dayton Airport. From Dayton, she would fly to New York. There she had a twelve-hour layover before changing airlines at Idlewild airport to fly to London. She had left a note telling Dad that it was difficult to get a seat on a plane, so she had to take what she could.

I went back to the set. I had a Spanish book on sentence structure I was studying. That was probably my weakest area. Since I wasn't part of this scene, I worked quietly. Ellen was arguing with her dad, the ranch foreman.

It was about Sir Nicklaus. It was funny hearing her praise me, while in the next scene after this, she would be giving me a hard time because I was stuck up.

Lunch was lunch. At least I could get around. I was still sore and wouldn't be jumping up on a horse, but I could do most things now.

The biology lab was fun, as usual. We were back to gooey stuff, as Nina referred to it. Today was a fish.

I'm looking forward to surfing on Saturday.

Back at the set, we walked through the scene where Ellen put me down. For some reason, while we were performing as required, the scene wasn't sending the message the director was looking for.

He wanted a teenage girl calling for attention from a teenage boy. The words looked good on paper but, when spoken, sounded like a fishwife scolding a kid.

Ron Dodge finally threw up his hands and called it a day. He sent the script back to the writers. He made a point of telling Ellen and me that the problem wasn't us. It was the script. We thanked him. From what I had been told, not all directors had this understanding of the root causes of problems.

I headed home after making a side trip to the supermarket. I couldn't believe how much food I ate and how many dishes I made dirty. A cleaning lady came on Tuesdays every week, but I was responsible for my food and dishes. Mum was handling six of us. I don't know how she could do it.

After dinner, I settled in with my Biology textbook. I was finally starting to feel comfortable with all the material that had to be covered in the ninth grade.

Mum called me at nine her time. She was at Idlewild airport, killing time until her flight at eleven. She wanted to know how I was doing. I assured her I was recovering nicely. To say she was unhappy with Paul Grant was putting it lightly. I talked to her until she sounded calmer.

She was going to call us again when she got to England and saw how Grandmum Newman was doing. Auntie Dell was in such a dither when she called that Mum wasn't certain how serious it was.

Ten minutes after I hung up, the fire alarms in the apartment started going off. I didn't see anything wrong in my unit, so I stepped outside. People were pouring out of their apartments and heading to the pool area, so I thought I had better do the same.

No one seemed to know what had caused them to go off. Since all of them were triggered, it had to be the front office. About that time, firetrucks showed up. The firemen began checking the area. Conversations started between neighbors. One thing I noticed was that almost no one knew anyone else. I guess this was a get-to-know-your-neighbor mixer.

I did notice one glaring lack. There were no other kids my age present, especially girls. My fellow tenants were in their thirties. Some of them had incredibly young children, but no teenagers were present. That meant no fun pool parties. I hadn't wanted to buy a house because I had no kids. This took care of that objection.

Word finally came down that a false alarm had been called to the front office. They had set the alarms off just in case. Dick, Janice, and I had reached that conclusion on our own. We had been there for an hour and seen no smoke. We were allowed to return to our apartments.

The phone was ringing when I opened the door. I was able to grab it in time. It was Dad. He wanted me to know that we had signed agreements with five out of the six showerhead companies. They were coming up with the ten thousand dollars upfront and our requested percentage.

The sixth one, Detroit Faucet, had visited Dad but couldn't come up with the money. The owner had just inherited half the company and bought out the other half from his sister, who wanted nothing to do with the business. Dad had visited his facility and described them as asset-rich and cash-poor.

"Would he consider a partner?"

"I've already asked him, and he would love to have someone bring money to the table. Otherwise, he is going to lose it all."

"Did you talk any dollars?"

"Of course I did. If we gave him the license and threw in another twenty grand, we would own thirty percent of the business."

"Dad, I think we should do it. I've another idea that could make us some real money."

"What's that, Rick?"

"On the sets out here, they have some very fancy faucets and other fixtures for the mansion sets. From what I've seen, no one makes them commercially. They are all special designs and orders. I think if we had an in-house designer, we could make designer faucets, and people would buy them. Please talk to this guy to see if he would be interested in something like that. What's his name, by the way?"

"Mark Downing."

"Well, if Mark likes that idea, I would like to buy in. I will pass if he wants to do business the same old way."

"I will talk to him and let you know, Rick. Anything else happening out there?"

I told him about the false alarm and the fact that no girls my age lived in these apartments."

Dad started laughing, "We knew that before you ever went to California!"

'Thanks a lot, Dad!"

"We didn't want too much temptation in front of you."

"As I said, thanks a lot."

"Anytime, Rick. I'll let you know what I hear from Mum."

"Thanks, Dad, and good night."

That night I reread a book I had read not long ago. This time it was in Spanish. The library had a copy right up front, and it caught my eye. This would certainly help me with sentence structure and vocabulary. Take that, windmill!

Chapter 38

Wednesday was better than the last two days. I could do all my exercises. I was stiff when I started, but it worked out. I was in full-blown Technicolor now. When I went over to Dicks for our run, he met me at his door and told me to come in.

"Have you heard?"

"Heard what?"

"About Paul Grant," Dick replied.

"What about Paul Grant?"

"He was killed last night, apparently in a gang war."

"What!"

"He and the two guys with him were gunned down as they were getting out of their car to go to a fashion show. It was in a parking garage. It is being compared to the St. Valentine's Day Massacre. Someone used a machine gun on them."

"A Tommy gun?" I asked.

"It was an L2A1 Patchett submachine gun. I have never heard of them. They shoot a nine-millimeter. They were riddled like Bonnie and Clyde. The police say it was a professional hit. The weapon had been wiped down, and the shell casings had no fingerprints."

"They did find a kilo of heroin in the car. They think Grant was doing business with one of the mobs. There has been a low-level fight going on for a while. It appears to be going hot now. At least you have an iron-clad alibi for last night. After your exchanges with Grant, you would have been a suspect."

"Who were the other two guys?"

"I think you may have met them, Boots Moran and Tiny Thompson. They were the gang who always followed him around."

"Oh."

While we ran, I tried to wrap my head around events. It seemed so unreal. No question, the guy had been a thug but a drug dealer and member of the mob! I think I was incredibly lucky to be alive.

The set was alive with speculation as almost everyone there knew Grant. I never knew how much he was disliked until people started talking. But then again, it was all after the fact.

The biggest question everyone had was whose show would replace *The Outlaw Kid*. It had a strong cleaning detergent sponsor that everyone would be chasing. I was starting to get a feeling about this predatory industry.

The Germans have a word, "Schadenfreude," which seems to cover this situation, pleasure at the misfortune of others. If others are suffering, then maybe you will benefit from their suffering. This event was more than the other team fumbling the football.

We still managed to get our shoot in. We finished at eleven-thirty. There were two detectives from the Burbank police department waiting for me. They were polite, but they had several questions for me at the request of the New York Police Department.

The lead detective, a guy named Friday, started with, "Since it was an early evening, I assume you were home by yourself, and no one saw you from the time you left the studio till you arrived this morning."

"Not correct at all, detective. Someone called in a false fire alarm at our apartment complex last night, and at least twenty people can testify I was there. Besides, how could I get to New York and back within that period?"

"Oh, so you think this is about Paul Grant's death?"

"I don't know what else it could be."

"Well, you are correct. The NYPD worked out that a jet could've got you there and back within those hours."

I saw Dick Wyman walking by, so I waved him over.

"Dick, please tell these gentlemen what occurred at the apartment complex last night."

"Dick proceeded to talk about the false alarm. He named half a dozen people that we had talked to. I'm glad he remembered their names; I had just met them.

Detective Friday thanked me for my time.

"As a formality, we will check with the apartment office, but it looks like you are in the clear. By the way, I liked your appearance on Jack Paar."

I had a quick lunch at the studio cafeteria. Their food was good. High school food wasn't bad in Bellefontaine, but you could tell the day of the week by what was on the menu. Here there was a real variety of tasty food. I mean, you could have pizza, tacos, hot dogs, or barbeque sandwiches for lunch! What's not to like?

In Biology, we had a project. Nina and I had to write down our parent's eye colors and ours, and then we had to predict what color the eyes of our children would be. Brown was the prediction, but that wasn't the issue. When we talked about what color our children's eyes would be, we both blushed and had trouble making eye contact. To say we were embarrassed would be putting it mildly.

The rest of our time was strangely quiet. I suspect Nina was thinking about being married, having a home, and raising children. Naturally, I was thinking of making children. Anyway, that assignment killed our conversation for the day.

Back at the set, the conversation was still about Paul Grant's being murdered. The more news that was released, the more it seemed he was a heavy-duty dealer. From the reports, he was dealing drugs before his TV career.

The gang war theory gained momentum when two gang members, who most likely killed him and his friends, were found shot to death. It looked like a war was underway.

In the meantime, I was able to do all my exercises. My swordplay was starting to get reflexive. I didn't have to think about the moves. I just did them. Sammy, who was teaching me, told me that I would practice against him next week. I now had the strength to hold the sword, at least a good start, and I knew the moves. Now I had to learn when to make them.

Mr. Palmer had me working out with the light bag at the gym. After that, he showed me how to punch through on the heavy bag. He told me it would still be several weeks before he let me in the ring to spar.

I checked back at the set when I was finished. It was a good thing that I had. They had some night scenes they wanted to do. They were simple but needed me. We ended up finishing at ten o'clock. On the way home, I stopped at the In-N-Out and called it a night.

Thursday morning, Dad called before I left for the studio. First of all, Grandmum was okay.

As Mum put it, "Auntie Dell got her knickers in a twist."

Mum would be staying for a week to visit. It had been ten years since Mum had been back to England. I was glad she had this opportunity and even happier that the Grandmum that I didn't know was alright. I hoped to see her this summer.

At the studio, it was work, work, and more work. Funny, it was like a vacation from school when I started acting. Now it was more like a very well-paying job, but still a job. The part that I liked was working with the stuntmen.

They were willing to teach me all the cool things that they did. It was the best part of the day. I enjoyed my time with Nina, but it was still school. Maybe we will have some real fun this Saturday.

We did film a neat scene. Sir Nick had a run-in with the Hole in the Wall Gang. It was some gunfight. It was really interesting how they made it seem real. I had seen real people die from gunfire, so I knew what it was like, which is nothing like the movies.

Even the fistfight I had with two of the bandits was much different than when I was jumped at the apartment. I wonder how many actors had never run into the real thing, so they thought this was real.

For a change, I went to Hollywood High right from my last set. I had been issued a card that would let me in the school and hopefully eat lunch there. I was looking for Nina. Talking to her outside of the classroom would help me start to know her better.

I didn't find her but was hungry, so I got in the serving line. Hot dogs were the meal of the day, so I went with two of those. There was an empty table in the corner, so I sat there. I had settled in when eight guys came up and told me that I was sitting at their regular table and to move on. With no desire to cause trouble, I stood up to go.

I hadn't given it any thought when I left the lot. I was still dressed as an 1890 cowboy. In other words, I looked like a hick. Two of the Neanderthals decided that my presence offended them, so they told me to throw my lunch out and leave.

Verbally insult me, okay, getting between me and my lunch is different. I kept walking away from the table, carrying my tray.

One of the brutes gave me a shove and said, "Hey, we were talking to you."

Thanks to my decent balance, I didn't fall over though I had to do a fancy hop, skip, and a jump. The guy who shoved me wasn't so lucky. When I started moving away from him, he was overbalanced. When I was a couple of feet away, he had no further support and went crashing to the floor.

There was quiet in the cafeteria. I figured I was dead.

Instead, the other thug said, "Did you see that judo move?" to the others.

"He could kill us!"

Some things are so good you should never try to resist them. I turned around and solemnly said.

"I'm required by law to inform you that my hands are registered as deadly weapons. If you attack me, I cannot be held responsible for any damage done to you."

I couldn't believe it. They all backed down. Even the kid on the floor mumbled, "Sorry."

I wrapped my hot dogs in a napkin and took them to the Biology Lab to eat. Wouldn't you know it; there was Nina, with the remains of a hot dog in front of her. She told me that she did this every day so she would have more study time.

We talked about school, which made an extremely limited conversation as this was the only class I was taking, and she was my only fellow student. In desperation to continue the talk, I told her I was going to be buying a house somewhere in the area.

She recommended that I look in Beverly Hills. Houses with a great view over LA were only around fifty thousand dollars. That would even include a pool. The best sites were over towards Bel Air.

I realized that maybe Nina and I came from different backgrounds. Not that the houses didn't sound nice, it was the price that I was choking on. This also set off an alarm. Maybe I should find out more about this girl before I got in too deep.

It was easy to direct the conversation to where she lived. She told me her dad's house, where she lived, was in Holmby Hills between Beverly Hills and Bel Air. She volunteered that her mother lived on the coast near Nice, France. This was money, real money.

"What does your father do?"

She gave me a funny look and told me, "You work for him."

"I do?" I dumbly asked.

"Dad is the CEO of Warner Brothers and a part-owner of the studio."

"Oh," was my brilliant rejoinder.

"Well, at least I know you haven't been trying to suck up to the boss's daughter."

"I haven't been trying to suck up at all!"

"Then why are you so nice?"

"Uh, I try to treat everyone like that."

"Then you are different from most guys I know."

I was saved by Miss Powell coming into the room. For some reason, Nina had a little smirk on her face for the rest of the class. I found it hard to make eye contact. I kept blushing.

After class, I booked out of there as quickly as I could. I headed for the safety of the studio and the stunt area. At least there, they were only trying to stab me, punch me out, or push me off a roof.

Before going to the stunt area, I did check in on the set. It was quiet as the stagehands rearranged, so I knew I was free for the day. I did my sword exercises and lifts.

The stuntmen were working on a fire scene. One of them was wearing a fire-retardant suit under his costume. His head was wrapped in the same fabric. They put some gunk on him and set it on fire. He ran across the corral in flames. Men with blankets were waiting to put him out. I asked about the fire suit he was wearing.

All they knew was the firesuit was treated with a lot of THPC, whatever that was, and it resisted burning. I was asked if I would like to try, but I declined. This was way beyond my Boy Scout firebug. Besides, I had been in a fire not that long ago.

After that bit of insanity, I went over to the boxing gym. I was fitted for a mouthpiece and a head protector. Then they taped my hands and fitted me with a pair of sixteen-ounce gloves. They felt like pillows.

I sparred with my coach. I found out they weren't pillows. He showed me how much I had to learn. He didn't tell me. He showed me by pounding on me. I stayed with him, but it was a rough session. Afterward, he told me that I had passed the real test. I could take a punch without wimping out.

I told Coach Palmer about the event at Hollywood High in the cafeteria. He thought it was funny. I asked him if his hands were even registered as deadly weapons. When he was done laughing, he told me Guam was the only place he had ever heard of it being done.

He had no idea why they did it. Since you got a certificate when you registered, maybe it was a bragging rights thing. He suggested that I not have lunch there anymore. I told him that I had already reached that conclusion.

After all, I didn't want these deadly weapons to put the high school kids in danger. I left him laughing hysterically.

I headed back to the apartment and added to my weekly letter. I then took another shower and headed out to drive around and find someplace to eat. I ended up eating at a little taco stand. I was getting addicted to Mexican food.

After that, I drove around learning the area. I stopped at a gas station and bought a Beverly Hills map for a quarter. I was amazed that they charged for maps. At home, they were free. The attendant pointed out this one marked all the movie star's houses. It still seemed like a lot of money for a map.

I drove aimlessly around, going ever higher up the hills and further into Bel Air. I passed Holmby Hill's housing but didn't go down any side streets. I was afraid Nina might see me and think I was following her. When it was too dark to see, I used the map to return home. I thought I would see some houses, but most of them had gates, and you could only see a portion of them from the street. This would give privacy and prevent people from grabbing you at your door.

That evening I read a translation of a French novel. If I were Vladimir, I would have given up waiting very quickly. It was obvious the guy was going to be a no-show.

Chapter 39

Friday was another beautiful day. As I was running, I realized that I hadn't touched a golf club in months. I instantly had the urge. I mentioned this to Dick and that I didn't know any golf courses. Also, sad to say, I was getting to be a golf snob. I didn't want to play on a poorly kept public course.

Dick didn't play but did have a suggestion.

"See your studio rep, Don Pearson. Part of his job is to take care of setting things like this up."

That was a good idea. I left a note for Mr. Pearson at the studio office when we went to work to the effect that I could use his help in finding a decent golf course to play on. That also meant that I had to buy a set of golf clubs and hit the driving range at my first opportunity.

The set was busy this morning. We worked hard with multiple takes. It felt like we were making progress in the movie, but I had seen this before. The director may decide this doesn't fit where he is taking the story, and it may all end up on the cutting room floor.

The film was developed overnight from the previous day's work. I wasn't invited to see the daily rushes, but since I wouldn't have much influence on the outcome of the movie, it didn't matter to me.

Lunchtime arrived in no time at all. That is the nice thing about being busy. After lunch at the studio cafeteria, I headed to Sheik Territory, Hollywood High. When I pulled into the parking lot, one guy standing there told me I had a nice car. We talked about the T-Bird for a few minutes, and we introduced ourselves. His name was Dick Perle. He seemed to be a decent sort and presented himself well.

Nina was already in our lab classroom. A friend of hers, Linda Evans, had stopped by. Linda checked me out, but I wasn't introduced as she left quickly. I wondered what that was all about.

Before Miss Powell showed up, we reconfirmed surfing on Saturday. Nina told me she had a surfboard and wet suit lined up for me. She gave me her telephone number and address.

I asked her if her Dad had any restrictions on when she could use the phone.

She told me, "Silly, this is the number of the phone in my room."

I had never met any kid who had their own phone before. This was a different world. It did occur to me that I had my phone, apartment, and car, so maybe I was fitting in.

I enjoyed being taught by Miss Powell. She kept things moving. Since there were only two of us, it moved quickly. I didn't intend to become a biologist of any type, but she turned a dry course into something enjoyable. Just her happy outlook on life made it fun.

She told me stories about Nina and two of her friends, Tuesday Weld and Stefanie Powers. It sounded like they spent more time in detention than in class.

In the movie, Sir Nicklaus is in trouble for one goat. They had set nine piglets loose in the school. Sir Nick got sent to America. They got sent to detention. I guess the moral is don't upset the queen.

Miss Powell lamented that they weren't like that nice Cathy Share, who was never in trouble and always had her work in on time, unlike some people she knew.

The class was fun, but I couldn't help wondering what the gang in Bellefontaine was up to.

When I returned to the lot, those crazy stuntmen were trying to drive a full-size car on two wheels. They had set up a ramp that tilted the car until the wheels on the driver's side were completely off the ground. When the car would get to the end of the adjustable ramp, it would crash back down, either flat on the driver's side or once on an early trial, tipping over on its roof.

They were discussing alterations they could make to the car. I thought about it and ventured a comment. "You are trying to balance the car on a very narrow point formed by the tires. Why don't you decrease the air pressure in the tires, so they are soft? Instead of balancing on a point, it would be a wider flat."

Then I had another thought, "Having a water tank inside might help when the car tips; the water would go to the downside of the tank, leaving more weight on the tires to keep it in place."

The lead mechanic said, "The kid is correct. Let's try the easy one first. Take the air in the tires down to ten pounds on the passenger side."

It only took a few minutes to set up the beaten wreck for one more trial. The car was a lot sturdier than its first appearance. It had a roll bar, the driver had an aircraft pilot seatbelt, and of course, the driver had a helmet. The studio fire department was on standby, along with an ambulance.

This time the car stayed on two wheels for twenty feet or so, which was twenty feet more than before. When I left to do my sword practice, they were sketching what the water tank setup should be like. The lead mechanic yelled, "Hey, kid, you should be an inventor or something."

That brought a small hidden smile to my face.

Sword practice was finally getting to the point where I was starting to counter moves by reaction rather than thought. This was not fencing which was a highly stylized sport. This was beating each other to death with a sharpened iron bar. We didn't use sharpened swords for practice. They were wood with dull edges. It still hurt through the padding when you took a hit.

The padding was two-inch-thick battening material, with frequent holes edged with brass grommets. If there were no holes, you would sweat to death in minutes. Sammy Dawson, my sword coach, told me that if there were a need, they would use me as an extra in a swordfight battle scene.

"I can appear as an extra in another movie on the lot?" I asked.

"Sure, you are under contract, but if you read the fine print, they can ask you to work in a minor role in others. You will be paid the minimum day rate for any extra work, but it is on top of what you already receive so it will be gravy. You will only be called on if it doesn't interfere with your shooting schedule."

I replied, "It sounds kind of cool."

"It is," he replied.

"I know my ex won't go to any movies because she might see me in the background."

Not knowing how to reply to that, I went over to do my weightlifting. I had been lifting weights for three weeks now. I could tell I was gaining strength, and my muscle groups were firming up but hadn't built up yet like I was told. It would take six weeks for me to notice a difference, according to Dick Wyman.

After the weights, I went to the boxing area. After warming up on the speed and heavy bags, I went into the ring with my gear on. This was not like my sword work. I had to think of my response counters. This took too long, so I beat the bags fairly well. Fortunately, Coach wasn't using full force on his body blows. It did feel like he was trying to take my head off. When I mentioned the force of his head hits, he asked me, "Are you still conscious?"

"Yes, I am."

"Then I'm not using full force."

Ouch!

As I was getting ready to leave, a runner from the front office, who looked like one of the kids I saw in the hall at Hollywood High, brought me a note. I had a tee time at the Calabasas Country Club at two o'clock Sunday afternoon. That meant I had better buy clubs and gear. The note included a map with directions and the name of the golf pro I was to ask for.

I met Dick in the parking lot as I arrived back at the apartment. I told him of my good fortune in getting to play. He told me, "Wait till you see who is in your foursome. Pearson probably has just dumped you on the pro without finding out the level of players you will be with or telling him how you play."

"We'll see."

I took a shower and put on clean clothes. Two showers a day were becoming the norm. After a hot, sweaty day on the set around horses and cattle, I needed it. I don't know how Ellen was able to stand to hug me in our last scene of the day. Nina and Miss Powell must wonder what I do on the set. They probably thought I shoveled bull crap all day. Come to think of it, I was in a movie, so that wasn't so far off.

There was a store off Wilshire that specialized in golf equipment. I'm certain I made the salesman's day. I spent a lot of money, but he spent a lot of time. He had me hitting balls into a net to make certain the length was correct and the shafts the right stiffness.

He told me they were considering buying a television camera that would save the pictures to tape. It was still too expensive for them, but he predicted every golf shop would have one to check your swing one day.

Tapes of golf swings made me think of transistors that had made my hairdryer possible. I wondered where they would take camera technology. Could they be made small enough to fit in a Dick Tracy-type watch? I shook my head. Of course not. It wouldn't hold the film.

After buying clubs, balls, shoes, tees, gloves, and golf towels and loading everything in the trunk of the T-Bird, I looked for dinner. I ended up at the little restaurant across from my complex. They now knew me and called me Movie Star. Someone had noticed the Warner Brothers parking sticker on my windshield. I told them I did odd jobs on the lot.

That night I called home for no particular reason. I just felt like hearing voices from home. Dad did have some good news. We were now thirty percent owners of Detroit Faucet. Mark Downing, the new young owner, liked the idea of trying new products. Dad apologized for not getting my buy-in before doing the deal, but it was good, and he didn't want to let it go. I agreed with him and thought he did the right thing.

I told Dad that I would get a camera and take pictures of the types of faucets I was talking about. He told me that Mark was looking for a design engineer. He preferred a recent female graduate, as she would better understand what women liked. Since she was female, he could pay her less, especially since she was a recent graduate.

"Dad, do you want to be the one who explains Downing's rationale to Mum?"

"No!"

"Then tell him we insist he pays the going rate for a man. You might want to contact an engineering school or someone who might know what that rate should be. If we are going to be in business, let's do it right."

"I agree. I hadn't thought about what he was planning. By the way, I talked to your mother. She is flying home this coming Wednesday. She has had a wonderful visit. She even had afternoon tea with your godmother."

"Wow, she saw the queen. How cool is that!"

"They were very friendly during the war. Your mum even made it to London on VE day while I was still laid up in Germany. She helped her friend Bets sneak out of Buckingham Palace, and they formed a conga line right through downtown London. Bets even led them through the Ritz. I guess that was a snoot full for the old fuddy-duddies."

I then talked to Eddy and Mary. Denny was at the movies with friends. Mary wanted to know when I was coming home as she missed me. I told her I missed her also. It was strange how my throat tightened up when I said that. I asked her to give the phone back to Dad.

"Dad, I think I just got hit by a bad case of homesickness."

"I'm not surprised. You are pretty self-contained, but you have always gotten along with your siblings, so I can see you missing them."

"It includes you and Mum."

"That is nice to hear, Rick. We also miss you."

"When Mum gets home, would you talk to her about a possible trip out here at Easter break? If we have a break in our schedule, I will fly home, even if it is only for a long weekend. Also, I need your opinion on my buying a house out here for security reasons. After last week I can see that I'm too open at this apartment."

"That's a lot to discuss, Rick. It may not be till next week."

"That's okay. Homesickness and the need for a different place to live just came up."

We said our goodnights. I felt better than I had all day.

I reread an old favorite. Mr. Angelo sold a Martian animal to Castor and Pollux. What a mess but lots of fun.

Chapter 40

Saturday morning, my usual exercise routine had more zest. I was getting to play today! I hadn't done anything fun with kids my age for what seemed like forever. I headed to Nina's house and arrived at the agreed-upon at eight o'clock. They had a gate across their driveway, and it was manned. Nina had left my name, so I was allowed right in.

She was ready to go. She suggested that I drive the family station wagon. Her older brother used it for hauling his surfboards around. It was a pretty beat-up 1937 Ford Deluxe Station Wagon. Before we could leave, I had to be introduced to her dad. I had seen Mr. Monroe at the studio but didn't know who he was at the time.

He was a pleasant late forties medium-sized guy with dark hair. He had a pencil-thin mustache, as you saw in the movies. Oh yeah, he made the movies, not in them, made them. He knew who I was. Nina had told him about me, and he knew I was working with Mr. Wayne.

He told me, "John likes you. He says you have a good work ethic and true grit. I'm not sure what he means by that, but I know it is a compliment."

"Thank you, sir. I enjoy working with Mr. Wayne and Warner Brothers."

"Okay, that's enough of the chit-chat. You kids have fun today."

On the way out to the car, Nina told me, "Daddy usually gives my boyfriends a hard time. He must like you."

Stop the presses, boyfriend? I accepted her comment and went with the flow. The car drove fairly well, not as good a ride as my T-Bird, but then I wouldn't want the mess of a day's surfing in it.

I wish I could tell the world that I was a natural on the surfboard and soon would be a world champion. I didn't drown. I had a lot of fun. I was told the waves at Santa Monica were okay but not great. I did manage several nice rides and even made it in once.

All in all, I would do it again. Higher, more frequent waves would be better. It seemed like we spent most of the day waiting for the right waves.

We started surfing at ten o'clock. Nina had their cook pack us a lunch which we ate on the hood of the car. We gave up at two o'clock because the tide had turned, and the waves were exceptionally low. We showered the salt off at the city's freshwater showers along the beach. We changed into street clothes using some fancy maneuvers in the car.

I accidentally got a flash of a breast. At least, I think it was an accident. It was only for a second, but I would think about it for days.

We strolled up on the Santa Monica pier. The amusement park was open, so we spent some time there. We even rode on the Ferris wheel at the end of the pier. That was cool, riding a Ferris wheel over the Pacific Ocean.

Even though it was February, it was a warm day, so I wore a golf shirt, shorts, and tennis shoes. I didn't even have socks; try that in Ohio in February!

We were eating cotton candy on our way back to the car when a small kid, maybe four years old like Mary, came running past us. His parents were chasing right behind him. "Stop, Billy," yelled his mom. Billy was enjoying the game, so he ran faster. Looking over his shoulder to see his pursuit, he veered to the right, right off the edge of the pier into the ocean.

As Dad had told me, there was a time to think and a time to act. I certainly didn't think, at least not linear thought. I dropped my wallet on the wooden deck and followed Billy into the water. He had run under the railing. I jumped over it.

On the way down, I grabbed my nose, as taught in Boy Scout lifeguard training, so I wouldn't break it when I hit the water.

Holding my privates, I managed to hit feet first, legs together, fairly straight in, so I plunged. I mean, I plunged like fifteen or twenty feet under the water. It was good because I ran into Billy just as my downward motion stopped, and I started back up. I grabbed him and kicked for the surface.

When we broke the surface, I put him in the standard life-saving grip with my arm around his chest and under his chin. I oriented myself and headed for the shore. Billy was coughing, so I knew he was going to be okay. He hung on to me like he was drowning. Then it occurred to me he had good reason to cling to me!

When I had him up to dry land, his parents were waiting. His mom grabbed him and held him. There were the tears that one would expect from both of them. Nina was also waiting. She'd had the presence of mind to pick up my wallet. The parents introduced themselves and thanked me profusely. Their last name was Gates. I didn't catch their first names.

A lifeguard was there and got all the details from us. He had to record all problems in his beach sector. He wanted to know where we lived, if we worked, and telephone number if they had to contact us. He looked up at me when I said I worked at Warner Brothers Studio.

"Are you an intern there?"

"He is starring in a movie with John Wayne," Nina proudly told him.

"Wow, that is cool. I would love to break into movies."

"Are you registered with Central Casting?" I asked.

"No."

"That is where most people get their start." I had been getting "I want to break into movies" comments more and more, so I had learned to give the Central Casting answer.

Who knew? If they registered, maybe, they would get work.

With Nina holding my wallet, I stood fully clothed under one of the beach showers. The saltwater was already starting to itch. I sat on a blanket as I drove us back to her house. Her dad was coming out of the door as we arrived. Since I looked like a drowned rat, he wanted to know what had happened.

Nina gushed about me being a hero. Mr. Monroe looked at me with a question in his eyes.

"I only followed my training. It wasn't that big of a deal."

"Yes, it was!" Nina yelled. "You don't know what great things that Billy Gates might grow up to do. If you hadn't saved him, the world might be worse without him."

Somehow, I doubted Bill Gates would be other than a normal person.

Mr. Monroe invited me to dinner. I declined because of my clothing situation. He said if I went home and changed, I could be back in an hour or so and join them. I told him that would work. Nina wanted to ride with me, but her dad wasn't wild about that idea. I wonder why a father wouldn't want his teenage daughter to go to the apartment of a boy who lived alone. I didn't blame him in the least.

With Nina pouting a little, I took off. At almost five o'clock, I returned all showered, shaved, and in clean clothes. I dressed up a little, wearing good slacks, a golf shirt, and a blue blazer. When I returned, I was really glad I did. There were other guests at dinner, and the guys were dressed like me.

There were two couples. I was introduced to them and then promptly forgot their names. As the dinner progressed, I figured out it was Jerry and Sally on my right and Marvin and Grace on my left. Not remembering the name of someone you were just introduced to is terrible. I vowed to pay more attention in the future.

The conversation was more of a local society update rather than an exchange of ideas. Since I didn't know most of the people involved, it was rather boring. I perked up once when Marvin started talking about John Wayne's conversion from one movie to another.

He was impressed with Wayne's business abilities on top of his acting.

Mr. Monroe let others know that I was involved in the halted film and the new one. This led to a few questions about how the new movie was going. I told them it was great but that Mr. Wayne seemed to enjoy throwing me in a water trough more than he should. After six takes, I had been informed on Friday that they would be redoing the scene, so I was in store for more.

That led to a discussion of the changes required in a scene like that, the logistics of clean clothes and getting dry between takes. This led Nina to ask how I had showered and dried my hair so quickly this afternoon. It didn't even look damp. I explained my hairdryer to the table at large.

The women all agreed they would want one like that. Even Mr. Monroe showed some interest as it would cut down the time between takes.

Nina said, "Besides being a lifesaving hero and actor, you are an inventor?"

That led to the discussion of the events at the Santa Monica pier. I told them that it wasn't such a big deal, my Boy Scout lifeguard training kicked in, and I did what had to be done.

Jerry followed up with, "In the army, they trained us all the time so that it was ingrained in us. We didn't have to think. We just did what we were trained to do. I know it kept me alive a few times."

That redirected the conversation to his war experiences. I think he was trying to be the center of attention. As he told of his adventures, it became apparent that he had never left California during the war. That was fine with me. I didn't want to be the center of attention.

Nina and I sat with the adults over coffee after the table was cleared. The conversation had returned to the social update, so I followed Nina's lead when she suggested we go for a walk. This got a sharp look from her dad, but he nodded his head.

We walked around the yard for a while, and then we sat on an outdoor swing by the pool. From the inside, they could see us, so I was hoping her dad wouldn't get his shotgun out. I wasn't too worried about that.

Nina and I talked about our different lifestyles growing up. She was shuttled between her mother in France and her dad in Hollywood, with stops in major cities like London, Paris, and New York along the way. This made my life in Bellefontaine seem so dull in comparison.

Nina told me Bellefontaine's life sounded wonderful, small-town America without the best-dressed competition of Rome or Paris. I didn't burst her bubble, but the competition between teenage girls in a small town seemed to me as vicious as any fashion center. It was on a smaller scale, but just as real.

I did agree that we didn't have traffic problems like LA or smog.

It was a pleasant evening, but I was getting tired, so I said good night to all and thanked Mr. Monroe for the dinner invitation. Nina walked me to my car. I kissed her good night. It was just a light brushing of the lips, but they were such nice lips. I thought about them all the way home and until I fell asleep.

Chapter 41

Sunday, Dick and I had agreed to sleep in, so we didn't do our run until seven o'clock. After that, Janice fixed us what she called a brunch. Since it was still early, I had no intention of giving up my lunch. After that, I returned home and finished off my weekly letter. I also decided to make my call as it would be late Ohio time when I finished my golf round. If I waited too long, Mary would be asleep.

As it turns out, I missed her anyway. She was playing outside with a neighborhood friend. They were building a snowman. I had forgotten that it was still winter. Here I was about to play golf, and they were playing in the snow. I had to give living here full-time some serious thought.

Denny and Eddie were fine. They wanted to know if I had been to Disney yet. I told them I had been too busy. I was told to get my priorities straight. Dad updated me on Jackson Housing. We now owned twenty units in Bellefontaine, and he was now looking to expand to Urbana to the south.

After that, he was already thinking of Kenton, Marysville, and Wapakoneta. We also discussed Russells Point, but both agreed that we didn't want to get into the vacation rental business yet.

He informed me that I had a package coming in the mail. It contained my first ten hair dryers. The prototype molds were finished, so Don Thompson and Paul Samson assembled the first dryers for my review. They had left them on for one hundred hours each, and they hadn't melted, caught on fire, or electrocuted them, so they thought they were safe to start using.

I left for the golf course and arrived at twelve. My name was at the gate, so I was allowed to drive on in. I unloaded my clubs at the caddie shack. Then I proceeded to eat my lunch. It was too many hours since my brunch! From there, I checked that my tee time was still two o'clock. A caddie took my clubs to the driving range for me. This was a level of service I had never had before.

I started on the range slowly with the smaller irons. As I limbered up, I was able to put more into them. After a half-hour, I was up to my driver and hammering them out to almost three hundred yards. This got me some looks on the practice tee, but no one commented.

The putting green kept me occupied until my tee time. These greens were faster than anything I had ever played on. I had heard the term slick used about a green. Now I knew what it meant. This course would be all about putting.

At two o'clock, I was in place at the first tee box. The starter introduced me to my foursome. They were three elderly gentlemen. They must have been in their sixties. After my loss of names at dinner last night, I paid attention today. When I shook hands with them, I made it a point of being polite.

"It is nice to meet you, Mr. Simpson, Mr. Acton, and Mr. Williams."

"Well, at least he has manners," one of them said.

"Can he play golf?" another asked as if I wasn't standing right there.

The guy that said that Mr. Acton turned to me and told me, "We can't hit it far, but we hit it straight. We don't want you to hold us up, so you can only take ten strokes a hole. After that, you pick the ball up."

I agreed with this restriction with a straight face. If I took a ten, I should pick the ball up, trash the clubs, and leave the state in shame.

They had been playing together for some years, so they had their routine down pat. They had their first tee lineup in order. No tossing tees to see who went first. I was informed I was last up. They had two carts, but I chose to walk. I would've carried my bag, but club rules made me have a caddie.

All three teed off and were straight down the middle of the fairway. If they played like that all day and had mastered these greens, I had my work cut out. After that, though, I had to laugh at myself. So much for a day of relaxation, the competitive drive had kicked in. Well, maybe that could be relaxing in a manner of speaking.

The first hole was only a 310-yard par 4, so I was waiting for the foursome on the green to move before I drove. I had a 3-wood out for my first shot to drive the green. The old guy who told me I had to pick the ball up if I took a ten now got on my case about not hitting. Rather than say anything, I changed the 3-wood for a 4-iron.

"Why are you using an iron?" I was asked.

"If I'm going to hit now, I have to lay up."

I then promptly hit the ball straight down the middle to within twenty yards of the green.

I noticed that the loudmouth had nothing to say after that.

As we walked towards the green, my caddie told me, "I loved it. That old man has been a pain in the butt for years. I hope you play that well all day."

I shared my concern about the putting, and he told me that they wouldn't be too fast as long as I hit the green so that the grass was bent towards me. He would tell me where I needed to be on each approach shot.

That was how the day went. My caddie directed me in each shot. I ended up a respectable 6-under for 18. Not a course record, but still good. The loudmouth had been quiet the whole round. One of the other old guys approached me in private.

"That was the most enjoyable round of golf I have had in years. You shut Todd up, and it was wonderful. Thank you, and I will play with you anytime."

I don't know where I dredged it up, but his name came to me,

"Thank you for letting me play with you, Mr. Williams. It was an enjoyable day."

I gave my caddie John Jacobs a twenty-dollar tip for his help. Without his guidance, my day would have been a disaster. I now knew why the pros used a caddie.

I returned home and spent some quality time with my Biology and Spanish textbooks, falling asleep early.

Chapter 42

I woke up at my regular time on Monday feeling good. I had an enjoyable weekend, and it looked like it would be a good week except for getting dunked in a horse trough some more. Dick and I did our regular run. My stamina was back up to where it was before my winter layoff. I began to appreciate why baseball had spring training.

After costuming and makeup, I found out they had been pulling my leg about redoing the water trough scenes. Everyone on the set was in on it. They all could see how tired I was getting of that particular scene. There were bets on whether I would show up today!

I felt a little insulted by those bets. I had been working since I was eight years old, first at home, then when I was ten, I had a paper route. You did your job unless you were sick. If I had skipped junior high school every time there was a test, or even worse, a school dance, I would never have graduated. If you had a job, you did it, taking the good with the bad.

Today was to be a walkthrough of a scene that was put in to lighten the movie up. They didn't want it to be all gunfire and fistfights. John Wayne and I were to install a water faucet on the ranch's new indoor plumbing system. This would result in us being soaked.

When I was told of the scene, I started thinking. I asked Mr. Wayne, "What sort of faucet are we installing?"

"I have no idea, just an older type they have in prop storage."

"Could we use a brand that was actually in production then?"

"What are you thinking, Ricky?"

I then proceeded to explain how our family, not wanting to say it was only me, owned thirty percent of a company, Detroit Faucet, that was founded in 1880. I thought it would be neat to have our product in the movie.

Wayne mused, "Since the faucet wouldn't have a name on it that could be read on the screen, we would have to say its name. That is called direct product placement. Since you were so good at the salary negotiations, I think we can do it for free."

"Mr. Wayne, I would like to take it further. I would like a clip to be included in the television special and then have Detroit Faucet be a sponsor of the show."

"Young man, I like the way you think. Let's make it happen."

Mr. Wayne got with the writers, and they changed some dialog. Now there was a reference to the Detroit Faucet that Mr. Wayne had found in the Sears catalog, being delivered by Wells Fargo. When Big Jim, the nickname of James Braxton played by John Wayne, had the faucet in hand, he made the statement, "This will be easy."

The next shot is of water pouring all over Big Jim and Sir Nick. They fixed this problem and turned the faucet on again. This time, Sir Nick takes the water flow in the face.

"Easy, huh?" asked Sir Nick, as he changed the water flow with his fingers right into Big Jim's face.

The scene ends up with Big Jim and Sir Nick laughing about their shared misfortune. This scene would be a makeup scene after the tough love Big Jim has had to show Sir Nick. It is the most lighthearted part of the movie. The rest of the movie is serious as outlaws and regulators are fended off.

We spent all morning on that scene. Getting wet, drying out, doing retakes. After four takes, the director, Ron Dodge, was happy with what he saw. He liked the addition of the faucet scene. He felt this modernization showed that they were living at the end of the Old West. The small modernization was a symbol of the much larger changes in the West, such as the Johnson County Range War.

Open ranges were coming under private control. This large change was at the root of the range war. After this war was finished, the Old West was no more. There would be minor incidents, but for all practical purposes, the West was won. I could see someone using this example in their Ph.D. thesis.

After my part was done for the day, I still had a little time before lunch, so I went to the prop master's office. Mr. Rodrigues was there, so I explained to him that I wanted to obtain pictures of some of the faucets in storage. What did I have to do to get them? I didn't go into detail why I wanted them, and he wasn't curious. He made a phone call. After fifteen minutes, a still photographer showed up.

We went to the shelves where they were kept. There must have been fifty types of faucets with multiple copies of each. I went through them and selected a dozen that looked good to me. I asked each of them to pick out some that looked nice to them. This added another eight faucets for a total of twenty.

I told the photographer, Mr. Grey, that I would like a picture of each. He asked if I needed the pictures right then or if he could take them elsewhere for proper lighting. I told him proper lighting would be better.

He said, "Okay, I should have them printed by tomorrow."

That sounded like a quick and dirty job to me, and that was all I expected.

"Thanks," I replied.

After lunch, I headed over to Hollywood High. This was my last week. I was eager to get it done and sit for my exams, so I was finished with ninth grade. I was more eager to see Nina. She was glad to see me if the greeting she gave was any sign. I was leaning in for a second kiss when Miss Powell entered the room.

"This is Biology class, not practice biology," she remarked.

Flustered, we backed off quickly. That was the end of it from Miss Powell. I shudder to think what would've happened if Mr. Hurley had caught us. I would be returning to school after graduation to work off my detention.

Miss Powell made a boring subject for me become interesting. I realized that I loved mechanical things but didn't get this living stuff. As I called it, this living stuff was much more complex than my simple mechanical thoughts. It was incredible. While I hadn't any desire to go into any form of organic science, I was developing a great respect for it.

It made me realize that anyone working on devices such as prostheses for arms and legs had to know how they interfaced with the human body. The logical next step would be to have a direct interface with the nervous system. Now that would be cool. Transistors' smallness was a tiny first step in that direction.

Nina had a verbal invitation from her father to a party at their house this Saturday. She told me all the movers and shakers in the movie industry would be there. She also told me not to be surprised with the afternoon paper.

The headline in the entertainment section would be, "Ricky Does it Again!"

Someone had an 8mm home movie of the whole Billy Gates rescue.

Nina's dad had followed up after dinner on Saturday night. He had his people check with the lifeguards. They, in turn, told of the people who had volunteered the fact that they had the film. From there, Warner Brothers purchased the film and released selected frames to the press along with the lifeguard report.

I hadn't told Nina or her father that I liked to avoid publicity and was ready to get angry, but I stopped and thought before opening my mouth. I must have been thinking for too long as Nina asked me what was wrong.

"Nothing," I said. "I was just thinking it through. I can see why your dad went to those lengths. His job is the publicity of his movies and their stars. While I don't like that sort of limelight because I don't see it as real heroism, I see why he did it."

"Ricky, you are a hero!"

"No, I'm someone who followed their training. I was never in danger. I didn't have to make a conscious decision to go into a known danger. Those are the heroes."

As I told her this, I imagined I heard machine-gun bullets rattling off a descending landing craft door. I was never there, but I would never forget the sound.

"The publicity won't cause me any harm, but I'm not making myself out to be something I'm not."

By the time I returned to the studio, the news was all over the place. One of the grips gave me today's *LA Examiner*. It had my rescue of little Billy Gates front and center on the entertainment page. It was a credible report. I liked the fact that they mentioned my Boy Scout lifeguard training.

I realized this might get me another lifesaving medal, but I didn't care. It certainly should help the Scouts' recruiting. I wondered briefly if they had a recruiting merit badge. I should qualify by now.

There was a story on the front page that caught my eye. The gang war in New York City had gone hot. There had been half a dozen killings in three incidents over the weekend. Whoever had killed Paul Grant had set something off.

After checking in on the set, I headed back to the stunt area. I took a little razzing from the guys.

I heard, "Help me, I'm drowning," several times, but it was all in fun.

My sword work was now credible. I wouldn't ever be a professional, but I now kept the pointy end aimed in the correct direction.

The records I was keeping on my weights and reps showed that I was improving all the time, and the tightness in my shirts was a testimony. I would have to buy new ones shortly.

Before I left the studio, I stopped at the office and asked if there had been any calls for me. They had a stack of call slips for me. All the usual news outlets wanted an interview. I returned one call; it was to the BSA National Headquarters. I was being put in for the Award of Merit. This would give me all three of the BSA lifesaving medals.

I was also told they intended to do a *Boy's Life* feature on me. I hadn't any problems with this as, without my scout training, I couldn't have saved those people. I owed the scouts and believed in the movement. As Baden-Powell called them, I wasn't a badge hunter, but I didn't turn down honors justly earned.

After I let myself into my apartment, I realized there had been no reporters lurking, so this story wasn't that big of a deal, or I was already boring them.

I did call home to let Dad know that everything was okay. He was glad to hear it. He also let me know that Mark Downing at Detroit Faucet had hired a female design engineer out of Michigan State. She had won several awards for her design work in school, so he had high hopes. Dad made a point of letting me know that the salary was the same as a man for the same job.

I told him about the pictures I had commissioned and hoped to see them tomorrow. They would give an idea of my vision. I didn't feel like cooking, so two peanut butter and jelly sandwiches made a good dinner. I am sure the food groups were represented somehow. To avoid dishes, I ate over the sink. Very efficient! I don't think I will tell Mum.

I watched TV for a while. They had a segment on the nightly news about me saving another life. They played it straight, reporting the news. I was half afraid I would become a comedy routine for Red Skelton or Jack Benny.

When I went to bed, I reread the book about Castor and Pollux. The story was fun, but the parts about asteroid mining made me wonder if it would ever be possible. A bigger question was with the expanding population of the earth, would it be a necessity?

Chapter 43

It was raining lightly on Tuesday morning, so I kept the top on my T-Bird. I noticed it was time to run the car through a car wash and vacuum out the front and back seats. Going to the beach last weekend had left it messy. That was even after using the woody station wagon. What a disaster if we hadn't.

On the set, the writers were in a tizzy. It turns out Yale had never admitted females in our movie's time frame. You would think it was a world-class disaster. Well, they would have to reshoot one scene where it was mentioned. They now had Ellen's character Lilly going to Bryn Mawr outside of Philadelphia.

Not only that, the writers had flunked math. The story started in 1889. Sir Nick died in 1918. How could he have been married for thirty-three years? Fortunately, that was an easy fix.

To say Mr. Wayne was pissed was an understatement. I wish I had something to write with as he tore into the writers. I heard so many useful phrases, but I wouldn't be able to remember them all. I also found out that Mr. Wayne was a hot burner. He got angry, let it out, and then got over it immediately.

If he had been drinking at lunch and got upset later, it could get nasty. They tried to shoot all his scenes in the morning to avoid this situation.

We worked hard well into lunchtime. I had to grab a sandwich and eat it on the go as I drove to Hollywood High. I tossed the wrappers in the backseat. Maybe this was why I had to get the car cleaned.

Before Miss Powell walked in, Nina and I hugged for a moment. She told me that slacks and a sports coat would be appropriate for Saturday night. I was to show up around six and help her make certain everything was ready. Also, since she was her dad's hostess, she would have to mingle with the guests. I could join her or entertain myself. I told her we would play it by ear.

I was feeling comfortable with the class material. I spent time with my textbooks while waiting on the set and early in the evenings. Not every evening but most. I was ready to start my official tests for the State of California tomorrow.

Returning to the set, we worked into the evening. Someone had left a newspaper, so I read the front page. The situation in New York was getting out of control. The FBI had just announced they had a gangster by the name of Joe Valachi in custody. He had named the head of the five major crime families. Before this, no one had ever talked.

In the meantime, the gangs were still gunning each other down. This week Daniel Garcia of the Norsemen was gunned down by members of the Italian Red Wings. Then the Mau Maus killed Anthony Lavonchino of the Italian Sand Street Angels. I never knew there were so many gangs in New York. Maybe they were like the minor leagues in baseball.

Whoever killed Paul Grant had upset the applecart in New York. It sounded like some long-delayed justice was being served.

As I was getting ready to leave for home, Mr. Grey showed up with the pictures he had promised. They were beautiful. Now that is a strange thing to say about water faucets, but they had cleaned and polished the faucets, then taken the pictures on what looked like black velvet. They were like works of art.

I thanked him profusely. He told me not to worry about it. He had fun doing it. Better than some of the studio jobs he had, trying to make some old woman look young and beautiful. At least the faucets couldn't swear at him if they didn't like the shots, and they held their poses as long as needed.

I thanked him once more and thought, "This guy needs to get a life!"

There were two sets of pictures, so I stopped at the studio office on the way out and mailed a set to my dad.

I was ready for a real meal, so I went home, cleaned up, and changed out of my Western shirt and jeans. After donning my new casual uniform of slacks, a golf shirt, which I still refused to call a polo shirt, and a sports coat, I went to the Brown Derby. I was surprised when Mr. Cobb recognized me and found me a table right away.

Mr. Baxter was there with his family. When he saw me, he took me over to his table and introduced me to his wife, daughter, and granddaughter. The little girl who they called Emmy was a delightful child. She was about the same age as Mary. Apart from being very pale, she appeared to be okay. She had energy.

Mr. Baxter must have sensed my noticing this because he said, "You should have seen her a month ago. It was enough to break your heart."

We talked for a few minutes more, never bringing up directly how I helped the family, but you could tell I had friends for life.

On the way back to my table, I mused that I had better never forget there were real people affected by my business dealings.

After a good steak and a Cobb salad, which I had found out the hard way, was invented by Mr. Cobb here at the Brown Derby. I had made the mistake of stating, on the set, that I met a man named after a salad. Boy, did I get razzed. It is a good thing that I liked the salads because one was put in front of me at lunch, in the cafeteria, every day for a week, compliments of Mr. Cobb.

I went over my Latin vocabulary that evening, as that was my weakest area. By the time I had done that for two hours, I was ready to go to sleep. I think I slept through my last two declensions.

Chapter 44

Wednesday, Thursday, and Friday afternoon had been set aside for me to take my exams for the State of California to see if I would graduate from the ninth grade. My first one was Biology.

I headed over to the set to find Mr. Wayne to show him the portfolio of faucet pictures. He wasn't there, but I was told that he would be in the cafeteria. He was but sitting with a woman whose back was to me. I was hesitant to interrupt, but Mr. Wayne saw me and waved me over.

As I approached the table, I heard the woman say, "John, I'm so bored. I have to find a new direction."

As I neared the table, I saw the woman's profile. It was the most elegant face in the world. At least, that is how *Time Magazine* had put it. The raven-haired beauty was none other than Anna Romanov, the actress.

Miss Romanov was the actress of choice if you needed someone to play a noblewoman or woman of great personal power. She was versatile in acting in comedies and dramas. She had performed on stage and screen.

It had been written that she was a cross between Katharine Hepburn and Grace Kelly. She was perfection. She was also my mum's age. Dang!

When Mr. Wayne made the introductions, I managed to not stutter and stammer or make a fool of myself. It was close. She was gracious in acknowledging me.

"Rick, what brings you here?" Mr. Wayne inquired.

I don't care how many times he tells me; he will always be Mr. Wayne to me.

"I wanted to share the faucet photos with you," I replied while opening the folder.

"Faucet photos?" inquired Miss Romanov.

I handed her the file. She leafed through them and then went back through them slowly.

"These are pieces of art. Where did you get them?"

Mr. Wayne said, "Pull up a chair, Rick, and share your whole story."

I told her about owning an interest in a faucet company, seeing these old pieces on the set and in the prop room here at the studio, my thought on doing a direct placement in the movie, tying it into the TV special planned around me, and then having Detroit Faucet sponsor.

I then told her that DF had just hired an award-winning designer to bring designs of this nature to our product line and that we would also be updating our catalogs. I crossed my fingers on all this because it was all in my head. I hadn't discussed it in any detail with Dad. To make matters worse, I had never had any conversation on any subject with Mark Downing, the majority owner.

Miss Romanov asked Mr. Wayne, "How old did you say this young man was?"

"I didn't, but he is fifteen going on forty."

"I was just telling John that I'm getting bored and that I need a new interest in my life. These pictures give me some ideas. I would like a few days to think things through, and I may have a presentation for you and your partners. May I have these photographs, please?"

"No!" Of course, I didn't say no. I said, "Why certainly, Miss Romanov, I can get another set easily."

I resolved to bring my parents and business partner up to speed as quickly as I could.

Miss Romanov stood up, and Mr. Wayne and I also rose.

"It was genuinely nice to meet you, Richard. I will be in contact with you."

She then walked away in that regal fashion of hers.

John Wayne said, "When she asked for those pictures, I almost thought I heard a no."

"You're kidding. She could have asked for my heart, and I would've ripped it out then and there."

"Yeah, she has that effect on men. I wonder what she is thinking of."

"I don't know, but I have some ducks to get in a row."

My first stop was Mr. Grey at the photo lab. He had ten more sets of prints. Overkill was the name of the job. He told me if I went over a hundred sets, he would have to have a charge code.

From there, I borrowed an office with a telephone. I did have to tell them to charge it to *Sir Nicklaus*. My first call was to Dad. I was in luck. He was about to leave for Dayton to pick Mum up at the airport. I filled him in on everything up to my conversation with Miss Romanov. He gave me Mark Downing's phone number and told me to update him on everything.

When I called Detroit Faucet, I told them this was Rick Jackson of Jackson Engineering calling for Mark Downing. I was put through immediately. Mark and I spent a few minutes getting to know each other. Dad had told him the patent holder was a teenager and was working on a movie with John Wayne. So, it wasn't all a shock.

When I told him about the photographs of the specially designed faucets, he was impressed. He got excited when I told him about the direct placement in the movie. Then I added that it would also be part of a TV special he was starting to stutter.

On top of that, I would provide the money for DF, as we both were now calling the company, to be a sponsor for the special. He was speechless at this point. When I suggested we update all the catalogs and have a special design section put together by our new design engineer, I could hear some strange sounds. I decided to wait for what Miss Romanov said before I told him. He sounded too young for a heart attack, but you never know.

I apologized for moving so quickly without consulting him. Did he have any problems with this plan? He got his voice back and told me it sounded fine to him. Would I please send him pictures of the faucets?"

I told him that would be no problem. I asked if he minded if I talked to the Warner Brothers CEO about using the faucet designs as is, or would we have to come up with variations."

"Can you get in to see him?"

"I'm dating his daughter and will be at his party at their house tomorrow night, so I will have a chance to talk to him, probably not at the party, but somewhere along the way."

"This opportunity is unbelievable. I will get to work with Sally as soon as we get the pictures."

"Who is Sally?"

"Oh, she is the designer we hired, Sally Enright. Rick, you need to come to Detroit and visit our facility."

"I will on my next trip east. We should have a break in a few weeks. Maybe I can make it then."

"Rick, I must say, a month ago I had just bought my sister's share of the business to keep control. I had no idea how I would be able to save it beyond that. Now it looks like DF is going to take off like a rocket."

"Mark, I just thought we needed the trademark on DF and a logo to go with it. Detroit Faucets is a good solid name, but in the world of fashion, it is too boring. We need to change the brand but not lose the heritage."

"You are right, Rick. I have been toying with a similar idea. I like DF because it came to us naturally in our conversation. If we have to, we can also say DF stands for Designed Faucets or some other variation."

"Good thought Mark. While we are throwing out ideas, think about a designer catalog in several languages such as Spanish, French, German, or Italian."

"We even could do it in British English and call them taps."

"Good one, Mark. My mum would love it." From there, the conversation descended to the inane, so we said our goodbyes. I knew I was going to like Mark, and ours would be a good relationship.

After taking care of my business communications, I went to the little schoolhouse on the lot. Hmm, that had a ring to it, *Little Schoolhouse on the Lot*. That would be a good name for a TV show, instead of a lot of use mountain, plain, lake, prairie, or something like that.

The schoolroom was busy with the little kids. Mr. Danson took me to a separate office where a very sour-faced person was waiting. We were introduced briefly. He was a state employee who was detailed to monitor my tests for the week. I could tell I would never be friends with this guy.

I knew I would never be a fan when he had me turn my pockets out. He thought I was going to cheat. He even made me roll up my sleeves and checked the inside of my cuffs and my arms to see if I had anything written on them.

I decided he was one of those petty bureaucrats who must be endured. I did not attempt to engage him in conversation, just listened as he explained the exam rules, mainly use a number two pencil, and be sure to put my name on the top of the answer sheet.

He asked me if I had any questions, and I replied, "No, sir."

Those two words were the extent of my conversation with him. I took the exam well within the allotted three hours. Two hours. I silently handed in my answers and left. Oh, joy!

From there, I went to what was becoming, more and more, my home away from home, the stunt area. I spent an hour on my sword work, an hour lifting, and then went on to the gym for my boxing workout. My work with the bags was going well. They had me skipping rope for several days but decided I didn't need that work.

My reflexes in the ring weren't where they needed to be. I learned to throw different punches such as hooks, jabs, and uppercuts. It was when to throw them and the defensive moves that weren't there yet. It was the same story every time I took up a new physical effort, learning to react automatically without having to think it through.

When I arrived home, there was a package on the doorstep. My hairdryers had arrived. I had to open them immediately. They were beautiful. This batch had white housings, but I knew they could do any color we asked for. I started thinking about who I would give one to out here.

I called home and found out that Mum had arrived okay. I told Dad about my conversation with Mark Downing and that he was on board with the faucet program; and how we both agreed that Detroit Faucet should become DF with a nice logo. From there, we talked about the dryers. I asked him to deliver one to Mrs. Bailey and mail it as a gift from them to each of my godparents.

I surprised him when I asked for two to be wrapped separately and taken to the school office for Miss Bales and Mr. Hurley and to include a note of thanks for all the help in school. I then thought of Miss Powell and Miss Sperry. I would present them with one also. Thinking of it, I had better give one to Mr. Danson for his wife, or he would feel slighted.

I had better have one sent to Mark Downing at DF and make certain that Don Thompson and Paul Samson, the engineers on the project, had one. Dad told me he planned to hand them out to my aunts and female cousins. I suppose this was the right thing to do, but they didn't thrill me as a group.

I talked to Mum for a few minutes. She was tired from her trip. She gave me greetings from my godmother and my grandmother.

She added that this was the most exhilaration she had had in years. I know a trip home to England would be exciting for her, but exhilarating?

She wanted to know how my bruises were from my beating. I told her they were a fading memory. In turn, I asked if she knew about what happened to Paul Grant, and she responded that she knew very well and good riddance to bad rubbish. My mum had never come across as the forgiving type.

I talked to Denny, Eddie, and Mary briefly. They all wanted to know why I hadn't gone to Disneyland yet. They couldn't understand why I hadn't gone on my first day in California. I told them it would be soon.

That night I dug into my stash of *Astounding Magazine,* which I had brought with me. I read about Slippery Jim di Griz robbing a bank and the Special Corp. That Harold Inskipp was certainly a dangerous one. It was pure space opera but a lot of fun.

Chapter 45

Thursday was work, work, and more work. I was in the scenes all morning long. One was a real surprise. It turned out my mother in the movie was being played by Anna Romanov. It was a cameo appearance for her. She had no lines. She just had to hug me as I was leaving the house to go to America. Of course, she did it in style. The look of tragedy on her face told the entire story of a mother's heartbreak and worry.

After that scene, I thought about how my mum would have played it. The answer was, she wouldn't. If you tried to do something to one of her children that she didn't care for, Hell wouldn't hold it.

By lunchtime, I was ready for a break. An afternoon of testing was looking good by comparison. I'm such a wimp!

My exams were in the same room with the same guy that looked like he had sucked on a lemon. He performed all but a strip search and gave the same dry instructions. When I was asked if I had any questions, I gave an original.

"None, sir."

I didn't want to be seen as boring and repetitious like some other people in the room.

It was such a relief to get to the physical part of my day. Who would have thought holding two swords out straight for ten minutes would be relaxing, that lifting one-hundred-pound weights soothing, or getting hit in the face repeatedly calming? Well, maybe getting hit in the face with a boxing glove isn't calming, but it was certainly more interesting than those exams.

On the way home, I stopped at a grocery store to pick up some items. It was surprising how fast things went and what they cost. I was spending close to ten dollars a week on groceries! There was a car wash on my route, so I ran the T-Bird through.

I decided that I had studied as much as I needed for my exams and gave myself the night off. I watched TV for several hours and then read. Tonight, it was about Lorenzo substituting for the Right Honorable John Joseph Bonforte, who was missing. I had read it before, but it was still a lot of fun. I could now relate to the actor.

Friday was fun. After my morning exercises and run with Dick, I stopped at his apartment and presented Janice with a hairdryer. She promised to try it this very morning. At the studio, I gifted one to each of the two make-up girls, then one to Mr. Wayne for his wife, and another to Anna Romanov. This left two, one for Nina and a spare for whomever I had forgotten. I would order another run of one hundred and present one to everyone on the set.

Miss Romanov's reaction was the most interesting. Everyone else received it as an interesting and probably useful device. She turned it on to see how it performed. She then told me that I was a highly intelligent person and that this would greatly influence her new idea.

We then went to work. Again, it was a serious day of filming. Every day the pace seemed to pick up. At the same time, I was becoming comfortable with the process. I paid attention to what the director was trying to achieve with each scene. Mr. Wayne told me that he tried to work with Ron Dodge whenever he could because he always had a clear vision of the movie in his head.

Having a vision of the story he was telling was a huge part of his success. Many a director was known for shooting as much film as possible, then trying to pull a story out of the mess. This usually failed.

Today I had a gunfight with one of the Hole in the Wall Gang. As could be predicted, I won. The only difference between this and most Westerns is I had to pretend to throw up afterward. This was the first time that Sir Nicklaus had killed a man, and Ron wanted it to be a defining moment. Sir Nicklaus could kill and do it very well, but it would never become normal to him.

Of course, this endeared him to Lilly, played by Ellen, even more. In the movie, this scene is followed by one where Big Jim, played by Mr. Wayne, tells him that is how real men feel. Only heartless killers felt no remorse. One more step towards Sir Nicklaus's growing up. These scenes left me extremely uncomfortable. I had killed two bank robbers and felt no remorse. Was I a heartless killer?

I must have looked troubled because Mr. Wayne later asked me what was wrong. I unburdened to him.

"Ricky, this is a movie, not real life. The scriptwriters wrote all our words. They are trying to convey a simple message. It would be a poor and boring movie if we explained everything in the detail it deserves. You know my biggest concern about some of the movies I've been in?"

"No, what?"

"That some poor kid out there will take things literally and pull some damn fool stunt he has seen in the movie thinking life is like that. They can't see what things we do behind the scenes or understand that our words are simplified to tell a story, and that is all it is, a story, not real life."

"I had never thought of what we are doing in that light. Should we be doing it?"

"Ricky, people have been telling stories that simplify life ever since Homer was a pup."

"I guess you are right, but I'm going to think of what stories I want to help tell in the future."

"Now you are getting it. You need to read scripts to see if they match your goals and if they match your beliefs. There are very few actors who can play a part that they don't believe in."

That was quite an insight that I had just received. This would give me food for thought for some time to come.

Speaking of food, it was lunchtime, and I was starved. No heavy thinking was going to put me off my food. After lunch, I headed to the office where I had been taking my tests. Mr. Congeniality was waiting. He was like a robot as he went through his routine when he asked if I had any questions about the examination.

I responded with, "No, *amigo*."

After all, it is my Spanish exam today.

It took longer than I expected, most of the three hours. When I turned my result in, I went to leave. Sour face cleared his throat and spoke.

"Mr. Jackson, I've been proctoring these exams for ten years. It has been a pleasure working with you. I cannot begin to tell you how often a student hasn't a clue about how to take an exam. They whine and repeatedly ask questions. Worse yet, there is about a fifty percent attempted cheat rate on these exams.

"I would wish you luck on your results, but I know luck has nothing to do with them in your case. You have earned them."

He then extended his hand. The weirdest thing was he had a smile. I didn't think that face was even capable of smiling.

I replied, "Thank you, sir," as I shook his hand.

As I walked to the stunt area, I thought about what had just happened. You just never know about people unless you know all about their backgrounds. I started laughing. That was the second serious thought I had for the day. I hope they didn't bump into each other in my head and get hurt.

When I reached my refuge from thought, the stunt area, where I just did things, I refused to recognize that this might be a third idea. I mean, my head is only so big, and there might be a traffic jam if I kept this up.

A quick bout with real swords cleared my mind. It is hard to think philosophical thoughts while someone is trying to beat on you with an iron bar that has a sharp edge and a pointy end.

After a good brisk workout with swords, I did my weightlifting. I was able to up the weights again. There was some wishful thinking going on, but I was getting some definition in my muscle groups, and from how my shirt sleeves felt a little tighter, I was bulking up.

The coach wasn't there to beat me up at boxing, so I had a good workout with the bags and called it a day. Once I was home, I was at loose ends, so I called Nina. She suggested I meet her at the Hamburger Hamlet in Beverly Hills. That's where she and her classmates hung out on a Friday evening.

I showered and shaved, not that I needed to shave. It just felt clean. Wearing the Hollywood teenage uniform of slacks, golf shirt, and blazer, I headed out. It is a good thing that I had bought that map. Between it and the yellow pages for the address, I was able to get there.

Chapter 46

The Hamburger Hamlet was a sit-down restaurant with booths. Unlike Don's in Bellefontaine, it had waitresses. Many of the waitresses would never have gotten a job in Bellefontaine. They were black! They were also good at their job and cheerful while doing it.

Nina was at a table with three friends, but they scooted another table up to it so I could join them. This also opened up seating for two more to join us promptly. Nina was with three girls; two guys joined me. It was like they had wanted to join the girls but were afraid to ask. Nina introduced me around. Even to the guys.

The girls had a hot round of gossip going, so I talked to the guys, Rob and Bob. They immediately reminded me of the two Toms in Bellefontaine. Here Bob was the class clown. I figured that out when he grabbed a bunch of straws and tore one end off. He then would blow into the straw, launching the wrapper towards kids at other tables.

They ignored him unless he got a good hit. That lasted until one of the waitresses slapped him lightly up the side of his head.

"Bobbie, how many times have I told you not to do that? Now get up and pick up all those wrappers, or I will tell your parents later."

It seemed Bob's parents were frequent customers, and the waitresses weren't going to put up with his nonsense.

Bob retrieved the straw wrappers while getting mostly good-natured comments from his classmates about crawling on the floor.

One of the girls remarked, "Bob, that is the second Friday in a row you have done this. It is time for you to grow up."

From the look on Bob's face, I knew this story. Bob had been trying to get her attention. He had, just not in the way he wanted to.

You could see Bob swell up to make a smart remark, which would have been anything but smart. He was sitting at the end of the

246

table next to me, so I distracted him by grabbing his arm and told him quietly, "Bob, Natalie is right. You need some new material."

He looked at me like a deer in the headlights.

I continued, "Natalie cares enough to notice what you are doing. Don't bore or embarrass her by being repetitive."

I wasn't going to criticize him for shooting straw wrappers across the room, which was good fun. However, he had achieved his objective and now had to move on, or in this case, move in on Natalie.

Bob was smart enough to shut up. Well, at least change the subject. He started telling us about how a friend of a cousin out in Riverside had seen two guys pull a trick on the cops. They had crept behind a patrol car that was sitting near a pole waiting on speeders. They put a heavy-duty cable around the rear axle and the pole, locking it in place.

They went back to their car and sped past the cop car. The cops started chasing them until it reached the end of the one-hundred-foot cable, which promptly stopped the car by the rear axle. The front end of the car kept going. Everyone at the table was listening to the story by the time he was finished.

I didn't burst his bubble by telling him that I had heard it had happened down the road from Bellefontaine in Urbana or how my Uncle Wally said it was done by the brother of a guy he knew back in the 1930s. The one thing in common with all the stories was it wasn't anyone they knew directly, and it had happened elsewhere.

It still made a good story, and I bet it would work, at least in a movie someday.

We ate burgers, surprise! We talked about nothing, well, the latest Hollywood gossip, which seemed strange because the girls in Bellefontaine discussed the Hollywood gossip. The only difference here was the kids personally knew the players and some of them were parents of those present.

When it was time to leave, I found that Nina had ridden with one of the other girls and would be delighted to have me take her home. She gave directions, and the next thing I knew, we were parked high above the lights of Los Angeles. A line of cars parked there was not that close to each other, but still quite a few. One thing led to another, and we were panting pretty hard when she broke away and told me we had better get home.

I asked her if she had a curfew, and she told me, "No, I'm afraid of what I want you to do."

What can you say to that? No comment that I could think of would do anything but cause trouble, so I kept my mouth shut. I was finding that to be a good tactic with women.

As we were leaving, a police car on patrol pulled up and started chasing the other parked cars out. I asked if the police had ever arrested anyone.

"Not very often. They come by at least once an hour, so you don't have a lot of time to get in trouble. They will haul you in only if you don't have any clothes on."

That was good information to have, but how did Nina know? I asked her, and she giggled as she let me know.

"All the girls share the best parking spots and the rules."

"Are there spots without rules?"

"Yes, but we must be serious before I show you those."

Open mouth, shut mouth. Remember good tactics.

At her house, I opened the trunk and pulled out a hairdryer which I had paid a woman in the front office to gift wrap. I walked her to her door, intending to hand it to her and say goodnight after a nice kiss. As usual, this plan went awry when her dad opened the door.

He invited me in and called out to Nina. He was about to leave us, but he noticed the present and inquired about it. Dads and guys giving their daughters a gift was an explosion waiting to happen.

Luckily for me, my gift was so unusual that it triggered curiosity questions. When I explained what it was and how it was used, Nina had to plug it in.

Her father wanted to know where I had found such a different item. When I explained that I had invented it and had the patents in the process, it led to an hour-long discussion. Along the way, I shared that I had designed and patented an adjustable showerhead and was collecting royalties. You could see him re-evaluating me.

I took the chance and explained the studio had a collection of faucets that interested me. I had taken pictures and intended to share them with my design person as inspiration.

"Your design person?"

That is when I told him about owning thirty percent of Detroit Faucet or DF as its new name would be. This led to the direct product placement in the movie, a clip in the movie in the TV special, and DF being a major sponsor of the show. He was nodding his head as I brought each point up.

Nina was beaming like her hunter had brought home a whole bunch of rabbits.

I was told that the prop men had checked, and there were no patent numbers on any of the faucets. They had been in storage so long no one knew where they came from. Most had been there since the 1920s, so if there were any patents, they had expired.

Mr. Monroe said, "Of course, I have to check all that out, but if it is true, I think we can strike a deal. In your catalog, you can use the name of the Warner Brothers movie they appeared in. You could list it as a style used in whatever movie it was. Giving the studio credit will be enough for us. It isn't like we make our money on faucets."

"That would be wonderful," I replied.

How I didn't run about the room making strange sounds, I don't know. This was wonderful.

Mr. Monroe mused, "As long as it wasn't a movie like a *Doorway to Hell*."

"That doesn't sound like a good fashion statement, Daddy," put in Nina.

"No, it doesn't, but that wouldn't have been the sort of movie that special props would've been made for. It was just an example."

"Rick, you are different from any other fifteen-year-old I've ever met. Why is that?"

"I had to grow up fast last summer."

"What happened last summer?" Nina's Dad questioned.

I told them the whole story, well, everything but the gold. For some reason, no one outside of my parents would hear about that. Mr. Monroe winced when I got to the bank robbers. Both he and Nina thought the rustler part was good. It turns out that Nina was a huge fan of the Beach Boys. She hadn't connected me with "Rock and Roll Cowboy". She had the grace to admit that she only listened to it because of the backup band.

I told her we both had something in common. We hated the song.

Nina turned to her Dad.

"This explains something my friends and I have noticed about Rick. Most of the time, he is as serious and as focused on things as you are. He is just another kid like the rest of us on a rare occasion like at the Hamburger Hamlet tonight."

"Rick, you are going to be an interesting person to watch," stated her father as he yawned. "As much as I have been fascinated by all this, it is my bedtime."

Looking at my watch, I realized it was past ten o'clock and fast approaching my bedtime also. We all said goodnight, and Nina walked me to my car. A quick goodnight kiss and I left for home and bed.

Chapter 47

The next morning, I was up at the normal time and ran with Dick Wyman. He asked me how things had been going. I gave him a small update as we circled the high school track. He told me he didn't understand how one person could get involved in so many things.

My morning was prosaic, to say the least. I stopped at the bank, the dry cleaners, and the library. From there, I went to the mall to pick up some new golf shirts as mine were getting tight. I went home and polished my boots and shoes. The housekeeper who stopped once a week didn't seem to have the same standards as I had been taught, so I spent some time cleaning the apartment.

At lunchtime, I went over to Larry's Chili Dog. Larry's is an outdoor stand with picnic tables to sit at. As far as I was concerned, they had the best Chili Dogs west of the Mississippi. Those at Crosley Field in Cincinnati were the best east of the Mississippi.

I read a book on economics and how the stock market works. I had picked it up at the library. I had a feeling that I would have to know about such things someday.

Later on, I took a nap because I had no idea how late Monroe's party would last. I also ate dinner before I went. I drove over to Sandwiches by Connal's in Pasadena for a quick meal.

I returned to my apartment to shower and shave. I wore my normal outfit of dark grey slacks, a yellow golf shirt, and a dark blue blazer. After dithering between my boots and shoes, I went with the boots. They seemed more natural to me these days, certainly more comfortable.

I arrived at the party at seven-thirty, a half-hour fashionably late. Nina had suggested this as most people would arrive about then. She was at the door greeting guests with her father. I got an air kiss on the cheek from her. Wow, were we fancy tonight. I cheated, though. As I was pulling away, I licked her ear.

In turn, she slugged me in the gut. Ain't love grand! Well, anyway, it was a little bit of fun. No one else noticed.

I went to one of the bar setups to order a Coke. After that, I snacked on appetizers for a while. The waiter informed me that the bacon-wrapped shrimp, or Angels on Horseback, were wonderful.

I finally found a corner to stand in and watch the crowd. I was joined by a young man who introduced himself as Jack McLeod in a strong Australian accent. He was here on business and knew some people who knew some people, so he got an invite. Well, at least he came with people who had an invite. He seemed like a good guy.

He was in the cattle business and was looking for bulls to improve his herd. He told me he couldn't wait to get home. This was okay, but he preferred the outdoors. We stood in the corner for the longest time and talked about the various guests. Naturally, we didn't know many of them, but we made up stories about them anyway.

Jack told me about his farm in Australia and invited me down under someday. He made it seem nice. It would be fun to take a bath in a tub set out in a field next to a windmill. Talk about a different world.

One of the people we talked about was a guy every bit as big as John Wayne and good-looking. Someone had pointed him out to Jack; he was a high-powered advertising man from Madison Avenue by the name of Don Drason or something like that. He sure liked his booze and women.

I wondered if DF would need an agency like that. If so, I think I would ask Mum to handle it. For some reason, I think she could hold her own with that crew. I wouldn't want to place Dad in that situation with his recent sobriety.

Standing there, I didn't notice a young lady who came up to me.

"Ricky, I am so glad to see you."

It was the beautiful Annette. We did the air kiss thing. What's wrong with a real kiss? At that point, Jack McLeod excused himself and walked away. Just as I was getting ready to have a good talk with Annette, another old acquaintance showed up. Paul Anka was there. I barely had time to introduce him to Annette; they were in another world.

Jack came back as they wandered away, "Puppy love if I've ever seen it."

Our corner was getting busy as now I was tapped on the shoulder by Anna Romanov. This time Jack did not attempt to leave, so I introduced them.

Anna told me that she was starting a design house. She would recommend products and even carry her brand names. Her first product was going to be a special line commissioned with DF Designs. She was interested in co-sponsoring my TV special and being in our catalogs. I told her I would have to talk to my partner Mark Downing and arrange a meeting to discuss terms.

She thought that was how we should proceed. About that time, John Wayne showed up and twirled her away.

Jack looked at me and said, "Mate, you certainly know some interesting people. Next, you will be introducing me to the queen."

"Both her and Eisenhower," I said with a straight face.

He looked at me. "Somehow, I think you could."

I just laughed at that, and we changed the subject. The corner was getting stuffy, so we took a walk around the parts of the house that were open to the public. One of the rooms was Mr. Monroe's office. In a glass case, there were cigars and cigar boxes on display. I recognized the box that had pride of place with its lighting.

It was a shabby-looking box that had been opened and had two dried-out cigars in it. I found interesting the picture of Teddy Roosevelt and the Rough Riders on the box. It was identical to the like-new unopened box I had found in Dad's office basement. I didn't say anything about it.

A young actor came into the office. While looking around, he introduced himself as Leonard Nimoy. We talked for a while. He joked that he might smoke one of Mr. Monroe's cigars. I didn't say anything, instead raising my one eyebrow at him. He loved it. He was going to practice it. He might be able to use it in a role someday.

At that time, Nina showed up freed from her duties. I introduced her to Jack. She seemed to lean towards him as they shook hands. I got her away from him as fast as I could. I suspected he was more of a ladies' man than that Don guy.

Nina and I went out by the pool, and that's where I found out where all the teens were hanging out. It was a fun party after that. We danced, ate, snuck in a kiss or two, ate some more, and danced. It was a great evening.

Around midnight people started to drift away. Nina told me only the hardcore drinkers would be staying, and some wouldn't leave till dawn. She was tired and wanted to go to bed, so I hunted up her father and thanked him for the great party. After that, Nina and I kissed goodnight, and I departed.

I wasn't five blocks down the road and the police had me pulled over for a sobriety test. I was able to walk the line and recite the alphabet backward, so they let me go. They did question my hardship license but bought my story.

I collapsed into bed without reading anything.

Sunday was a sleepy day. I was too late to run with Dick, so I did the route myself. Lunch was at Bob's Big Boy in Burbank. I made my tee time with the same old guys I played with last week. The mouthy one wasn't so mouthy this week.

I had longer to warm up this week and knew the course better. John Jacobs was my caddie once again. This time I managed an eight-under, still not a course record but getting there. I think I owed it to Mr. Williams just to help keep the mouth of the nasty one closed.

After a day out golfing and a late night for me, I was ready for a quiet evening. I called home and talked to everyone. I had to apologize that I hadn't written a letter this week. No one was upset, but it would be missed. Mum told me more about her trip to England and how the family was getting along. Even though Grandmum was okay with this trip, the sooner we made it over, the better.

She also wanted to know if I had any further problems like last week. I told her no, and she told me she thought those problems had gone away. That must have been wishful thinking on her part, as she had no way of knowing.

I asked Dad to mail me the box of unopened cigars that were in my closet with the picture of Teddy Roosevelt on them. He said he would but would like me to check out the Rowland-Workmen families in the City of Industry, especially seeing if I could find anything out about the last Spanish governor of California. I promised him I would do it next weekend.

After saying "Hi" to my brothers and sister and explaining that I had yet to make it to Disney and, yes, I would get there soon, I hung up with a round of I love you's.

I then called Nina, and we talked about the party last night and what a good time we had. I told her about getting stopped, and she told me that several people at the party had spent the night in jail, and her dad wasn't happy. He had talked to the mayor earlier, and now the mayor wasn't happy. Soon the mayor would talk to the chief of police, and he wouldn't be happy.

I tried to imagine Sergeant Woodruff of the Bellefontaine Police Force worrying about making anyone unhappy but couldn't picture it. I chalked it up to another difference between Hollywood and the real world.

I was glad to get to bed. I wondered what the next week would bring. I was finished with school for the year and would be on the set all day.

Finished for now....

Back Matter

Continued In:

Book 4: In the Movies The Richard Jackson Saga[1]
https://www.enelsonauthor.com/

For information on hiring Janet E. Rupert to edit your fiction project, email:

janeteditorrupert@gmail.com

---

1.   https://www.amazon.com/gp/product/B07WNJVV67

Other books by Ed Nelson

The Richard Jackson Saga

Book 1 The Beginning

Book 2 Schooldays

Book 3 Hollywood

Book 4 In the Movies

Book 5 Star to Deckhand

Book 6 Surfing Dude

Book 7 Third Time is a Charm

Book 8 Oxford University

Book 9 Cold War

Book 10 Taking Care of Business

Book 11 Interesting Times

Book 12 Escape from Siberia

Book 13 Regicide

Book 14 What's Under, Down Under?

Book 15 The Lunar Kingdom

Book 16 First Steps

In the Richard Jackson World

Mary, Mary

Stand-Alone Story

Ever and Always

Cast in Time

Book 1, Baron

Book 2, Baron of the Middle Counties

Book 3, Count

Book 4, Earl

Book 5, Earl of the Marches

Did you love *Hollywood*? Then you should read *In the Movies* by Ed Nelson!

The Richard Jackson Saga, Book 4 In the Movies has Rick firmly in the movies where he grows in his capabilities. Rick finds that fame may not be all it is cracked up to be. Finding girls is not hard, but he has his hands full between the boss's daughter, an old flame, and a bad girl from Hollywood. Joined by his family in California, they buy a mansion with hidden secrets. The adventure continues ranging from a stampede to a group of bank robbers running into the Square of Death. For the young this is a coming-of-age adventure; for those who lived it, a trip down memory lane, and for those with a search engine, Easter eggs galore. This tongue-in-cheek saga is all true, give or take a lie or two.